Juniperclaw let out a hiss of fury and reared back to pounce on top of Twigpaw, who dodged to one side, swiping at his flank. But Juniperclaw jumped back quickly enough that Twigpaw's blow never landed. Growling fiercely, Twigpaw leaped toward her adversary, throwing up a paw to block the ShadowClan warrior as he slashed at her shoulder.

Excitement flooded through Twigpaw as her body remembered all the fighting moves she'd learned in training. *This feels natural . . . it feels* right. *I'm fighting for my Clan!*

WARRIORS

THE PROPHECIES BEGIN

Book One: Into the Wild

Book Two: Fire and Ice

Book Three: Forest of Secrets

Book Four: Rising Storm

Book Five: A Dangerous Path

Book Six: The Darkest Hour

THE NEW PROPHECY

Book One: Midnight

Book Two: Moonrise

Book Three: Dawn

Book Four: Starlight

Book Five: Twilight

Book Six: Sunset

POWER OF THREE

Book One: The Sight

Book Two: Dark River

Book Three: Outcast

Book Four: Eclipse

Book Five: Long Shadows

Book Six: Sunrise

OMEN OF THE STARS

Book One: The Fourth Apprentice

Book Two: Fading Echoes

Book Three: Night Whispers

Book Four: Sign of the Moon

Book Five: The Forgotten Warrior

Book Six: The Last Hope

Warriors: The Ultimate Guide
Warriors: The Untold Stories
Warriors: Tales from the Clans
Warriors: Shadows of the Clans
Warriors: Legends of the Clans

MANGA

The Lost Warrior
Warrior's Refuge
Warrior's Return
The Rise of Scourge
Tigerstar and Sasha #1: Into the Woods
Tigerstar and Sasha #2: Escape from the Forest
Tigerstar and Sasha #3: Return to the Clans
Ravenpaw's Path #1: Shattered Peace
Ravenpaw's Path #2: A Clan in Need
Ravenpaw's Path #3: The Heart of a Warrior
SkyClan and the Stranger #1: The Rescue
SkyClan and the Stranger #2: Beyond the Code
SkyClan and the Stranger #3: After the Flood

NOVELLAS

Hollyleaf's Story
Mistystar's Omen
Cloudstar's Journey
Tigerclaw's Fury
Leafpool's Wish
Dovewing's Silence
Mapleshade's Vengeance
Goosefeather's Curse
Ravenpaw's Farewell
Spottedleaf's Heart
Pinestar's Choice
Thunderstar's Echo

Also by Erin Hunter

SEEKERS

RETURN TO THE WILD

MANGA

SURVIVORS

THE GATHERING DARKNESS

Survivors: Tales from the Packs

NOVELLAS

BRAVELANDS

A VISION OF SHADOWS

WARRIORS

SHATTERED SKY

ERIN HUNTER

HARPER

An Imprint of HarperCollinsPublishers

Special thanks to Cherith Baldry

Shattered Sky
Copyright © 2017 by Working Partners Limited
Series created by Working Partners Limited
Map art © 2017 by Dave Stevenson
Interior art © 2017 by Allen Douglas

www.harpercollinschildrens.com
Library of Congress Control Number: 2016960410
ISBN 978-0-06-238647-2
Typography by Ellice M. Lee
19 20 21 22 CG/BRR 10 9 8 7 6
❖
First paperback edition, 2018

ALLEGIANCES

THUNDERCLAN

LEADER

BRAMBLESTAR—dark brown tabby tom with amber eyes

DEPUTY

SQUIRRELFLIGHT—dark ginger she-cat with green eyes and one white paw

MEDICINE CATS

LEAFPOOL—light brown tabby she-cat with amber eyes, white paws and chest

JAYFEATHER—gray tabby tom with blind blue eyes

ALDERHEART—dark ginger tom with amber eyes

WARRIORS

(toms and she-cats without kits)

BRACKENFUR—golden-brown tabby tom

CLOUDTAIL—long-haired white tom with blue eyes

BRIGHTHEART—white she-cat with ginger patches

THORNCLAW—golden-brown tabby tom

WHITEWING—white she-cat with green eyes

BIRCHFALL—light brown tabby tom

BERRYNOSE—cream-colored tom with a stump for a tail

MOUSEWHISKER—gray-and-white tom

POPPYFROST—pale tortoiseshell and white she-cat

CINDERHEART—gray tabby she-cat

LIONBLAZE—golden tabby tom with amber eyes

ROSEPETAL—dark cream she-cat

BRIARLIGHT—dark brown she-cat, paralyzed in her hindquarters

LILYHEART—small, dark tabby she-cat with white patches, and blue eyes

BUMBLESTRIPE—very pale gray tom with black stripes

IVYPOOL—silver-and-white tabby she-cat with dark blue eyes

APPRENTICE, TWIGPAW (gray she-cat with green eyes)

DOVEWING—pale gray she-cat with green eyes

CHERRYFALL—ginger she-cat

MOLEWHISKER—brown-and-cream tom

SNOWBUSH—white, fluffy tom

AMBERMOON—pale ginger she-cat

DEWNOSE—gray-and-white tom

STORMCLOUD—gray tabby tom

HOLLYTUFT—black she-cat

FERNSONG—yellow tabby tom

SORRELSTRIPE—dark brown she-cat

LEAFSHADE—a tortoiseshell she-cat

LARKSONG—a black tom

HONEYFUR—a white she-cat with yellow splotches

SPARKPELT—orange tabby she-cat

QUEENS (she-cats expecting or nursing kits)

DAISY—cream long-furred cat from the horseplace

BLOSSOMFALL—tortoiseshell-and-white she-cat with petal-shaped white patches

ELDERS	(former warriors and queens, now retired)
	PURDY—plump tabby former loner with a gray muzzle
	GRAYSTRIPE—long-haired gray tom
	MILLIE—striped silver tabby she-cat with blue eyes

SHADOWCLAN

(REFUGEES LIVING WITH THUNDERCLAN)

LEADER	**ROWANSTAR**—ginger tom
DEPUTY	**TIGERHEART**—dark brown tabby tom
WARRIORS	**TAWNYPELT**—tortoiseshell she-cat with green eyes

WINDCLAN

LEADER	**ONESTAR**—brown tabby tom
DEPUTY	**HARESPRING**—brown-and-white tom
MEDICINE CAT	**KESTRELFLIGHT**—mottled gray tom with white splotches like kestrel feathers
WARRIORS	**NIGHTCLOUD**—black she-cat
	APPRENTICE, BRINDLEPAW (mottled brown she-cat)
	GORSETAIL—very pale gray-and-white she-cat with blue eyes
	CROWFEATHER—dark gray tom
	APPRENTICE, FERNPAW (gray tabby she-cat)
	LEAFTAIL—dark tabby tom, amber eyes

EMBERFOOT—gray tom with two dark paws
APPRENTICE, SMOKEPAW (gray she-cat)

BREEZEPELT—black tom with amber eyes

LARKWING—pale brown tabby she-cat

SEDGEWHISKER—light brown tabby she-cat

SLIGHTFOOT—black tom with white flash on his chest

OATCLAW—pale brown tabby tom

FEATHERPELT—gray tabby she-cat

HOOTWHISKER—dark gray tom

HEATHERTAIL—light brown tabby she-cat with blue eyes

ELDERS   **WHITETAIL**—small white she-cat

RIVERCLAN

LEADER   **MISTYSTAR**—gray she-cat with blue eyes

DEPUTY   **REEDWHISKER**—black tom

MEDICINE CATS   **MOTHWING**—dappled golden she-cat

                                       WILLOWSHINE—gray tabby she-cat

WARRIORS   **MINTFUR**—light gray tabby tom

                                       DUSKFUR—brown tabby she-cat

                                       SHADEPELT—dark brown she-cat

                                       MINNOWTAIL—dark gray-and-white she-cat
APPRENTICE, BREEZEPAW

                                       MALLOWNOSE—light brown tabby tom

                                       PETALFUR—gray-and-white she-cat

BEETLEWHISKER—brown-and-white tabby tom

CURLFEATHER—pale brown she-cat

PODLIGHT—gray-and-white tom

HERONWING—dark gray-and-black tom

SHIMMERPELT—silver she-cat

APPRENTICE, NIGHTPAW (dark gray she-cat with blue eyes)

LIZARDTAIL—light brown tom

FOXNOSE—russet tabby tom

HAVENPELT—black-and-white she-cat

PERCHWING—gray-and-white she-cat

SNEEZECLOUD—gray-and-white tom

BRACKENPELT—tortoiseshell she-cat

JAYCLAW—gray tom

OWLNOSE—brown tabby tom

ICEWING—white she-cat with blue eyes

QUEENS **LAKEHEART**—gray tabby she-cat (mother to Harekit, Dapplekit, Gorsekit, and Softkit)

ELDERS **MOSSPELT**—tortoiseshell-and-white she-cat

ROGUES

(DARKTAIL'S "KIN")

LEADER **DARKTAIL**—a strong, muscular tom, with white fur broken up by black spots around his eyes

MEDICINE CAT **PUDDLESHINE**—brown tom with white splotches

THE "KIN"

RAIN—long-furred gray tom with green eyes

RAVEN—long-furred black she-cat

ROACH—silver gray tom

NETTLE—brown tabby tom with long, spiky fur

NEEDLETAIL—silver she-cat

SLEEKWHISKER—sleek yellow she-cat

JUNIPERCLAW—black tom

SPIKEFUR—dark brown tom with tufty fur on his head

YARROWLEAF—ginger she-cat with yellow eyes

STONEWING—white tom

STRIKESTONE—tabby tom

DAWNPELT—cream-furred she-cat

BEENOSE—plump white she-cat with black ears

SCORCHFUR—dark gray tom with slashed ears

BERRYHEART—black-and-white she-cat

CLOVERFOOT—gray tabby she-cat

RIPPLETAIL—white tom

SPARROWTAIL—large brown tabby tom

MISTCLOUD—spiky-furred, pale gray she-cat

BIRCHBARK—beige tom

LIONEYE—yellow she-cat with amber eyes

SLATEFUR—sleek gray tom

GRASSHEART—pale brown tabby she-cat

PINENOSE—black she-cat

VIOLETPAW—black-and-white she-cat with yellow eyes

QUEENS   **SNOWBIRD**—pure white she-cat with green eyes (mother to Conekit, Gullkit, and Frondkit)

ELDERS   **OAKFUR**—small brown tom

RATSCAR—scarred, skinny dark brown tom

GREENLEAF
TWOLEGPLACE

TWOLEG NEST

TWOLEG PATH

TWOLEG PATH

CLEARING

SHADOWCLAN
CAMP

SMALL
THUNDERPATH

HALFBRIDGE

GREENLEAF
TWOLEGPLACE

HALFBRIDGE

CAT VIEW

ISLAND

STREAM

RIVERCLAN
CAMP

HORSEPLACE

MOONPOOL

ABANDONED
TWOLEG NEST

OLD THUNDERPATH

THUNDERCLAN
CAMP

ANCIENT OAK

LAKE

WINDCLAN
CAMP

BROKEN
HALFBRIDGE

TWOLEGPLACE

THUNDERPATH

KEY
To The
CLANS

THUNDERCLAN

RIVERCLAN

SHADOWCLAN

WINDCLAN

STARCLAN

NORTH

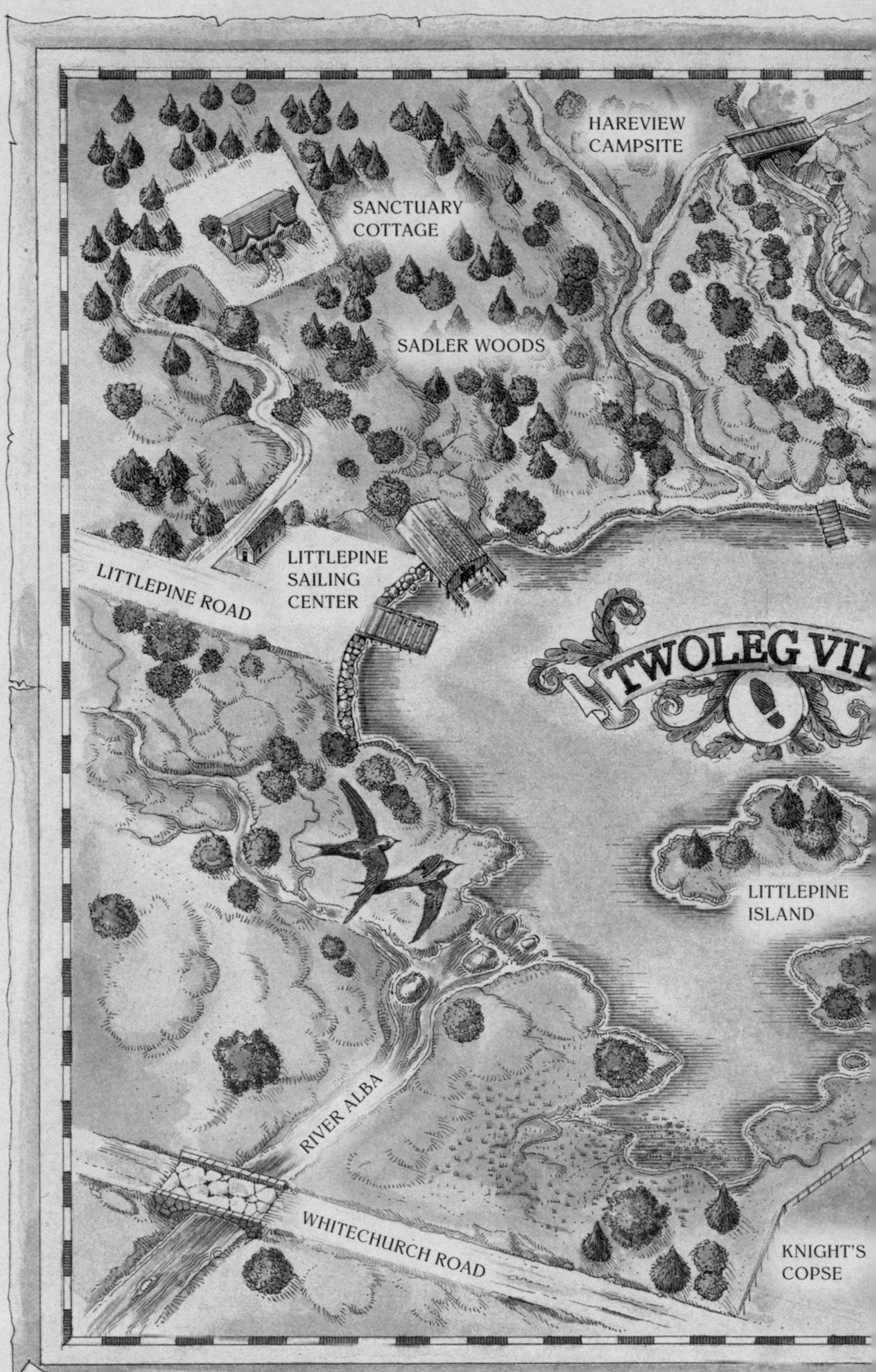
HAREVIEW CAMPSITE
SANCTUARY COTTAGE
SADLER WOODS
LITTLEPINE SAILING CENTER
LITTLEPINE ROAD
TWOLEG VIL
LITTLEPINE ISLAND
RIVER ALBA
WHITECHURCH ROAD
KNIGHT'S COPSE

PROLOGUE

The sun edged its way above the horizon, casting a flood of golden light over the grassy hollow where Alderheart stood. Blinking in the dazzling rays, he glanced around and tried to work out where he was. He couldn't remember ever having visited this hollow before, and a pang of apprehension seized him as he wondered if he had managed to wander away from Thunder-Clan territory without realizing it.

In the bottom of the hollow was a small pool, the surface glittering in the sunlight. Straggling bushes surrounded it, and when Alderheart looked more closely he spotted a group of cats huddled in the shelter of the branches. A small, silver-gray tabby she-cat lay stretched out in their midst. Alderheart thought he had seen her somewhere before, but the other cats were all strangers to him.

Hesitantly, Alderheart began padding down the slope into the center of the hollow. "Greetings!" he called out as he drew nearer to the group of cats. "Can you tell me where . . . ?"

His voice trailed off as none of the cats reacted to his approach—it was as if they could neither see him nor hear him. A spark of excitement fizzled through Alderheart.

I must be having a vision! Are these the cats of SkyClan? But I don't really recognize any of them....

Eager to know what his vision had to tell him, Alderheart drew closer to the clump of bushes, noticing that his paw steps did not even bend the grass blades beneath them.

As he padded forward, Alderheart could see that the silver-gray tabby had a long gash down her flank. The flesh around it was swollen, and pus oozed from the wound. The tabby was very thin, her pelt dull and almost colorless; her breathing was shallow, and her eyes looked glassy with fever. Once again he felt that odd sense of familiarity, as though he really ought to recognize her.

I wish I could help this cat, Alderheart thought. *Chervil or marigold for the infection, some borage leaves to bring down her fever a little . . .*

But in his vision he was helpless, with no way to communicate with these cats or find the herbs for them. All he could do was watch as one of the tabby's companions dipped a scrap of moss into the pool and held it to her mouth so that she could drink.

"Is there anything we can do for you?" one of the other cats asked her.

Wearily, the silver tabby shook her head. "Maybe dandelion or borage," she murmured. "But I don't know where you would find them here. My time is almost up. The infection is too strong. . . . There's nothing any cat can do now."

Her eyes closed. One of the other cats bent over her and gave her ears a gentle lick.

Alderheart almost thought that the tabby had died, but a

moment later she roused again.

"I wish I could protect you all," she mewed, her voice shaking and filled with guilt. "We're so far from the gorge . . . and we haven't been able to find the home that StarClan wishes for us." Suddenly she startled, looking over her Clanmates' heads. "Frecklewish! Have you found us at last?"

The other cats looked eagerly in the direction she was staring, but disappointment clouded their eyes when they saw no cat there. Alderheart understood that the tabby's fever was causing her to hallucinate. The cat who had been licking her said gently, "She's not here. You know we never found Frecklewish after we were driven from the gorge. I fear that she must be dead."

Another cat nodded. "We looked everywhere."

Alderheart realized that the dying tabby must be their medicine cat. Pity for her Clanmates clawed at him: they looked so thin and ragged, and it sounded as if they had struggled hard to find themselves new territory.

They've been through so much, he thought. *And losing their medicine cat will only make things more difficult.*

The cat's name was on the tip of Alderheart's tongue, and suddenly it felt vitally important for him to remember it. But he was distracted when the silver-gray tabby let out a gasp and struggled to sit up. Her eyes widened, her gaze fixed on something on the horizon. Alderheart wanted to turn and see what it was that she saw, but he couldn't tear his gaze from her face.

"They're coming . . . ," she whispered, seeming to relax; then she forced herself upright again, her legs trembling and her tail flailing. "You must look for the blood trail in the sky! Follow the blood trail!" she rasped out.

The effort had taken the last of the tabby's strength. She sank back onto the grass, her eyes fluttering shut. Her breathing slowed, then stopped.

"Echosong!" The cats who surrounded her flung back their heads and sent wails of anguish up to the sky. "Echosong!"

Echosong! Alderheart's suspicions were confirmed. *No wonder she looks familiar—I've seen her in a vision before! And I know her name . . . Sandstorm spoke of her. She's SkyClan's medicine cat . . . which means these cats are all that's left of SkyClan.*

The vision began to fade into a swirling gray mist, and as he lost sight of the grieving cats, Alderheart felt certain that SkyClan still desperately needed help—more than ever, now that they were without a medicine cat.

Opening his eyes in the apprentices' den, Alderheart saw pale dawn light filtering through the ferns that screened the entrance. He lay still for a moment. His vision had convinced him not only that his Clan *must* help SkyClan, but that SkyClan definitely had something to do with the prophecy.

It's time to do something, Alderheart thought, hauling himself to his paws and shaking moss and bracken out of his pelt. *I'll talk to Bramblestar about it as soon as I can. But I'm afraid that won't be until after this morning's battle. . . .*

CHAPTER 1

❧

Cats of all four Clans were massed as one on the ShadowClan border. All around her, Twigpaw could hear the faint rustling, as their paws shifted in the grass, and taste their mingled scents. "So many warriors!" she whispered. "All four Clans together . . ."

The cats of ThunderClan were clustered around Twigpaw, their gleaming eyes and bristling fur showing that they were ready for battle. Twigpaw let her gaze travel over them: the Clan leader, Bramblestar, with his deputy, Squirrelflight, beside him; Lionblaze, his muscles rippling under his golden tabby pelt; Cloudtail with his mate, Brightheart, and their daughter Whitewing; Larksong and his littermates, Leaf-shade and Honeyfur, proudly awaiting their first chance to fight for their Clan as warriors.

Twigpaw pressed close to Ivypool's side, nervously sheathing and unsheathing her claws. The dawn light was growing stronger, but shadows still lurked under the trees, making the ShadowClan territory ahead look even darker and scarier than usual.

Ivypool dipped her head to speak softly into Twigpaw's ear.

"After the Great Storm, Bramblestar proposed a new addition to the warrior code." Her eyes shone with pride in her Clan leader. "He said that though the Clans must all remember their separate histories and traditions, in times of dire need all should stand together so that no Clan should ever fall. And if this isn't a time of dire need," she added wryly, "I don't know what is."

"Do you really think we can drive the rogues out of ShadowClan territory?" Twigpaw asked. She tried to stop her voice from shaking, even though her mouth was dry and her heart pounded so hard that she thought every cat must be able to hear it.

Ivypool brushed her tail reassuringly over Twigpaw's shoulders. "Your first battle is always tough," she meowed. Her silver-and-white pelt was as neat as if she had just groomed it, and her voice was full of confidence. "But stick close to me, and I'll look after you."

Relief flooded through Twigpaw, and she blinked gratefully at her mentor. *I'm so happy to be Ivypool's apprentice,* she thought. *She always has my back.*

"Cats of all Clans . . ." Bramblestar's voice rang out across the assembled cats. "The time has come to take the rogues by surprise and force them out of ShadowClan territory."

"Yes," Rowanstar agreed. The ShadowClan leader's voice was quiet but invited no argument. He stood at the front of the crowd, his ginger fur beginning to glow as the light strengthened. His mate, Tawnypelt, had positioned herself close beside him. "We must get rid of the rogues *once and for all.*

The future of the Clans depends on it!"

Onestar, the leader of WindClan, glared at Rowanstar and gave an irritated lash of his tail. "That's an interesting order," he meowed, "coming from the cat who allowed the rogues to live on his territory for moons, until finally most of his Clan decided they would rather follow Darktail! Maybe, Rowanstar," he added, "you could stop issuing orders to cats who are cleaning up *your* mess."

Rowanstar's neck fur bristled and he drew his lips back in the beginning of a snarl. "And just maybe," he retorted bitterly, "WindClan cats could mind their own business."

"You made it our business!" Onestar snapped.

"Enough!" Mistystar of RiverClan thrust her way between the two furious leaders, holding herself with authority. "What hope do we have if we fight among ourselves? Rowanstar is right about one thing: the rogues must be driven out. They killed Furzepelt, they enticed ShadowClan warriors away from their Clan, and now they've stolen ShadowClan's territory. It's time to get rid of these fiends once and for all."

"Exactly," Bramblestar agreed, his voice level. "So please can we stop blaming one another, and work together to drive out these rogues?"

He glanced from Rowanstar to Onestar and back again. Onestar dipped his head in acquiescence, while Rowanstar turned aside, breathing heavily and shaking out his fur.

Seeing the leaders fight like that only made Twigpaw more nervous; she felt as if she had a belly full of mice that were chasing one another's tails.

"Are you ready?" Ivypool asked.

Twigpaw hesitated. "I'm worried about my sister," she confessed at last. "Poor Violetpaw is with the rogues now, and she's bound to be caught up in all of this. What if she gets hurt?"

"Violetpaw is strong and smart." A new voice chimed in; Twigpaw turned her head to see the ShadowClan deputy, Tigerheart, standing just behind her, with her Clanmate Dovewing by his side. "She'll be okay," Tigerheart continued reassuringly. "And none of the cats here would seriously injure an apprentice."

"Thank you." Twigpaw gave the dark brown tabby cat a grateful glance, though she noticed her mentor's tail-tip twitching back and forth in irritation. *I wonder why Ivypool doesn't seem to like Tigerheart.*

Bramblestar waved his tail as a signal for the assembled cats to move. His muscles rippled under his dark tabby pelt as he led the way. Padding forward as one cat, the combined forces of the four Clans slid silently after him through the long grass and crossed into ShadowClan territory. Twigpaw shivered as the reek of the border markers wafted over her.

Every cat kept quiet under the shadow of the trees, paw steps soundless on the thick layer of pine needles that covered the ground. They spread out as they headed toward the ShadowClan camp.

But before the bushes that surrounded the camp came into view, Twigpaw spotted movement among the trees ahead. A patrol emerged: four of the ShadowClan cats who had chosen to remain on their own territory with the rogues. Sleekwhisker was in the lead.

The patrol halted as they spotted the crowd of cats stalking purposefully toward them. They stared as if they could not believe what was in front of them.

Sleekwhisker was the first to recover from the shock. "Intruders!" she screeched. "We're under attack! All cats—back to camp, now!"

She whirled around and vanished into the trees, her patrol hard on her paws.

Harespring, the WindClan deputy, looked at his paws and shook his head. "There goes our chance of surprising them," he muttered.

"Into your groups!" Bramblestar ordered.

Before they'd left the ThunderClan camp, every cat had been assigned to a group that would fight together in the battle. Now Twigpaw knew exactly where she was supposed to be. Still nervous, and amazed at how fast everything was happening, she raced forward, following Lionblaze. Her paws hardly touched the ground as wind flowed through her fur. Ivypool, Dovewing, and Tigerheart pelted along beside her.

The mingled scents of many cats told Twigpaw that they were now very close to the ShadowClan camp. At the same moment, cats began to stream out of the bushes ahead. Twigpaw's eyes widened, and for a heartbeat her flying paws faltered, as she realized just how many rogues there were now that former ShadowClan cats had joined them—far more than she had seen or heard of before.

The silence of the forest was split by yowls and caterwauling as the two groups of cats clashed. Twigpaw found herself face to face with Juniperclaw. For a moment she hesitated, unsure what to do, until the ShadowClan tom swiped at her, claws extended and jaws gaping in a snarl. Instinctively Twigpaw ducked underneath his outstretched leg and raked her claws across Juniperclaw's underbelly, her fighting lessons with Ivypool echoing in her mind.

Juniperclaw let out a hiss of fury and reared back to pounce on top of Twigpaw, who dodged to one side, swiping at his flank. But Juniperclaw jumped back quickly enough that Twigpaw's blow never landed. Growling fiercely, Twigpaw leaped toward her adversary, throwing up a paw to block the ShadowClan warrior as he slashed at her shoulder.

Excitement flooded through Twigpaw as her body remembered all the fighting moves she'd learned in training. *This feels natural . . . it feels right. I'm fighting for my Clan!*

She dashed at Juniperclaw again, bunching her muscles to leap upon his back. But at the last moment Juniperclaw reared onto his hind legs and twisted to one side, pinning Twigpaw to the ground. The ShadowClan warrior's glaring eyes and sharp teeth were less than a mouse-length from her face.

"You're good, apprentice," he hissed. "But not *that* good."

Unable to breathe under his weight, Twigpaw tried to bring up her hind paws to bat at the ShadowClan cat's belly, but Juniperclaw was too heavy; Twigpaw couldn't push him far enough away to get any strength behind her blows.

What do I do now? she wondered, fighting off panic.

Suddenly a silver-and-white blur flashed across Twigpaw's vision as Ivypool leaped right over her, knocking Juniperclaw away. The ShadowClan cat fell to the ground, paws flailing, while Ivypool followed up her leap with a couple of hard blows across his shoulders.

"Scram, flea-pelt!" she snarled.

Juniperclaw scrambled to his paws and fled; Twigpaw lost sight of him among the battling cats.

"Thanks, Ivypool," she gasped, forcing herself upright again.

"My pleasure," Ivypool mewed swiftly; then she hurled herself toward Lionblaze and Dovewing, who were battling three of the rogues.

Her chest heaving as she fought to catch her breath, Twigpaw took a moment to look around. Everywhere cats were locked in combat. Her spirits rose as she realized that the Clan cats seemed to be winning the fight. She saw Bramble-star knock Rain to the ground, while Cherryfall was darting to and fro, slashing at Sleekwhisker, whose efforts to defend herself grew feebler with every heartbeat.

Twigpaw was about to leap back into the fray when she spotted Onestar, who had Darktail pinned to the ground. Onestar's forepaws pummeled at Darktail's face, leaving bloody slashes across his cheeks. Darktail barely struggled, gasping for breath.

Onestar must be taking revenge for his lost life, Twigpaw guessed.

But as she watched the two leaders fight, Darktail heaved himself up and tumbled Onestar to the ground. He staggered toward Onestar and murmured something, his mouth close to the WindClan leader's ear. Onestar's eyes widened into a horrified stare as he rose to his paws and drew away from the rogue. His message—whatever it was—delivered, Darktail sagged to the ground again. Twigpaw could see that his white fur was smudged with red from injuries on his sides and chest.

She tensed, expecting Onestar to lunge at Darktail and deliver a killing blow. But the WindClan leader backed away. *Why doesn't Onestar finish Darktail off?* Twigpaw wondered. *That's the whole point of this battle!*

Instead Onestar raised his head to let out a loud yowl. "Cats of WindClan! Retreat! Back to the camp!"

Twigpaw let out a gasp. She couldn't understand why Onestar would call his cats out of the battle, especially when he had been so adamant that they drive the rogues out at last.

What could Darktail possibly have said to him?

"WindClan! Retreat!" Onestar yowled again.

Twigpaw caught no more than a glimpse of the WindClan cats breaking off their tussles with the rogues before something hard hit her in the back and bowled her over, knocking the breath out of her. Too late she realized that she shouldn't have been staring at Onestar instead of paying attention to the battle around her.

Summoning every scrap of her strength, Twigpaw twisted around to see Yarrowleaf glaring balefully down at her, the hostile she-cat's breath riffling Twigpaw's whiskers while her claws dug into her shoulders. Twigpaw heaved upward and managed to dislodge the ShadowClan cat so that she could rake her hind paws across her belly. But Yarrowleaf still kept a grip on her and bent down, jaws parted to sink her teeth into Twigpaw's throat.

Twigpaw strained away from her, bracing herself for pain. Then Ivypool appeared once again, fastening her claws into Yarrowleaf's neck and hauling her bodily away.

After flinging Yarrowleaf to one side, Ivypool crouched to pounce on top of her, but before she could move, Tigerheart appeared, thrusting himself between the two cats and giving Yarrowleaf the chance to scramble away.

Ivypool straightened up, glaring at Tigerheart. "What in StarClan's name do you think you're doing?" she snarled. "Yarrowleaf isn't your Clanmate now. You're supposed to be on *our* side!"

Tigerheart cast an anguished glance after the fleeing Yarrowleaf. He opened his jaws to answer, but before he could speak he was interrupted by an angry yowl from Lionblaze. The WindClan cats were streaming away from the ShadowClan camp in the paw steps of their leader, leaving the remaining warriors at a serious disadvantage.

"Stop!" Bramblestar yowled.

"You can't leave us! We agreed!" Mistystar added.

Rowanstar was tearing up clumps of grass with his claws, his fur bristling with rage. "Traitors!" he screeched after the departing WindClan cats. "Cowards!"

While the leaders were distracted, Twigpaw spotted one of the rogues looming up behind Mistystar. Her belly clenched in anxiety and she let out a screech, but her warning came too late. The hulking tom barreled into Mistystar and knocked her to the ground in a whirl of waving paws. Several River-Clan cats raced up to defend their leader, and more of the rogues piled in, viciously swiping at the RiverClan warriors.

Ivypool and Tigerheart exchanged a swift glance, their argument forgotten for now, and dived back into the battle.

Twigpaw glanced from side to side, anxiously watching her battling Clanmates. Even she, an apprentice fighting in her first battle, could see clearly that the tide had turned. The Clan cats were losing. WindClan had fled, the RiverClan warriors were giving way under the pummeling of the rogues, and like Tigerheart, the ShadowClan cats were hesitant to attack their own former Clanmates.

This is a disaster! she thought despairingly. *And we planned it so carefully! How did it all go wrong?*

As Twigpaw turned around, wondering what she could do now to help her Clan, she spotted a small black-and-white cat emerging from the shadows underneath a bush. "Violetpaw!" she gasped.

Her sister halted, and the two she-cats stared at each other for a moment. Twigpaw could see that Violetpaw looked thinner and taller than when she had seen her last. Blood trickled from a scratch on one of her ears, but to Twigpaw's relief she looked mostly unhurt.

"Are you okay?" Twigpaw blurted out after a moment.

Violetpaw's eyes widened at the question. She didn't reply, and for a couple of heartbeats neither cat moved. Twigpaw knew that she should spring into attack, but every hair on her pelt shrank from the thought of hurting her sister.

"I miss you," she whispered.

Violetpaw's jaws parted as if she was about to speak, but just then a snarl came from behind her.

"What are you waiting for?"

The long-furred gray rogue, Rain, ducked out from beneath the same bush, followed by Needletail, who had grown larger and more formidable since Twigpaw had last seen her. They separated, moving to either side of Twigpaw, their eyes menacing. Twigpaw flinched back, trying to keep all three cats in view.

"She's the *enemy*," Needletail hissed to Violetpaw.

Twigpaw could hardly believe what she was hearing. *Is this the same cat who used to bring Violetpaw to play with me when we were kits?*

Rain draped his tail over Violetpaw's shoulders. "We're your kin now," he growled.

Violetpaw gave one desperate glance from Needletail to Rain and back again. Then she gathered herself and sprang at Twigpaw, claws outstretched to slash at her shoulder.

For a heartbeat, Twigpaw could do no more than stare at her, stunned; then she recovered enough to stumble backward, out of range. But before she could take more than a couple of paw steps, one of her hind paws caught in a hole behind her. She fell heavily onto her side, wrenching her leg, and she let out a screech as hot pain clawed through her body. Violetpaw stood over her, staring down with her teeth bared.

Twigpaw knew that she couldn't fight anymore. *This is when*

I go to hunt with StarClan. Oh, Violetpaw, how did we end up like this? Are you really going to strike the blow that kills me?

Then a yowl rang out from behind her and Lionblaze raced past, flinging himself on Rain and the ShadowClan cats. All three of them flinched backward in the face of his ferocious attack.

Twigpaw stared after her sister's retreating form. *Violetpaw doesn't care about me anymore,* she realized miserably. *She thinks I'm her enemy! She attacked me!*

All around Twigpaw, the battle was still raging. She could see that the Clan cats were being driven back, but she could hardly bring herself to care. Guilt flooded over her; she knew she ought to be panicking at the defeat of the Clans. But all she could think about was her sister.

CHAPTER 2

❧

The sun was dipping behind the trees at the top of the hollow, the slanting rays filtering into the medicine cats' den, as Alderheart laid one last piece of cobweb on Birchfall's shoulder wound. "It will heal well," he reassured the older warrior. "Do you want a poppy seed for the pain?"

"No." Leafpool turned from where she was tucking fresh moss around Twigpaw's drowsing form. "We need to save the poppy seeds for the cats with more serious injuries."

"That's okay," Birchfall meowed. "It doesn't hurt much anyway. Thanks, Alderheart," he added. "I'll be fine." He brushed past the bramble screen at the entrance to the den and headed out into the camp.

Alderheart joined Leafpool beside Twigpaw, who was dozing uncomfortably in her nest of moss and bracken close to the sleeping Briarlight. The apprentice's fluffy gray fur was barely visible among the thick bedding. Occasionally she let out little murmurs of pain.

"I'm worried about her," Alderheart confessed to Leafpool. "Her leg was twisted badly."

"At least it's not broken," Leafpool responded. "And the stick you and Jayfeather bound onto it will give it some support. She'll just have to stay off the leg completely until it gets better."

"That's going to take a few days," Alderheart mewed gloomily.

He was concerned about Twigpaw's other injuries, too, the long scratches on her sides and face that he had treated with marigold to protect against infection. But what worried him most of all was the heartbroken expression on Twigpaw's face before the poppy seeds had helped her to drift into sleep. He remembered her anguish as she'd told him how Violetpaw had attacked her. He knew how terrible he would feel if Sparkpelt had turned on him like that.

And Twigpaw has never had any kin but Violetpaw, he mused. *I'll do my best to look after her.*

Alderheart's thoughts were interrupted as Bramblestar stuck his head around the bramble screen.

"We're getting ready to leave for the Gathering," he meowed. "I want at least one medicine cat, but you can decide which of you is going."

He withdrew again without waiting for a reply.

"You and Jayfeather should go," Leafpool suggested immediately. "Jayfeather!" she called. "Do you want to go to the Gathering?"

Jayfeather emerged from the cleft at the back of the medicine cats' den, where he had been checking on the remaining herb stores. "I suppose," he muttered, not sounding enthusiastic. "If you're sure you can cope by yourself."

"I was coping before you were kitted," Leafpool reminded

him tartly. "I'll check on the injured warriors, and I want to keep an eye on Blossomfall. Her kits are due any day now."

"Okay," Jayfeather agreed. "Come on, Alderheart. Let's see if Onestar has any excuse for what he did during the battle."

The sun was gone, and twilight filled the stone hollow as Alderheart followed Jayfeather out into the clearing. The other cats who were to go to the Gathering were emerging from their dens to join Bramblestar. The Clan deputy, Squirrelflight, was there, along with Lionblaze and Dovewing, all of them with minor injuries from the fight that morning. Alderheart's former mentor, Molewhisker, a long gash running across his back, stood beside his sister, Cherryfall, whose tail was bound up with cobwebs. Sparkpelt trotted up to them, a clump of fur missing from her shoulder.

We really are a battered group, Alderheart thought. *A battered Clan . . .*

As he padded across the clearing to join his Clanmates, Alderheart spotted the three elders emerging from their den. Graystripe and Millie headed toward the crowd of cats around Bramblestar, but Purdy broke away from them and sidled up to Alderheart.

"I've got a bit of a bellyache," he confided in a low voice. "Do you reckon you could get me some chervil, or maybe a juniper berry, before we go?"

"You should go see Leafpool," Alderheart responded, angling his ears in the direction of the medicine-cat den. "She's staying behind to keep an eye on Blossomfall and the injured warriors."

Purdy took a step back. "I won't bother her if she's busy," he mewed. "Maybe I'll just skip the Gatherin' and sleep off the bellyache."

"If you're sure . . ."

"I'll be fine, young 'un," Purdy insisted. "You'll tell me what I missed, right?"

"Of course," Alderheart promised. "Have a good rest, Purdy."

As the old tabby tottered back toward the elders' den, Alderheart realized that Bramblestar was already heading for the thorn tunnel, leading his warriors out of the camp. The ShadowClan cats who were living with ThunderClan—Rowanstar, Tawnypelt, and Tigerheart—had joined the group and were padding along just behind Bramblestar.

As Alderheart followed his Clanmates down to the lake and along the shore, he reflected on what he had heard about the battle that morning. No cat had expected so much blood to be shed, and most of the ThunderClan warriors were blaming Onestar, who had ordered the WindClan cats to retreat and given the rogues an unexpected advantage.

Mistystar had suffered a serious wound, and many of the RiverClan warriors who had jumped in to defend her were in bad shape too. When Leafpool heard that, she had offered to go to RiverClan to help Mothwing and Willowshine treat the injured cats, but Bramblestar had forbidden it.

"Mothwing and Willowshine can handle their own Clan," he had meowed. "Leafpool, you're needed here, in *our* camp, to care for your Clanmates."

Leafpool had dipped her head in acquiescence, though Alderheart had realized she was still deeply worried about the RiverClan cats. He wondered how bad their injuries were. *Might Mistystar have lost a life?*

As he padded along the lakeshore, which was silent except for the lapping of waves against the pebbles, Alderheart could imagine the yowls and screeching of ferocious cats, the hot reek of blood, and the flashing of teeth and claws. *So much blood—and we didn't even achieve our goal.*

Still the rogues hold ShadowClan's territory.

The ThunderClan cats talked among themselves as they traveled around the lake, but they grew quiet as they approached the end of the tree-bridge that led to the island. Alderheart could see exhaustion in the faces and bodies of his Clanmates, though they raised their heads proudly as they padded along the tree trunk and jumped down on the opposite shore. He knew that they would do their best to hide any trace of weakness from the other Clans.

When the ThunderClan cats pushed their way through the bushes that surrounded the central clearing, they saw that RiverClan had already arrived. Alderheart suppressed a gasp of shock and pity when he saw Mistystar's wound, a gash running from her neck almost to her hind leg. She winced at every movement, and her eyes were filled with pain. Duskfur, Mintfur, and Reedwhisker clustered closely around her, wounds visible on their bodies too. Yet all of them stood proudly; Alderheart admired their determination to be strong.

Chatter broke out among the cats of both Clans, but it sank into silence a moment later as Onestar led the cats of Wind-Clan into the clearing.

They've got a few scratches, Alderheart thought, gazing at them with disgust. *But none of them are hurt as badly as our cats, or River-Clan's.*

From the glare of contempt that Mistystar gave Onestar, she was clearly thinking the same thing.

Alderheart and Jayfeather padded closer to the Great Oak in the center of the clearing, murmuring greetings to Mothwing and Willowshine, who were already sitting there. Kestrelflight, the WindClan medicine cat, joined them a few heartbeats later. Alderheart flashed him an awkward glance; the rest of the cats simply ignored him. Kestrelflight crouched down a tail-length away, clearly embarrassed, and said nothing.

Bramblestar and Rowanstar leaped into the branches of the Great Oak, followed closely by Onestar, who scrambled out onto a branch far away from the other two. Alderheart thought Mistystar would never make it into the tree, but she clawed her way up, her teeth set in grim determination, and collapsed onto a low branch.

"Is Rowanstar even a Clan leader anymore?" Sparkpelt whispered to Cherryfall. "The only other cats in his Clan now are his mate and his kit."

Overhearing his sister, Alderheart shifted uncomfortably. He knew that she was wrong. StarClan had given nine lives to Rowanstar, and nothing could take that away: Rowanstar had every right to sit with the other leaders. But that didn't change the fact that ShadowClan was in trouble.

Even worse trouble, after today, Alderheart reflected, a terrible thought filling his mind. A thought he could barely believe possible. *Is this the end of ShadowClan?*

"I think we all know what we need to discuss tonight," Mistystar announced, after Bramblestar had called for attention from the cats in the clearing. "Onestar, what got into you this morning? You cost us the battle when you fled and took your cats with you. And RiverClan took the worst of the damage."

"So you say," Onestar snapped.

"And how would you know?" Mistystar flashed back at him. "You weren't there, you coward! Perchwing was *killed*, and many more of my warriors were injured. All to solve a problem we did nothing to cause!"

Alderheart was startled. He hadn't realized that any cat had died in the battle. Now he understood even better the scathing contempt in Mistystar's eyes and voice as she faced the WindClan leader.

"Perhaps I should do the same as you," Mistystar went on, "and just close my borders when I don't agree with other Clans. It would certainly be easier than fighting their battles for them!"

"Mistystar, no cat wants you to do that," Bramblestar broke in, clearly trying to stay calm. "But we certainly don't blame you for feeling as you do. Onestar, in StarClan's name, *why* did you order your cats to retreat?"

"I don't have to tell you anything," Onestar meowed

defensively, his neck fur bristling. "I had my reasons."

"Yes," Rowanstar growled, "that you're a coward."

"I am *not*! But I shouldn't have to see my Clan destroyed rescuing ShadowClan from its own incompetence. My only responsibility is to WindClan."

But he didn't retreat to save his Clan, Alderheart thought. *From what Twigpaw told me, he gave the order because of something Darktail told him. Onestar is hiding something, and I would really like to know what it is.*

"But you gave your word that you would help us drive out the rogues," Rowanstar meowed. "And then you broke that word. How can any cat trust you again?"

"You're a fine one to talk!" Onestar snarled. "You and the ShadowClan cats with you were trying to protect your *former* Clanmates, the cats you were supposed to be fighting! Don't blame *me* for losing the battle!"

Rowanstar's shoulders sagged and his tail drooped, but there was still pride in his tone as he replied. "That is true, Onestar—but I do not believe that we lost our honor because we could not bring ourselves to attack our true Clanmates. Once the rogues are driven out, ShadowClan—"

"Thanks to you and Onestar," Mistystar interrupted, her voice full of bitterness, "right now the rogues don't seem anywhere close to being driven out. First of all we held back from getting rid of them because of the prophecy that told us to embrace what lay in the shadows."

"And every Clan agreed with that," Rowanstar pointed out.

Mistystar sniffed disdainfully. "It was ShadowClan who assumed they should let strange cats move onto their territory!

If you ask me, Rowanstar, you brought this on yourself."

"But—" Rowanstar began.

"We've waited too long to drive out the rogues," Mistystar retorted. "Perhaps we were once confused by the prophecy, but its meaning seems clear now: the rogues are not 'what you find in the shadows.' The rogues are what we must drive out to clear the sky!"

Rowanstar had no answer to that, and in the moment's silence that followed, Mallownose of RiverClan sprang to his paws.

"But *how*?" he asked. "The lost kits that ShadowClan and ThunderClan took in don't seem to be part of the prophecy, either," he pointed out. "We thought that by embracing them, we would find the answer. But they've been with the Clans even longer, and things here beside the lake are only getting worse."

Alderheart cast an unfriendly look at the RiverClan tom, his neck fur beginning to bristle. *Violetpaw and Twigpaw were innocent kits! You can't expect them to solve a problem like Darktail.*

At the same time, Alderheart could not help feeling frustrated. *I know what the prophecy is about—SkyClan! I just have to convince Bramblestar.*

Arguments were springing up all over the clearing, drowning out the voices of the Clan leaders. The cats sounded increasingly desperate, worrying about what the prophecy might mean.

"What if the sky *never* clears?" some cat wailed plaintively.

Snarls and hisses rose up around Alderheart. Cats were

leaping up, their fur fluffed out and their ears flattened in rage. He felt that, at any moment, the truce of the Gathering might be broken.

"Jayfeather, we have to—" he began.

Before he could get more words out, Alderheart realized that the light in the clearing was growing dim. Looking up, he saw that a cloud had begun to drift across the moon, obscuring the shining silver circle.

"Look at the moon!" Bramblestar's voice rose above the clamor in the clearing. "StarClan is angry! This Gathering is at an end."

Instantly the four leaders jumped down from the Great Oak and began to call their Clans together. The hostile snarling died away as the cats glanced anxiously up at the darkening sky and hurried to leave the island across the tree-bridge. But they still glared at one another; there were none of the friendly farewells that marked the end of an ordinary Gathering.

Alderheart felt uneasy. He wished the Gathering had lasted long enough for the Clans to work out their differences.

But then, he reflected, *that probably wouldn't have happened if we'd kept on arguing all night.*

This rift between the Clans was too deep to be easily healed. It made him more certain than ever that he had to persuade Bramblestar to tell the other Clans the truth. *For the sake of SkyClan, too,* he added to himself, remembering the wretched cats from his vision.

Alderheart was unable to relax until his Clan had crossed the bridge and was heading back to ThunderClan along the

WindClan lakeshore. Then he slipped away from Jayfeather and quickened his pace until he caught up to Bramblestar at the head of the group.

"May I speak to you?" he asked.

Bramblestar blinked at him in surprise. "Yes, of course," he replied. "If you have anything useful to say about this mess, I want to hear it."

"I think the time has come to tell the other Clans about SkyClan," Alderheart began. "No, please listen to me," he continued, when Bramblestar looked as if he was about to protest. "SkyClan lies in the shadows, hidden from all of us—and helping them would 'clear the sky.' Right?"

He realized anxiously that his leader looked taken aback, and not at all sympathetic to the idea he had suggested.

"Don't we have enough problems on our own territory," Bramblestar asked, "without taking on another difficult quest?"

"I had another vision," Alderheart told him. "The SkyClan cats are still wandering, lost and homeless—now they don't even have a medicine cat. They need our help, and I don't think StarClan would be giving me these visions if we weren't *meant* to help them." Encouraged to see that Bramblestar had begun to look more thoughtful, he added, "If the prophecy is about SkyClan, then every cat should know about them. After all, the prophecy was given to *all* the Clans, not just to me."

Bramblestar hesitated before replying, and Alderheart felt his belly tense with worry. *I'm sure it's time for the secret to be told,* he thought, *but what if Bramblestar refuses? Can I go against the orders of my father, of my Clan leader?*

Eventually Bramblestar let out a long sigh. "Perhaps you're right, Alderheart," he mewed. "I've been so ashamed of the way the Clans treated SkyClan, I never wanted any other cat to know, but maybe—with your vision guiding us—we can put things right."

Alderheart swelled with pride to see the respect in his father's eyes as Bramblestar gazed at him. *He really listened to me!* New confidence and relief surged through him like a stream released from the icy grip of leaf-bare. *Now at last we can work toward fulfilling the prophecy!*

Sunhigh was approaching as Alderheart waded through the stream that marked the border with WindClan, following Bramblestar and Squirrelflight. Lionblaze and Dovewing brought up the rear.

Facing the swell of moorland that they had to climb, Alderheart felt exhausted, hardly able to put one paw in front of another. He had barely slept the night before. After they'd returned from the Gathering, Bramblestar had told the rest of ThunderClan, and the three ShadowClan cats, all that he and Alderheart knew about SkyClan. They had all stayed up until the moon had almost set, the other cats questioning Bramblestar and Alderheart—along with Cherryfall, Molewhisker, and Sparkpelt, who had been told about SkyClan when they accompanied Alderheart on his quest—about every detail of the story.

"I'd have something to say to Needletail, if she was here," Rowanstar had meowed with a lash of his tail. "She never said a word about visiting SkyClan territory! I knew I should never have trusted her."

"She only kept it a secret because I asked her to." Alderheart had tried to defend the cat who had been his friend, especially as he still hoped that she might abandon the rogues and help the Clan cats drive them out. "I thought it was for the best."

Rowanstar had been unimpressed. "Her first loyalty should have been to ShadowClan," he growled.

As soon as the sun was up, Bramblestar had led their patrol over to RiverClan to tell them the truth. Alderheart had been very apprehensive, remembering Mistystar's justified anger at the Gathering the night before. But to his relief, the meeting had gone better than he had anticipated.

"Just what I'd expect from ThunderClan," Mintfur had snapped. "Thinking they should keep this secret to themselves—that they're the only Clan that matters!"

But Mistystar had silenced her warrior with a wave of her tail. "Is it true that you don't know how to find SkyClan?" she asked Alderheart.

Alderheart nodded. "Not yet."

"Not ever, I should hope," the elder Mosspelt muttered. "There are enough cats around the lake already."

Mistystar looked relieved at Alderheart's response. "In that case, I don't see what we can do," she mewed, then added to Bramblestar, "Just don't expect RiverClan to solve any more problems for the Clans right now. We need time to lick our wounds."

Alderheart had felt disappointed that RiverClan hadn't shown any more enthusiasm for finding the lost Clan, but at least they hadn't been upset or hostile. And he thought that Bramblestar seemed to be more relaxed, breathing more easily, now that he wasn't carrying the burden of the secret.

But how is Onestar going to react? Alderheart wondered as he toiled up the moorland slope in the paw steps of his leader. *He's been so unpredictable lately.*

A stiff breeze was blowing from the crest of the moor, flattening Alderheart's whiskers against his face. It carried the scent of many cats, fresh but distant, coming from the direction of the WindClan camp. Then, before the ThunderClan patrol had traveled more than a few fox-lengths from the border stream, a stronger scent wafted over them, and a WindClan patrol appeared from behind an outcrop of rocks.

The dark gray tom Crowfeather was in the lead, followed by Larkwing, Emberfoot, and his apprentice, Smokepaw.

Bramblestar halted and signaled to his patrol to do the same as Crowfeather stalked up to them. The WindClan cat's eyes were cold and unfriendly.

"What are you doing on WindClan territory?" he demanded. "You're not welcome here. Onestar does not want to see any cats from other Clans."

Bramblestar dipped his head politely to Crowfeather, ignoring his hostility. "I believe Onestar will want to know—" he began.

"Then you believe wrong!" Crowfeather retorted. "Onestar

is *very* upset about the accusations that were made at the Gathering."

"But we've come on important Clan business," Bramblestar argued.

"Yes," Squirrelflight added, "and it has to do with a medicine-cat vision. Come on, Crowfeather, this is us you're talking to. Have you forgotten how we all made the journey to the sun-drown-place together? You should know that we wouldn't lie to you."

Crowfeather looked briefly uncomfortable, then dug his claws hard into the rough moorland grass. "That was a long time ago," he snapped, "and I have my orders from Onestar now. Turn back, and get off our territory. Now."

Bramblestar exchanged a frustrated glance with Squirrelflight. Alderheart was afraid they would have to obey Crowfeather and leave, when he heard a yowl coming from the top of the hill and saw another WindClan patrol racing down toward them.

"What's going on?" Gorsetail, the cat in the lead, asked Crowfeather as she halted beside him. "What do these cats want?"

Her companions, Oatclaw and Featherpelt, stood a pace behind her, eyeing the ThunderClan cats warily. *We're outnumbered if it comes to a fight,* Alderheart thought.

"They say they have to speak to Onestar," Crowfeather replied. "But Onestar won't want to speak to *them*."

"We have important information for him," Bramblestar put in swiftly.

Gorsetail gazed at the ThunderClan leader for a heartbeat, drawing a gray-and-white paw over one ear. "Maybe Onestar will want to hear what another Clan leader has to tell him," she meowed eventually. "We'd better escort them to the camp."

Crowfeather looked outraged. "Are you mouse-brained?" he demanded. "You were standing right next to me when Onestar told us to keep *all* other cats out."

"Mouse-brained yourself, Crowfeather," Gorsetail responded. "Bramblestar wouldn't be here if this weren't something Onestar needed to know. I'll take responsibility, if it bothers you so much."

Crowfeather opened his jaws for a stinging retort, then clearly thought better of it. "Suit yourself," he snarled with an angry shrug. "If Onestar claws your ears off, don't come crying to me."

"I'll take the risk," Gorsetail mewed dryly.

Without bothering to respond, Crowfeather waved his tail to gather the rest of his patrol, and headed downhill toward the border.

Gorsetail watched them go, then turned to Bramblestar and the others. "Come on, ThunderClan cats," she ordered. "This had better be good."

Flanked by Oatclaw and Featherpelt, Bramblestar followed her up the slope, with Alderheart and the rest clustered behind him. As they climbed farther up, Alderheart glanced down in the direction of the horseplace and was surprised to spot a third WindClan patrol heading along the lakeshore.

Why are their borders so heavily guarded? he wondered.

When they drew close to the camp, Gorsetail sent Oat-claw racing ahead to warn Onestar of their arrival. By the time Bramblestar and his patrol crossed the lip of the hollow where WindClan had their camp, Onestar was waiting for them outside his den. As they padded down toward him, more WindClan warriors surrounded them, suspicion and hostility in their eyes and their bristling fur.

If we put one whisker out of place, I'm sure they'll tear our pelts off, Alderheart thought uneasily.

"Well, Bramblestar? What is it that you want?" Onestar demanded as Bramblestar drew closer, facing off with the WindClan leader. "If it's about the battle, you can turn around right now and get off my territory."

"This has nothing to do with the battle," Bramblestar meowed calmly. "There's something important that you ought to know. Do you remember, seasons ago, back in the old forest, when Firestar left ThunderClan for a while . . . ?"

Alderheart watched Onestar closely while Bramblestar told the story that no other Clan had heard until now: how Firestar had been led to the gorge by a vision of a SkyClan ancestor and had helped renew the lost SkyClan. Outrage grew on the WindClan leader's face with every word that Bramblestar spoke.

"So ThunderClan has been lying all this time?" he burst out when Bramblestar had finished. "I should have known you couldn't be trusted, Bramblestar—you or Firestar before you!"

"No cat has lied to any cat!" Squirrelflight retorted, stung. "But Firestar saw no reason to spread the story around, and neither did Bramblestar—until now."

Onestar let out a snort of disgust. "So what has changed?"

For answer, Bramblestar gestured with his tail for Alderheart to step forward. Alderheart's belly roiled with nerves as he faced the WindClan leader's hostile stare, but he managed to keep his voice steady as he explained about his visions.

"I'm sure that the prophecy is StarClan's way of telling us that we need to help SkyClan," he finished.

Onestar's lips curled back in the beginning of a snarl, and he gave a furious lash of his tail. "So you want my support to help some strange Clan that only ThunderClan has ever heard of?" he rasped. "Are you planning to bring them here and give them WindClan territory? You won't get the chance!"

Angry growls came from some of the listening WindClan warriors. Alderheart saw Lionblaze and Dovewing slide out their claws, and he knew that they were bracing themselves in case Onestar gave the order to attack the visitors.

"We don't intend that at all," Bramblestar responded, still managing to stay calm. "Alderheart, tell Onestar about your quest."

Still uneasy, Alderheart began the story of how he and his Clanmates had made the long journey to the gorge where Sky-Clan had their camp, only to find that they had been driven out by rogues.

"They were the same rogues who attacked you here in WindClan," he explained. "The same who have taken over ShadowClan territory."

As he spoke, Alderheart saw the anger in Onestar's eyes be

overtaken by shock and horror. For a heartbeat, the Wind-Clan leader seemed too frozen even to speak. "So Darktail was to blame for SkyClan being driven from the gorge?" he asked eventually. "And nearly destroyed?"

Alderheart nodded.

Onestar was silent for a few heartbeats more. Then rage seemed to fill him up and spill over like water from an upturned leaf in pelting rain. "WindClan owes SkyClan nothing!" he screeched. "And you ThunderClan cats need to get out! Go on—get off my territory! WindClan's borders are closed!"

Alderheart exchanged a stunned look with Bramblestar and the rest of the patrol. *What's all that about?* he asked himself. *What's making Onestar so furious?*

Though Bramblestar tried to protest, Onestar refused to listen. His warriors gathered around the ThunderClan leader and his patrol, herding them back up the side of the hollow and onto the moor.

"I'll escort you to the border," Gorsetail meowed, beckoning a few more cats to join her with a whisk of her tail.

The ThunderClan cats headed downhill in silence; clearly there would be no point in trying to talk to the WindClan warriors. As he padded along beside his leader, Alderheart couldn't forget the horrified look on Onestar's face.

I thought so before, but now I'm sure of it, he told himself. *Onestar is hiding something!*

CHAPTER 3

❧

Violetpaw grimaced at the reek of mouse bile as she dabbed the scrap of soaked moss on one of Oakfur's ticks. The ShadowClan elder let out a sigh of relief as the tick dropped off.

"That's better, youngster," he meowed. "I only wish we could put everything right in ShadowClan as easily as we deal with these pesky ticks. Nothing is the same as it used to be. With Rowanstar gone, no cat treats elders with respect."

"Darktail says we're not ShadowClan anymore," Violetpaw responded grimly. "He says we're Kin now."

"I'll be ShadowClan until I die," Oakfur declared with an angry twitch of his ears; alarmed, Violetpaw glanced around to make sure that none of the rogues were listening. "Loyalty is important; that's what some of you young cats don't understand."

"That's true," Ratscar agreed. He paused for a moment, scratching furiously behind one ear with his hind paw, then added, "Cats aren't what they were in our day. These kits Snowbird just delivered—I wonder what sort of world they'll grow up in."

Violetpaw flinched. Perhaps she should be worrying about

the tiny kits Puddleshine had helped deliver, but instead, she couldn't help remembering the battle and the look in Twigpaw's eyes when Violetpaw had attacked her. *I hurt my own sister!* she thought, sure that she would never shake off the guilt. *Would I actually have struck her while she was injured?* She couldn't answer that question, and felt wretched. *Oakfur must be right: young cats like me don't understand loyalty.*

There was a flurry of paw steps, and the bramble tendrils that overhung the elders' den waved wildly as Needletail barged inside.

"I've been looking for you everywhere!" she meowed to Violetpaw, ignoring the two old toms. "Why are you messing around with that gross mouse bile and ticks? You should come with me and have something to eat."

"Dawnpelt told me to come and help the elders," Violetpaw explained, dropping the twig with the bile-soaked moss.

Needletail flicked her tail dismissively. "Dawnpelt isn't the boss of you anymore," she pointed out. "Darktail and Rain are right—the elders need to start looking after themselves. We don't have room for cats who don't contribute."

Ratscar fixed her with a glare. "There was a time Shadow-Clan didn't have room for rude little flea-pelts," he rasped.

"*I'm* not the one who has fleas," Needletail sneered. "Are you coming, Violetpaw?"

Violetpaw cast a guilty look at the elders. "Okay," she mewed.

"Hey, you haven't finished!" Oakfur protested. "There's a huge tick right down my back next to my tail. I can feel it!"

Violetpaw would rather have stayed to help, but Needletail was waiting for her, her tail-tip giving impatient twitches.

"Sorry," Violetpaw whispered, and followed her friend out into the camp.

Needletail led the way to the fresh-kill pile, where Thistle, a muscular gray rogue, was sniffing around the edge, taking his time to choose. Needletail picked out a blackbird for herself. Violetpaw spotted a plump vole and whisked it away; her jaws watered as she crouched beside Needletail to eat it.

But before she had taken more than a mouthful, Thistle bounded toward them. Violetpaw eyed him warily. She didn't know him very well, as he and some other rogues had only recently arrived. She couldn't help wondering how many more cats Darktail would welcome into camp as "Kin."

Where will it all end?

Thistle padded up and halted beside Violetpaw, his cold blue eyes fixed on her succulent piece of prey. "That was *mine*," he snarled, obviously expecting Violetpaw to step back and let him take it. "I saw it first." He took a pace forward, looming over Violetpaw.

Violetpaw would have given him the vole to avoid a fight, but before she could move, Needletail broke in.

"Hey, back off, mange-fur!" she challenged Thistle, baring her teeth and letting out a furious hiss. "Prey is not yours until you take it."

"Okay, okay," Thistle meowed. "Keep your fur on." With a furious glare he headed back to the fresh-kill pile and started pawing over the prey again.

"Thanks, Needletail," Violetpaw murmured. "I wish there weren't so many rogues in camp these days. Some of them look kind of scary."

"Huh!" Needletail snorted around a mouthful of blackbird. "They're all meow and no claws, if you ask me. But you don't need to worry, Violetpaw. I'll look out for you." She tore off another mouthful, swallowed, and then added more thoughtfully, "Mind you, Rain is suspicious of some of these new rogues, just like you."

Violetpaw wasn't sure what to make of that. *I know Needletail likes Rain, but I'm not sure I trust him, either. He challenged Darktail and got blinded for his trouble. I'm still not sure whether he's supporting Darktail now. Is he still questioning him?*

She gulped down her vole, casting sidelong glances at Needletail as she did so.

"Have you got something on your mind?" Needletail asked. "Spit it out!"

Violetpaw hesitated for a moment, then took a deep breath. "I can't stop thinking about hurting Twigpaw," she confided shyly. "I feel so bad about it. I didn't *mean* to hurt her, but she was trying to get away from me and she hurt her leg. What if . . ." Under Needletail's intent gaze she found words for her greatest fear. "What if I've crippled my sister?"

Needletail touched her nose reassuringly to Violetpaw's ear. "No cat ever got crippled from a little fall like that," she stated. "Twigpaw will be fine. You *had* to fight her, Violetpaw. ThunderClan and the other cats attacked *us*, didn't they? The Clan cats are our enemies now. And that includes Twigpaw."

Violetpaw listened, knowing that what her friend was saying made sense, but still unable to shake off her feeling that
something was terribly wrong. *How can my sister be my enemy?*

"You did what you had to do," Needletail went on. "And
now you need to forget about Twigpaw. We're your kin now—
me and the rest of the cats here. We're the ones who care
about you."

Violetpaw couldn't find words to protest. *But whatever
Needletail says, I can't forget my sister!*

"I'm going to take a mouse to Puddleshine," Violetpaw
announced when she had finished her prey. "He's working so
hard, looking after the injured warriors, and I'm sure he's not
taking time to eat."

"Good idea," Needletail meowed. "I'll come with you. I
want to see how Darktail's doing."

Violetpaw tidied up the fresh-kill pile, which Thistle had
left scattered, and found a juicy-looking mouse for Puddleshine. Needletail padded beside her as she carried it to the
medicine-cat den.

Puddleshine's den lay in the farthest corner of the camp,
where the bushes and bramble tendrils didn't cluster so
thickly. But there was a sheltered space under a slanting rock,
the ground thickly covered with moss and bracken, where
Puddleshine and any injured cats could sleep.

When Violetpaw and Needletail entered by a tunnel
through the brambles, the only cat there apart from Puddleshine was Darktail. He lay stretched out on the bedding,
his chest heaving with each breath. Violetpaw had heard how

badly Onestar had injured him in the battle; now she could see the pain in his slitted eyes. Needletail padded over and sat beside him; he could barely raise his head to see which cats had come to visit him.

"Puddleshine, I brought you this," Violetpaw mewed as she set the mouse down in front of the medicine cat.

Puddleshine fixed the mouse with a hungry gaze. "Thank you, Violetpaw! I'm starving—my belly thinks my throat's been clawed out!" He crouched and began to gulp down the mouse with ravenous bites.

"Violetpaw," he mumbled a moment later, around a mouthful of prey, "could you chew up some of that coltsfoot for me? It should help Darktail with his breathing." He pointed with one paw to a small heap of coltsfoot flowers at the foot of the rock.

"Sure." Violetpaw padded over to the coltsfoot and began chewing some of the flowers into a pulp; they had a sharp, quite pleasant taste.

"That's fine." Puddleshine joined her a moment later, swiping his tongue around his jaws as he swallowed the last bite of mouse. "Now let's give it to Darktail."

The rogue leader managed to raise himself and lick up the pulp, then sank back into his bedding with a grunt. "That mange-pelt Onestar really hurt me," he growled. "He was a far fiercer fighter than I expected from our last battle."

He took a few deep breaths, seeming to find it easier after the coltsfoot, and turned his head to give Violetpaw a long stare. Her pads prickled with apprehension. *What does*

Darktail think about me now?

"You fought well in the battle," the rogue leader mewed at last. "You're a credit to the Kin here."

Relief that he wasn't angry flooded over Violetpaw. Her pelt warmed at her leader's praise, even though she felt that she didn't deserve it.

"Violetpaw's worried about wounding her littermate," Needletail put in.

Violetpaw's nervousness returned, an even sharper prickling. She wished Needletail hadn't mentioned that. *What if Darktail gets angry now?*

But Darktail gave her an understanding nod. "I know it must have been hard to choose between your littermate and your new Kin," he told Violetpaw. "I'm proud of you for making the right choice."

Violetpaw dipped her head, flattered. *Maybe Darktail's not so scary after all.* She felt her guilt over Twigpaw ease a little. *Twigpaw and I were born together, but these cats have chosen me to be their Kin. Maybe Darktail and Needletail are right: I chose to fight for the cats who are important to me.*

A rustling sound came from the tunnel through the brambles, and Rain pushed his way into the den. Violetpaw noticed that his injured eye was almost healed. "Greetings, Darktail," the gray tom mewed, with a nod to his leader. "How are you feeling?"

"Better," Darktail replied. "I'm glad you came; there are some things I need to discuss with you. What did you think about the way Grassheart fought in the battle?"

Rain shrugged. "Well, I've seen fiercer cats," he responded.

Darktail's tone sharpened. "Do you think she's a traitor?"

Rain hesitated for a moment, then shook his head. "No, I think she could just do with a bit of extra training. Now, Dawnpelt . . . there's a cat who needs watching."

"You think so?"

Violetpaw's pelt itched uncomfortably, as if ants were crawling through it, as she listened to the two rogues discussing her Clanmates. *Do they ever talk about me like that?* she wondered.

While Darktail and Rain were conferring, Needletail crept out of the den, but Violetpaw lingered a little longer, easing herself back into the shadows. Though she didn't like what she was overhearing, she was pleased to see how well the two cats were getting along.

It hasn't been that long since Rain challenged Darktail for the leadership and Darktail half blinded him, she reflected. She felt warmed and comforted at the thought that the larger group of cats—the ones Darktail had started to call their Kin—was more important to them than their rivalry.

Darktail's comments and replies to Rain grew shorter as the wounded leader grew tired, and eventually he settled down to sleep.

"I ought to go and check on some of the other injured cats," Puddleshine meowed when he was settled, "but I don't want to leave Darktail alone." He was turning to Violetpaw, as if he was about to ask her to stay, and Violetpaw would have been happy to offer, but Rain forestalled them before either of them could speak.

"Don't worry, Puddleshine. I'll stay until you come back."

"Thanks, Rain." Puddleshine gathered a few herbs and went out.

Violetpaw followed him and wandered around the camp for a while, wondering if she ought to go back and finish off the elders' ticks. But she knew she would only get another lecture about how worthless the young cats of today were, compared with Oakfur and Ratscar when they were young.

Finally she decided to find a good piece of prey and take it to Darktail for when he woke up. *He's pretty badly hurt, and he was really kind to me about how I fought in the battle. He ought to eat well so he can build up his strength while he's recovering.*

Violetpaw headed for the fresh-kill pile and took her time picking out a plump shrew. She spotted Puddleshine on the far side of the camp, making Scorchfur stretch out his leg to show how his injured shoulder was healing. Carrying the prey in her jaws, she headed back to the medicine-cat den.

But when she emerged from the bramble tunnel, she halted in shock, letting the shrew drop from her gaping jaws. Rain was lying on top of Darktail, his paws over the rogue leader's nose and mouth. Darktail was struggling feebly and making a terrible choking noise.

Violetpaw stifled a gasp of horror, realizing that Rain was trying to cut off Darktail's air and kill him. *Rain hasn't forgiven Darktail at all!*

Frozen by the sight in front of her, all Violetpaw could do was watch as Darktail's struggles grew slower. When the big tom was finally still, blood staining the fur around his nose and mouth, Rain rose to his paws, turned, and spotted Violetpaw. His green eyes narrowed, and he began to stride slowly toward her.

Violetpaw had never been so frightened in her life. Her heart thrummed in her chest and she could barely breathe. *I wasn't supposed to see that,* she thought, terror turning her muscles to stone so that she couldn't even flee. *Now he will kill me, too!*

Before Rain could reach her, he was attacked by a flash of white.

Darktail was not dead.

Violetpaw flattened herself to the ground as the rogue leader reared up over Rain. She didn't want to watch, but she couldn't tear her gaze away as Darktail hurled himself forward and drew his claws across Rain's throat with a single powerful slash.

Rain staggered, his mouth opening and blood spilling over the fur on his chest. The stench of it filled the medicine-cat den. Then Rain's legs gave way and he dropped at Darktail's paws. Choking back a screech of terror, Violetpaw flinched away to avoid the sticky stream of blood that flowed from his throat.

Darktail looked down at the long-furred gray tom's spasmodically jerking body, then raised his head to meet Violetpaw's horrified gaze. His voice was rough and hoarse as he spoke.

"I always knew that Rain would betray me."

CHAPTER 4

Alderheart passed his paws carefully down Twigpaw's leg, feeling the muscles and bone beneath. The young she-cat didn't react at all, just stared dully at nothing.

"How is she doing?" Leafpool asked, looking up from where she was helping Briarlight with her stretching exercises.

"Much better," Alderheart replied. "Her leg was only badly wrenched, after all, not broken. Did I hurt you just then?" he asked Twigpaw, who just shook her head in answer.

"That's great!" Briarlight meowed cheerfully. "But I'll miss you, Twigpaw, when you go back to the apprentices' den."

"I'm sure Twigpaw will come back to visit," Alderheart reassured her.

Twigpaw only sighed; Alderheart wasn't sure whether she was actually listening. He wished he knew what he could do or say to cheer her up: the young apprentice had been depressed ever since her encounter with Violetpaw during the battle.

"Tell me again about Blossomfall's kits," Briarlight begged. "I can't believe she's a mother now! It seems like it was only yesterday she and I were playing together in the nursery."

"She'll be a good mother," Leafpool mewed. She stifled a

yawn. She and Alderheart had been up half the night helping to deliver the new litter. "It's good to see new life beginning. It gives me hope, even in the middle of all this trouble among the Clans."

"Are their eyes open yet?" Briarlight asked.

"No, it'll be a few days," Alderheart told her, keeping an eye on Twigpaw as he spoke. "But all four of them seem healthy and strong."

"Let me see if I can remember their names," Briarlight murmured. "Stemkit, Eaglekit, Plumkit . . . and what's the fourth one? Oh—Shellkit! They're beautiful names, and I'm sure the kits are beautiful, too. I can't wait to see them!"

Alderheart stifled a *mrrow* of laughter. "You should have seen Thornclaw last night. We had a hard time keeping him calm while Blossomfall was giving birth."

"True." Leafpool's amber eyes gleamed with amusement. "He might be a senior warrior, but this is his first litter of kits, and it made him as nervous as an apprentice on his first hunt."

All the time he had been talking, Alderheart had watched Twigpaw. He had thought she would surely be interested in the new kits, but once again she hardly seemed to be listening.

"You'll be fine now, Twigpaw," he mewed, rising to his paws and feeling himself sway a little with weariness.

"If you're done checking on her, you might as well duck into the apprentices' den to get some sleep," Leafpool suggested. "I was able to get some rest this morning, but you've been on your paws ever since Blossomfall's pains began just after moonhigh."

"Okay," Alderheart agreed, feeling more tired than ever at the thought of collapsing into sleep.

"On the way, you could find Jayfeather and tell him to come back," Leafpool meowed. "He left to get something to eat, but he's had enough time to go to the horseplace and return."

Alderheart nodded, though privately he doubted that he— or any other cat—could make Jayfeather do anything he didn't want to. Despite this, he dutifully padded out into the clearing and looked around for the other medicine cat.

The first cat he spotted was Purdy, drowsing in a patch of sunlight near the fresh-kill pile. Remembering the old cat's bellyache on the night of the Gathering, Alderheart hurried over to him.

"How are you feeling, Purdy?" he asked.

Purdy blinked up at him. "Better, thanks," he replied. "The bellyache comes an' goes, y'know?"

"Should I get you some juniper berries now?"

Purdy flicked an ear. "No, I'll manage. At my age, a bit o' bellyache is nothin' to worry about. I'll just take it easy at the fresh-kill pile for a couple o' days."

"If you're sure . . . ," Alderheart mewed.

"Sure I'm sure. Herbs can't fix everythin', young whipper-snapper. I remember one time . . . ," Purdy began, but the rest of the story was lost in a massive yawn.

"Well, make sure you come to the medicine-cat den if the pain gets any worse," Alderheart told him.

Purdy let out a rumbling purr. "I will . . . I know I can count on you." He rested his nose on his paws and drifted into sleep.

Alderheart looked down at him for a moment until raised voices distracted him. He turned and let out a groan as he spotted Rowanstar and Bramblestar, nose to nose and in the middle of an argument.

"Not *again*," he muttered.

"It's obvious what we have to do now!" Rowanstar snapped. "We must organize another attack, and take back Shadow-Clan territory."

"I don't disagree with that." Bramblestar sounded as if he was finding it hard to hold on to his temper. "But we have to take our time and make a plan, instead of just dashing in like foxes after a rabbit."

Rowanstar glared at him. "You're just making excuses."

"Excuses?" Bramblestar's tone grew cold. "Have you forgotten that WindClan has closed its borders, and that RiverClan has refused to commit to more fighting, at least for now? You're expecting ThunderClan to carry this battle alone."

As the leaders spoke, Alderheart noticed that Jayfeather was sitting close by, with his brother, Lionblaze, and Lionblaze's mate, Cinderheart. Jayfeather and Cinderheart were openly following the argument, their ears pricked with interest, while Lionblaze simply looked embarrassed; the golden-furred tom was pretending to groom himself, though Alderheart could tell from how he would break off after every tongue stroke that he was paying close attention to the two leaders. Tawnypelt, too, was listening, a couple of tail-lengths away from the others.

Alderheart padded over to join his Clanmates, and

Cinderheart brushed a friendly tail over his shoulder as he sat next to her.

"I would never have thought that ThunderClan could be such *cowards*," Rowanstar hissed nastily.

At once, Lionblaze stopped his grooming and half rose to his paws, glaring furiously at the ShadowClan leader. He only sat down again when Cinderheart leaned closer to him and murmured something into his ear.

"And *I* would never have thought I'd hear that from you, Rowanstar," Bramblestar retorted. "If you and the other ShadowClan cats hadn't hesitated to attack your former Clan-mates, maybe the battle would have gone better." Whirling to face Alderheart and Jayfeather, he added, "Tell this excuse for a leader that my warriors are too badly injured to stage another attack."

Alderheart nodded, while Jayfeather replied, "Send them into battle again before their wounds are healed, and you will have *dead* cats on your conscience, Rowanstar."

Before Rowanstar could retaliate, Tawnypelt rose to her paws and took a step forward. "There must be another way . . . ," she began.

Both her brother and her mate glared at her. "Keep out of this," Rowanstar snapped.

"Yes, this is leaders' business," Bramblestar added.

Tawnypelt gave a single lash of her tail. "Are you complete mouse-brains?" she snarled. "This is every cat's business. I still have *kin* in that camp, in case you've forgotten!"

By now, Alderheart realized, more of his Clanmates were gathering around to listen. Most of them looked furious: he guessed this was because they had heard Rowanstar accuse them of being cowards.

As his gaze passed over them, Alderheart spotted one cat who was glaring in another direction: Ivypool was watching Tigerheart and Dovewing, where they were sitting together, and she looked both irritated and anxious.

I wonder what that's *all about.*

"Rowanstar's got a lot of nerve," Cinderheart mewed quietly to Lionblaze, "expecting ThunderClan to fight his battles for him." With a flick of her tail she added, "If most of the ShadowClan cats want Darktail to be their leader, maybe ThunderClan shouldn't be fighting for Rowanstar at all. Is it really our business?"

Shock and confusion spread through Alderheart from ears to tail-tip. *StarClan chose Rowanstar to be leader, and gave him nine lives,* he thought. *To refuse to defend that would be a violation of the warrior code.*

The camp began to blur in front of Alderheart's eyes. He blinked to clear his vision, realizing how weary he was.

"Jayfeather, Leafpool wants you in the medicine cats' den," he meowed, and added to the other cats, "I'll see you later."

Then he headed to the quiet of the apprentices' den, behind its barrier of ferns, where he settled into his nest and closed his eyes. He sank at once into sleep, as if he were gently falling into a dark lake.

* * *

Alderheart opened his eyes and found himself on the edge of a large group of cats.

The other cats were thin, their pelts ragged, and they lay stretched out or curled up, sleeping, as if they were all exhausted. Suddenly Alderheart recognized them.

These are the cats of SkyClan. I'm having another vision!

Although he looked closely, he could not see Echosong among them. Sorrowfully, he realized that she must really have died when he'd seen her in the hollow beside the pool.

Glancing around, Alderheart tried to work out where they were. At first he was confused. Walls of gray stone rose up all around him, with light slanting in from narrow openings near the top. The floor was hard stone, too, covered with heaps of straw.

This must be some kind of Twoleg den.

Then he remembered the place where he and Needletail had sheltered from the rain on their way back from the gorge, where Sandstorm had visited him in a dream and told him to find a different path. This could be the same yellow barn. There were no horses here now, but the wooden barriers dividing the den into sections were in the same place.

If this is that barn, then the SkyClan cats aren't so far away!

Movement in the shadows caught Alderheart's eye, and he saw a gray tom emerge from behind one of the heaps of straw, the limp body of a mouse in his jaws. He padded across the stone floor and laid the mouse down beside a queen whose belly was swollen with kits.

Alderheart had never noticed this particular cat before. He must have overlooked him, distracted by Echosong's suffering, in his previous vision. He had the same gray pelt as Twigpaw, and when he looked up after laying down the mouse, Alderheart saw that he had amber eyes the same size and shape as Violetpaw's.

Excitement tingled through Alderheart's fur, his heart beating harder.

Every cat is sure that Twigpaw and Violetpaw's mother must be dead, he thought. *But could this cat be their kin? Are the two kits lost members of SkyClan?*

Alderheart sprang to his paws, wanting to observe the gray tom more closely. But at the same moment, harsh sounds fell on his ears, and he startled awake to find himself back in the apprentices' den.

He let out a hiss of annoyance at the raised voices coming from outside. This time they belonged to Ivypool and Tigerheart, but the topic was still the same: whether ThunderClan should attack the rogues again.

Frustration coursed through Alderheart at the sudden interruption of his vision, especially when he felt he had been on the verge of discovering vital information. He squeezed his eyes tight shut, committing every detail of the vision to memory so that he could be sure not to forget a single thing.

Then he opened his eyes again, already knowing what his next move must be.

Could Twigpaw and Violetpaw be SkyClan cats? I need to talk to Bramblestar!

CHAPTER 5

❧

Twigpaw lay in her nest in the apprentices' den. Daylight still filtered in through the screen of ferns, but her leg was aching and she felt like going to sleep.

It's not like I've got anything better to do, she thought. She had been excused from her apprentice duties until her leg was stronger, and she couldn't work up any enthusiasm for finding something to eat or talking to any of the other cats.

The only cat I really want to talk to is Violetpaw, and that's not going to happen.

Twigpaw loved the Clanmates she had grown up with, but Violetpaw had always been the most important cat in her life. They were each other's true kin.

"Isn't that what matters?" she sighed aloud. She wished she could ask Violetpaw if she really believed what Needletail had said. Did Violetpaw really think that they weren't kin anymore?

Twigpaw was curling up to sleep when she heard Bramblestar's voice ringing out across the camp.

"Let all cats old enough to catch their own prey join here beneath the Highledge for a Clan meeting!"

In spite of her gloomy thoughts, Twigpaw was intrigued. She brushed her way through the ferns and limped into the clearing to hear what was going on.

Bramblestar stood on the Highledge outside his den, with Squirrelflight flanking him on one side and all three medicine cats standing on the other. A buzz of speculation rose from the ThunderClan cats as they gathered beneath the ledge in the rock face to hear what their leader had to say.

"This *has* to be important," Whitewing meowed as she sat beside her mate, Birchfall. "Maybe Bramblestar has thought of a way of getting rid of the rogues at last."

"Watch out for flying hedgehogs," Birchfall responded, flexing his wounded shoulder.

Twigpaw went to sit beside Lilyheart, who had been her foster mother when she first came to ThunderClan. The small tabby she-cat turned to her with a *mrrow* of welcome and gave her shoulder a friendly lick.

"Are you feeling better?" she asked.

Twigpaw didn't want to share her worries with any cat, even Lilyheart. "My leg will be fine," she replied.

"Cats of ThunderClan!" Bramblestar began to speak, and the chatter in the clearing died down. "The time for secrets is past. Alderheart, tell the Clan about your latest vision."

Alderheart stepped forward, looking slightly embarrassed to be addressing the whole Clan from the Highledge.

"I have seen the SkyClan cats again," he announced. "I believe I know where they are: in a barn where I took shelter on the way back from my quest, not very far from here.

I think that ThunderClan should send out another search party to find the lost SkyClan cats. They looked so skinny and exhausted; I fear that they need our help, urgently."

Pity for the cats Alderheart described flowed through Twigpaw, but at the same time, she wondered what kind of help the Clans could give. *Haven't we got enough trouble right now?*

Alderheart's last words were almost lost as the cats in the clearing began to yowl out questions and protests. Rowanstar sprang to his paws, his eyes glaring with outrage.

"I've never heard such a load of bat droppings!" he exclaimed. "We should be focusing on what's going on *here*—the rogues taking over ShadowClan."

"That's right," Birchfall meowed, while several of the other Clan cats murmured their agreement. "We have to deal with what's in front of us before we rush off on a new adventure."

"Yes," Berrynose added, giving a dismissive flick of his tail. "The *last* journey cats went on because of Alderheart's visions didn't turn out so well, did it?"

Twigpaw felt as if her insides were being clawed out by badgers when she heard Berrynose's words and realized that many of his Clanmates agreed with him. *Are they saying that they regret finding me and my sister?*

She felt sorry for Alderheart, too, as he looked down at his paws, even more embarrassed. Sparkpelt, who was sitting next to Berrynose, gave the cream-colored cat a hard shove.

"It's easy for a cat to say that when all *he* did was stay at home getting fat on prey!"

Berrynose turned his head to hiss at Sparkpelt, but said nothing more.

"I don't agree." Whitewing spoke up, with an apologetic glance at her mate, Birchfall. "It's obvious to me—SkyClan must be the sky that will clear from StarClan's prophecy. Surely we *need* to find them? If we learned anything from the battle against the Dark Forest, it's that living cats must listen to StarClan."

Some of the cats were nodding, clearly appreciating what Whitewing had said, but Twigpaw spotted Larksong and Hollytuft exchanging a dubious glance, and even Alderheart looked doubtful for a heartbeat. Twigpaw could understand that. Like her, the younger cats hadn't been born at the time of the Great Battle. It was hard to imagine fighting with spirit cats on your side, and even harder to think of facing their claws and teeth in combat.

"There's something else," Alderheart continued, raising his voice to be heard above the discussion going on in the clearing. "One of the cats in my vision looked so much like Twigpaw, I think he might be her kin."

Twigpaw stared at him, feeling as if a massive rock had just hit her in the belly. For a few heartbeats she couldn't even breathe. *I might have* kin, *besides Violetpaw?* She was sure that her mother was dead, and she had never even thought about other kin. *I might have a father out there! Or my mother or father might have had littermates who would be glad to know me.* A warm, confused feeling rushed over her. *Maybe I'm not as alone as I thought.*

"If this cat is kin to Twigpaw," Alderheart went on, "then

the lost kits have always been linked to SkyClan. The prophecy might depend on us bringing them together."

Twigpaw flexed her claws in and out with excitement. *Not only kin, but perhaps a whole Clan out there that's tied to me!*

But to her dismay, none of the other cats seemed to be much affected by Alderheart's announcement.

"There are a lot of ifs and perhaps in what you're saying," Cloudtail pointed out, lifting a paw to examine his claws. "If you ask me, all this talk of visions is a lot of thistle-fluff. You had a vivid dream, that's all."

"Excuse *me*," Jayfeather snapped from where he stood beside Alderheart. "Medicine cats know the difference between dreams and visions."

"Sure, and I'm a starling," Cloudtail muttered, but not loud enough for his words to carry up to the Highledge.

"Well, *I* think we should take this vision seriously," Dovewing meowed, with an exasperated glance at Cloudtail. "I think we should send a patrol to look for SkyClan and offer them whatever help we can. I'd be happy to lead it."

"I'll join you," Lionblaze added, though he didn't sound as certain as Dovewing. "If you think we can be spared from defending the Clan, Bramblestar."

"I could go with them." Sparkpelt's eyes were gleaming with excitement. "I remember where that barn is."

"I'll go, too," Tigerheart volunteered, touching Dovewing on the shoulder with the tip of his tail.

Instantly Rowanstar sprang to his paws. "You will not!" he growled.

Tigerheart was unmoved by his leader's anger. "You don't want ShadowClan to have a paw in this affair?" he asked. "After all, the prophecy was made to all the Clans, so it should not be just ThunderClan that investigates."

Rowanstar's only response was a bad-tempered snort. He sat down again, his tail twitching to and fro.

"I think you're all wrong!" Ivypool had risen now; Twigpaw was surprised by the depth of passion in her voice. "I'd like to find Twigpaw's kin as much as any cat, but we can't be sure that the cat Alderheart saw is connected to her. And right now we're in the middle of a fight with the rogues. They've taken over ShadowClan; what if they come for *us* next? ThunderClan doesn't have any responsibility to SkyClan—we owe no Clan anything, and I think we should focus on our own problems right now. It's not like any of the Clan cats who originally drove SkyClan out of the forest are still around."

Twigpaw's excitement ebbed away, leaving behind a vast well of hurt and confusion. *Ivypool's my mentor. I thought she would always have my back. Why is she turning against me like this?*

"Ivypool's right," Poppyfrost meowed. "This is no time to weaken our Clan by sending warriors away."

"Yes." Thornclaw spoke up from where he sat at the entrance to the nursery. "If the rogues attack us here, what's going to happen to my kits?"

"Can we afford to help SkyClan when we're in such danger ourselves?" Cherryfall added.

Twigpaw felt even more hurt that more cats were agreeing

with Ivypool. *Don't they understand how important this is—not just for me, but for the whole Clan?* Her belly felt as hollow as if she hadn't eaten for a moon. "But what about *me?*" she asked suddenly, without really planning to. Several stunned faces turned toward her—some having the decency to look a bit guilty. "Don't I have the right to find my kin, if they're out there?"

Lilyheart, her foster mother, stepped forward and looked at Twigpaw with sympathy. "Of course you do, Twigpaw," she said gently. "But"—Twigpaw felt a pang in her heart with that *but*—"when you're part of a Clan, you must put your needs aside for the good of the Clan. Perhaps right now is not the best time for you to look for your kin."

Twigpaw could feel her ears turning hot with embarrassment and hurt. She looked down at the ground, unable to believe that her Clanmates were seriously going to prevent her from finding her kin. When the discussion had continued for a few moments more, Bramblestar took a pace forward and raised one paw for silence. "I've heard the arguments on both sides now," he began. "Alderheart, I'm grateful that you've shared your vision with us. Eventually I mean for us to do everything we can to help these cats. And Twigpaw, I do understand how important it is for you to find your kin—someday. But the Clan has spoken, and I agree with the majority of our warriors. For now, we must put our own safety first. We will not go to look for SkyClan." He raised his paw again to cut off protests from Dovewing and Tigerheart. "We need all our warriors to stay on ThunderClan territory until we know what the rogues are going to do next. Alderheart, let me know if you have any more visions."

Bramblestar turned away and went back into his den, followed by Squirrelflight. The three medicine cats made their way down the tumbled rocks, while the rest of the Clan began to disperse.

For a moment, Twigpaw couldn't move at all. She felt utterly miserable and betrayed, as if she were sitting at the center of a gray storm cloud. Then she spotted Ivypool heading toward her with a look of concern and apology on her face. But Twigpaw didn't want to talk to any cat. She rose to her paws, turned her back on Ivypool, and limped away.

First Violetpaw, then Ivypool, and then Lilyheart, she thought wretchedly. *Now I know for certain: I can't expect any cat to be on my side. . . .*

CHAPTER 6
❧

"Tell me again." Needletail's *voice was* taut with desperation. "Tell me again what happened."

Violetpaw flinched. She didn't want to revisit the horror of what she had witnessed in Puddleshine's den, but she knew that she had to tell her friend the truth.

"Rain tried to kill Darktail while he lay injured," she replied. "He pressed down on top of him and tried to stop his breathing. He thought he'd done it, but when he turned his back, Darktail reared up and . . . and he clawed out his throat." Her voice shook, and she had to make a massive effort to continue. "I'm sorry, Needletail, but Darktail was only defending himself, just like he told every cat. And he defended me, too," she added. "I'm sure Rain would have killed me, because I saw what he tried to do."

Needletail didn't reply; she just crouched at the foot of a pine tree, looking miserable.

"I know how much you cared about Rain," Violetpaw went on. "And I know that this must be very hard for you. Come on," she mewed, trying to encourage Needletail. "Let's go on looking for prey. You know Darktail wanted us to bring back as much as we can find, and we've already caught quite a bit. You're such a terrific hunter, I'm sure you can find more."

Needletail's neck fur began to bristle. "I don't want to catch prey because *Darktail* says so," she muttered.

"But it's important for us to show our loyalty to the Kin right now," Violetpaw pointed out.

Needletail glanced up, alarm in her green eyes. "Do you think Darktail doubts my loyalty?" she asked.

Violetpaw shook her head. "No." *I hope he doesn't,* she added silently to herself.

With a sigh, Needletail rose to her paws and headed farther into the trees. Violetpaw followed her, ears pricked for the sound of prey, parting her jaws to taste the air. A few heartbeats later, Needletail halted and angled her ears toward a spot where the ground fell away into a small hollow; at the bottom, ferns grew around a pool. Violetpaw saw the ferns twitching slightly, just before she picked up the scent of vole.

Needletail dropped into the hunter's crouch and crept silently forward, her paws seeming to float over the ground, her sleek, silver-gray pelt no more than a drifting shadow. When she reached the top of the hollow, she launched herself into an enormous pounce. As she dived into the ferns, Violetpaw heard a thin shriek of terror, abruptly cut off. Needletail emerged with the limp body of the vole in her jaws.

"Great catch!" Violetpaw mewed admiringly.

"It'll do," Needletail mumbled around her prey.

As she and Needletail headed back to where they had left the rest of their prey hidden under pine needles, Violetpaw was glad that Needletail had agreed to keep hunting. She knew the truth was that Needletail was too scared of the rogue leader to do anything else.

I'm scared of him too, Violetpaw thought, *even though he's only been nice to me since I backed up his story about how Rain died.*

She couldn't ignore how Darktail looked coldly at Needletail every time the young she-cat crossed his path, and how, in spite of her usual impudence, Needletail hadn't twitched a whisker against his orders since Rain's death.

Violetpaw stifled a sigh. Things had changed in camp after that day. Darktail seemed more suspicious and unfriendly toward every cat. Her paws tingled with apprehension every time he turned that brooding, cold look on Needletail.

It's obvious: because Needletail was so close to Rain, Darktail thinks that she might—or will—betray him just as Rain did. What if Needletail is the next cat he strikes down?

Violetpaw wished that she could help her friend, but she had no idea what to do, except to try to keep Darktail happy with them both. Her fur prickled at the sense of trouble approaching, like a storm cloud swelling on the horizon, ready to release something terrible on the Kin.

She and Needletail were padding alongside a small stream, on their way to their prey cache, when Violetpaw spotted movement among the vegetation that overhung the water. The scent of frog flowed into her jaws. Almost without thinking, she flashed a paw down into the clump of plants and drew it up again with the frog wriggling on her claws. Swiftly she killed it with a bite to its neck.

"Good job," Needletail commented. "And now we really do have to take our prey back to camp. We'll need to make two trips as it is."

Violetpaw's heart grew a little lighter as she followed Needletail through the trees, all the prey she could carry dangling from her jaws. *I'd never tell Needletail this,* she thought, *but I always thought that Rain was a little bit . . . scary. And Darktail only killed him because he* had *to. And at least it happened before Rain could get Needletail into serious trouble.* She hoped that she could help Needletail keep her head down until Darktail wasn't suspicious of her anymore. *Then we'll both be safe, and everything might be okay.*

When they reached the ShadowClan camp, more cats were approaching from the opposite direction. Roach and Thistle were escorting three cats Violetpaw had never seen before. All three were plump, with glossy pelts, and they were eyeing their surroundings nervously as they entered the camp.

Violetpaw exchanged a shocked glance with Needletail. "Those are *kittypets!*" she exclaimed.

"Do Roach and Thistle have bees in their brain, bringing them here?" Needletail muttered.

Padding across the camp to drop her prey on the fresh-kill pile, Violetpaw saw Darktail emerge from his den, and she braced herself for an explosion of anger. She was grateful that neither she nor Needletail would be the ones in trouble this time.

But to Violetpaw's astonishment, Darktail bounded across the camp and dipped his head to the kittypets. "Greetings," he meowed. "Welcome to our camp."

What? Darktail actually wants *kittypets here?*

Violetpaw could see that the ShadowClan warriors weren't as pleased as Darktail to see the newcomers. They crowded around with expressions of shock and annoyance.

"What's going on?" Pinenose asked Darktail. "What are kittypets doing on our territory?"

"Come on, Pinenose." Darktail's tone was light, but Violet-paw thought she could detect an underlying menace. "Don't be so unfriendly. These are our guests. And the Kin here will always be *kind* to guests, won't they?"

Violetpaw willed her foster mother not to argue, and to her relief, Pinenose had the sense to back down. "I guess so," she muttered.

The rest of the ShadowClan warriors had gotten the message, too; no other cat protested about the kittypets' presence in camp.

Darktail beckoned with his tail for his cats to gather around him, then raised his voice to address them. "As the cats living on the territories around us—the so-called *Clan* cats—have proved so hostile, and attacked us—"

Violetpaw spotted some of the ShadowClan cats exchanging glances at the rogue leader's words, but none of them made any comments.

"—I've decided that the Kin could use some friends from the Twolegplace," Darktail continued. "And here they are. We've promised them hunting lessons and adventure; they'll see what fun it is to live with us." His glance raked across the cats around him. "I'm sure that all of you will show them a good time," he purred.

A good time? Violetpaw felt thoroughly alarmed. She was sure that whatever Darktail intended, showing kittypets a good time was the last thing on his mind.

"Come and introduce yourselves," Darktail invited, waving his tail at the kittypets to encourage them to come forward.

A young black tom glanced around shyly and ducked his head. "My name's Loki."

"And I'm Zelda." An even younger tabby she-cat—she looked around the same age as Violetpaw—gave an eager little bounce as she spoke. "It's great to be here!"

"And I'm called Max." An older black-and-white tom stepped forward, puffing out his chest. "Those other wild cats had better not mess with you while *I'm* around."

"It was so exciting when Roach invited us here," Loki mewed, with a grateful glance at the silver-gray tom.

"Yes, we've heard stories about the cats who live around the lake from our friend Minty," Zelda added. "But we never thought we'd meet you, and we wanted to, so much! Minty stayed here when her housefolk's den was flooded, and she said she'd never had so much fun in her life."

"Well," Darktail meowed cheerfully, "I think that we should swear a promise of friendship, to protect each other from the wild cats—the *vicious* wild cats—by the lake."

The visiting cats looked surprised, but they didn't protest, and willingly followed Darktail to the center of the camp. Violetpaw's sense of unease was growing. It was obvious that

Darktail didn't just want to make friends with these kittypets. She wondered whether any other cat could detect the underlying menace in his words.

"Now, say this after me," Darktail began. "'I swear to be a friend to the Kin . . . to share what I have with them . . . to defend them and help them and be one with them . . . for as long as I live.'"

The three cats repeated the phrases Darktail spoke. Zelda's voice in particular rang out clearly, as if she meant every word she said. Violetpaw wondered whether she had any idea of what she was promising.

"Now we ought to seal the pact with blood," Darktail announced.

The three kittypets exchanged alarmed glances, shifting from paw to paw as their shoulder fur began to bristle. "I don't know about that . . . ," Max began.

"Only a drop," Raven reassured them. "It won't hurt at all."

After a moment's hesitation, all three kittypets nodded agreement, though Max still looked doubtful. Violetpaw wondered whether Darktail's rogues had been through this ritual. It was so different from the warrior ceremonies of the Clan cats.

Each kittypet in turn raised a forepaw, and Darktail lightly pierced one of their pads with his claw. Each of them winced, and Loki let out a squeal of surprise, but it was soon over, and Raven had told the truth: it was only a drop of blood, and as they licked their paws the three kittypets' eyes were still shining with enthusiasm.

"Each of you must have a guide to show you around," Darktail meowed. "Raven, I want you to look after Max. Sleekwhisker, you can take charge of Loki. And . . ." He hesitated, then gave Violetpaw a nod. "Yes. Violetpaw . . . I think you and Zelda might have fun together," he told her.

Surprised, Violetpaw exchanged a glance with Needletail, wondering why Darktail had chosen her. Then she stepped up to stand next to the kittypet.

Violetpaw took Zelda with her to collect the remaining prey that she and Needletail had caught earlier, then spent the rest of the day showing her around what had once been ShadowClan territory. Together they climbed a tree that overlooked the Twolegplace, and Zelda tried to work out which of the Twoleg nests was hers. She warned Violetpaw about big dogs who lived in one of the nests nearby. Violetpaw asked her what a dog looked like, since she'd never seen one herself, and Zelda told her of a savage, slobbering brute whose housefolk seemed unable to control it. It loved to chase cats, she said. "Luckily, he's too heavy to catch us!"

Violetpaw thanked her for the warning, even as she thought: *I hope I don't ever have to get too close to a dog.* She tried to teach the kittypet some hunting techniques, and was impressed by how attentively Zelda listened. *She might have made a good apprentice.* Even though Zelda didn't catch any prey, and didn't seem to know *anything*, she never lost her enthusiasm or good humor. Violetpaw found she was enjoying their time together. *I feel so sorry for her,* she thought. *It must be so boring, being a kittypet.*

Still, Violetpaw realized that there were worse things than being bored. *We're having fun now. . . . I could almost stop worrying about what Darktail is up to.* But the apprehension that was gnawing at her belly wouldn't entirely go away.

Finally Violetpaw led Zelda back to camp and brought her back to the fresh-kill pile so they could eat together.

"I've never eaten an *animal* before," Zelda mewed, tucking in enthusiastically to the shrew she had chosen. "I *love it!*"

Violetpaw's eyes widened in surprise. "What do you eat, then?" she asked. "Grass, like the cows Needletail told me about?"

Zelda let out a *mrrow* of laughter. "No, my housefolk give me hard pellets to eat. They're pretty tasty, but not as delicious as this shrew!"

Pellets? Violetpaw thought. *Weird . . . and gross. It must be like eating mouse droppings.* She wished Zelda didn't have to go back, and could stay with the Kin always and be her friend. *But she's a kittypet, and a kittypet is better off with her Twolegs.*

As Violetpaw was finishing the blackbird she had taken from the fresh-kill pile, Max and Loki padded up, escorted by Raven.

"Help yourselves," the rogue meowed, waving her tail at the pile.

"Thanks!" Max replied, dragging out a vole and starting to gulp it down. "'S good!" he exclaimed around a huge mouthful.

Loki was more hesitant, but after an encouraging prod from Zelda he began nibbling cautiously at a mouse. Raven watched for a few heartbeats, then withdrew to talk to Darktail, who was standing a few tail-lengths away.

"Have you had a good day?" Zelda asked the two other kittypets. "Violetpaw showed me *everything*! It was *fantastic*!"

Max nodded. "I've had fun."

"I never knew how many of you there were," Loki added. "And you have such a great place to live. I'm glad that we got to see it."

"Now *we've* got stories to tell Minty!" Zelda mewed with a wave of her tail.

"But we ought to be going now." Max sounded reluctant as he swallowed the last of his vole. "It's starting to get dark, and our housefolk will be looking for us."

Loki gave a sharp mew. "Mine will probably try to feed me when I get back, but I'm so *full* already."

Zelda gave a nod. "I'm still going to eat. Whenever I don't, my housefolk get so worried. They just . . . *stare* at me. I never like it when they do."

Relief crept through Violetpaw like the sky paling toward dawn. *If the kittypets go now, then nothing bad will have happened to them.*

"It was great, showing you around," she meowed to Zelda. "Maybe I'll come find you in the Twolegplace sometime."

"That would be—" Zelda began enthusiastically, then broke off as Darktail loomed up beside her.

"What's all this talk about leaving?" the rogue leader rumbled. "We still have so much more to teach our new kittypet friends—isn't that right, Violetpaw?"

The menace that glittered in Darktail's eyes as he turned

his head toward her told Violetpaw that she ought to agree with him. She could just manage a scared little nod, even though she wanted the kittypets to get out of Kin territory and safely back to their Twoleg dens.

"Don't you want to stay with us?" Darktail asked. His tone was warm and friendly; Violetpaw could see that he was doing all he could to win over the kittypets. "You're very welcome."

"Thanks, but no," Max replied. "We really have to be getting back now."

"Yes," Loki added. "My housefolk kit likes me to sleep on her bed."

Darktail looked surprised and a little offended. "Have you forgotten that you swore an oath of kinship to the cats here?" he asked.

"We did," Loki replied, looking puzzled, "but how can we be part of your Kin when we're not actually *kin* to you?"

That's a good question, Violetpaw thought.

Darktail's voice was cold and calm as he replied. "The blood that bonds cats as kin is nothing compared to the blood a cat is prepared to spill to protect those around them. That means so much more, don't you think?"

For a couple of heartbeats the kittypets were silent, and Zelda exchanged an uncertain glance with Violetpaw.

The blood a cat is prepared to spill? Is Darktail planning another battle?

Then Loki shrugged. "I guess so," he mewed.

"I just need you to stay for a few more days," Darktail continued smoothly. "Tomorrow you'll start learning how to fight, in case those fiendish Clan cats attack again."

At the idea of fighting, the kittypets looked even more uncertain. "Is that likely to happen?" Zelda asked.

"Anything can happen," Darktail responded.

"Well," Max meowed after another moment's hesitation, "I guess if it's just for another day or two, we'll stay. I remember once I got lost, and it took two days for me to find my way back to my housefolk. I'm pretty sure they won't panic—as long as I'm not away from the den for too long."

Loki and Zelda both nodded. "Okay," Loki agreed.

Violetpaw felt a twinge of anxiety in her belly. She remembered the night she had spent with the rogues when she was in ShadowClan, and how that had led to the rogues moving into ShadowClan territory.

What is Darktail planning now? she wondered.

Raven and Sleekwhisker padded up to escort Max and Loki to dens for the night, leaving Zelda with Violetpaw.

"Come on," Violetpaw mewed to her new friend. "I'll show you where to sleep."

"Good night," Darktail purred, dipping his head and watching them as they went.

Violetpaw took Zelda with her to the apprentices' den. *Or what was the apprentices' den, back when we had apprentices and mentors. These days, most Kin cats sleep where they like.*

Together the two she-cats settled into Violetpaw's nest of moss and bracken. Zelda was soon asleep, curled up with her tail over her nose and letting out little snores. But Violetpaw stayed awake as twilight deepened into night. It felt good to have Zelda cuddled up next to her, reminding Violetpaw of the time when she'd had her sister, Twigpaw, with her in the ShadowClan camp.

But as she gazed up at the stars between the branches that overhung the den, Violetpaw's anxiety still gripped her like a badger's claw.

Why does Darktail want these kittypets? Why does he need more cats willing to spill blood for him?

CHAPTER 7

The early morning sunlight slanted through the trees, shedding blotches of golden light on the forest floor. Alderheart enjoyed the warmth on his fur as he scoured the ground outside the camp, sniffing at each clump of new growth. Now that his Clanmates' injuries from the battle were beginning to heal, the medicine-cat den was much quieter; Alderheart had taken the chance to restock the herb stores.

He spotted a tuft of comfrey, nipped off a few stems with his teeth, and headed back through the thorn tunnel into the camp. As he passed the apprentices' den, he hesitated for a moment, then padded over and stuck his head through the barrier of ferns that screened the entrance.

It took a moment for his eyes to adjust from the strong sunlight outside, but then he could make out the mound of Twigpaw's back where she lay curled deep in her mossy nest.

She was so disappointed yesterday, when Bramblestar decided not to send out a patrol to look for SkyClan, he remembered. *She has always wanted to have kin in the Clan. I was disappointed myself, but I can understand. There is a lot going on with the Clans right now.* He let out a long sigh. *Perhaps we can go look for SkyClan when we've dealt with the rogues.*

"Do you *really* think that the cat you saw in your vision could be my kin?" she had asked Alderheart then.

Alderheart could see the desperation in her eyes. "Yes, I do," he assured her. "And even though Bramblestar can't send out a patrol just yet, we are not going to ignore SkyClan."

However, Alderheart had seen that Twigpaw was still upset when she went to sleep the night before. He wasn't surprised that now she seemed to want to stay curled up in her nest for as long as possible.

Then a breeze stirred the ferns at the mouth of the den, and a beam of sunlight from the entrance struck the mound of Twigpaw's sleeping form. Alderheart suppressed a gasp. He slid into the den, clawed the bedding aside, and realized that the heaped-up moss and leaves he was gazing at were no more than an empty lump. Twigpaw was gone!

Heart thumping, Alderheart drew back from the apprentices' den and bounded across the camp.

You're being stupid, he told himself. *She must be around here somewhere.* But then he realized that Twigpaw must have deliberately piled up her bedding to make it seem as if she was still there. *She has to be hiding something!*

Brushing past the bramble screen into the medicine cats' den, Alderheart found Briarlight doing her exercises, raising herself up on her forepaws while Jayfeather supervised her.

"One more, and then rest," Jayfeather instructed her.

Briarlight obeyed, then let herself flop back into her nest. "Phew! I'm exhausted!" she panted.

Jayfeather turned to face Alderheart, alerted by the sound

of his fur brushing against the brambles. "What's going on?" he asked. "Your breathing sounds as if you ran all the way from RiverClan. Is it the rogues?"

"No," Alderheart responded, dropping his stems of comfrey. "It's Twigpaw. She's not in her nest. I thought she might be here."

Jayfeather shook his head. "Not since last night," he replied. "You could ask Leafpool. She's over at the nursery, checking on Blossomfall." As Alderheart turned to go, he added, "Don't worry. Twigpaw will turn up."

Hoping he was right, Alderheart left the den and headed across the stone hollow toward the nursery. All around him, the camp was waking up to the new day. A few warriors were emerging from their den, blinking in the strong sunlight, while the first of the hunting patrols was already returning, carrying their prey across the clearing to the fresh-kill pile.

Close to the pile, Alderheart spotted Berrynose and Tigerheart standing nose to nose, their shoulder fur bristling and their tails bushed up to twice their usual size. They were hissing at each other, clearly furious, though Alderheart couldn't make out what it was all about. His heart sank at the thought of yet another argument between ShadowClan and ThunderClan cats.

He had decided that it was none of his business when he saw Purdy get up from where he was dozing in a patch of sunlight and thrust his way between the two quarreling cats.

"Stop it, stop it, both of you," he began. "This is no time for fightin' among ourselves. We—"

Purdy broke off, then gasped out a few more words that Alderheart couldn't understand. The plump brown cat's limbs jerked and spasmed, and he fell to the ground as if some cat had attacked him. But there was no attacker in sight.

Berrynose and Tigerheart sprang apart, letting out yowls of alarm. By then Alderheart was racing across the camp, heart pounding harder than ever in panic. More cats gathered around, wailing in dismay or asking Purdy what was wrong. Alderheart had to push through the crowd to reach the old cat's side.

"Keep back!" he snapped. "Let him breathe!" Turning to Berrynose, he added, "What happened?"

It was Tigerheart who replied. "We were arguing, and Purdy was trying to break it up. Then suddenly he said that one of his forelegs hurt, and he . . . he just collapsed."

Alderheart crouched down and put his nose close to Purdy's. The old tom's eyelids were fluttering, but he was still conscious. Relief began to trickle through Alderheart. *Maybe he'll be okay.*

"What's wrong? Is it the indigestion?" Alderheart asked, remembering how the elder had been complaining of belly-ache. "How can I help?"

Instead of replying, Purdy began struggling to get up, then had to give in, flopping back onto his side. "Can't . . . can't manage it," he gasped. "Hurts too much."

Alderheart began to examine him, running his paws over Purdy's chest and side, though he wasn't sure what he was looking for. He could feel the old cat's heartbeat, laboring and irregular, and fear gripped him deep within.

"I haven't been feelin' quite myself lately." Purdy's voice was weak, and he had trouble forcing out the words. "But I just thought . . . it was normal. I'm an old cat, after all, and I expect to get some aches an' pains. . . . I didn't want to cause trouble, not with so much goin' on."

"Helping you wouldn't have been any trouble!" Alderheart protested, trying to sound confident, aware of the ring of anxious faces that surrounded him and the elder. "But don't worry, Purdy. I'm going to help you now."

It'll only make things worse for Purdy if I admit the truth, he thought, fighting back panic. *I have no idea what's going on, or what Purdy needs me to do.*

"Go get Jayfeather!" he ordered Berrynose, who instantly shoved his way through the watching cats and streaked across the camp toward the medicine cats' den.

Alderheart's fears peaked as he turned back to Purdy and saw the faraway look in his amber eyes. It was almost as if he had already crossed the border into StarClan territory. Yet as he gazed up at Alderheart he seemed as calm and good-humored as ever.

"You're a good medicine cat, young 'un," he murmured. "You've got some big paw prints to fill, but I reckon you're goin' to be just fine."

Then he let out a long sigh and lay motionless, his eyes still open as if he was gazing at something far away.

No! He can't be dead! Alderheart thought, every hair in his pelt rising up in denial of what he was seeing. "Purdy . . . ," he choked out.

Jayfeather had reached his side, along with Leafpool, who must have dashed across from the nursery.

"What's happening?" she asked.

"I don't know," Alderheart replied, forcing down the wail of a lost kit. "Purdy complained of indigestion earlier—and just now he said he had a pain in his foreleg. Then he collapsed, and . . . and he's not breathing. But he has to be okay," he finished, anguished. "Purdy can't be gone!"

Jayfeather bent over to examine the elder, sniffing carefully from his ears to his tail-tip. Then he shook his head sadly and reached with a gentle paw to close Purdy's eyes.

"No!" This time Alderheart couldn't suppress his wail of grief. "There must be something we can do," he insisted. "Maybe we can chew up some chamomile, put it in his mouth, and rub his throat so he swallows it. Maybe we can push his chest to make his heart start beating again!"

But when Alderheart reached out to touch one of Purdy's legs, he could feel that it was already beginning to stiffen.

"Don't, Alderheart." Jayfeather's voice was surprisingly sympathetic as he hooked a paw around Alderheart's neck and pulled him away. "Purdy's gone. He was very old and lived a long life, and now that life is done. Part of being a medicine cat is knowing when you have to let go."

Alderheart stared at Purdy, who had been alive and speaking only moments ago—and now lay dead on the ground like a piece of prey. "I didn't help him," he whispered.

Jayfeather touched his tail to Alderheart's flank. "Sometimes you can't."

Alderheart shuddered, feeling waves of heat and cold pass through him. *Will I ever get used to seeing cats die?* he asked himself. *Especially an elder like Purdy, who was such an important part of Thunder-Clan?* He turned away, his head and tail drooping. *Purdy said I'd be just fine . . . but will I?*

Graystripe and Millie moved Purdy's body to the center of the camp, where more of his Clanmates gathered around to share tongues with him one last time, grooming his pelt to make him ready for burial. The rest of the Clan sat nearby, silently grieving as they waited for that night's vigil to begin. The ShadowClan cats joined in, too, sitting together at a respectful distance.

Alderheart felt like the fog of regret and sorrow that surrounded him would never lift. He padded quietly over to Bramblestar, who was sitting close to Purdy's body, with Squirrelflight by his side.

"Bramblestar," he began hesitantly. "Purdy was never a warrior. Do you think he'll be allowed to walk with StarClan?"

Bramblestar gazed at him, not replying for a moment. When he spoke at last, he didn't seem to be answering Alderheart's question. "We first met Purdy when we made the journey to the sun-drown-place," he meowed. "He saved us from a dog, and then showed us where we could find food."

Squirrelflight nodded. "I'll never forget that. Without

Purdy, we might not have made it to the meeting with Midnight—and without her, we might never have known to leave the old forest and find our new home here."

"When he came to join us," Bramblestar went on, "he fit into the elders' den like he had always been living with us. He cared for Mousefur when she was ill and dying."

By now, most of the cats who were clustered around Purdy's body had turned to listen to their leader.

"He was always good with the apprentices," Ivypool put in. "Do you remember, in the Great Storm, how he looked after them and kept them out of trouble?"

"And he told the best stories!" Ambermoon added.

"And he joined in when we fought against the Dark Forest," Squirrelflight pointed out. "He may have been a kittypet once, but he was a brave cat and a true member of ThunderClan."

Bramblestar nodded, his amber eyes warm as he met Alderheart's gaze. "Alderheart," he mewed. "Which of us deserves better than Purdy to walk with StarClan? I know he'll be there, watching over us."

"Thank you," Alderheart whispered.

But Bramblestar's assurance did little to ease Alderheart's grief. He still felt as if there should have been something he could have done to save Purdy. *It's okay to think that he'll watch over us from StarClan, but he watched over us while he was here.* Sighing, he rose to his paws and headed back toward the medicine cats' den.

Halfway there, he halted. The stress of Purdy's death had

driven everything else from his mind, but now he remembered what he'd been worried about when he found him.

Twigpaw . . .

If she had come back to the camp, Alderheart knew she would have come out to pay her respects to Purdy.

That means she really must have left. And I have a horrible feeling that I know where she went.

Alderheart turned and raced back to where he had left Bramblestar beside Purdy's body. "I'm sorry to interrupt," he murmured, so as not to disturb the other cats. "But this is an emergency. I need to talk to you."

Bramblestar didn't protest, but rose to his paws and gestured with his tail for Alderheart to follow him to a spot near the entrance to the warriors' den, out of earshot of the grieving cats. "Well?" he asked.

"Twigpaw is missing," Alderheart announced. "I'm afraid that she may have gone out on her own to look for SkyClan and the cat who might be her kin."

Bramblestar slid out his claws and dug them hard into the ground. "Great StarClan!" he exclaimed, exasperated. "Could Twigpaw have chosen a worse time to run away?" Then he shook his head, clearly trying to recover his calm. "We'll send out a patrol to look for her," he meowed.

Bramblestar turned back to where the rest of the Clan was sitting. "Cats of ThunderClan!" he called, and as his Clanmates' faces turned toward him, he continued, "Yesterday we decided that we would not send out cats to look for SkyClan. But now Twigpaw is missing, and Alderheart and I believe that is where she has gone—to find her kin. The journey is too dangerous for an apprentice traveling alone, and so we must bring her back."

As he spoke, Ivypool sprang to her paws. "This is all my fault," she mewed, her blue eyes filled with distress. "I spoke out against sending a patrol, and I know that upset Twigpaw. But I didn't realize she would react like this. I should have known . . . ," she finished miserably.

"Don't blame yourself," Bramblestar told her. "We *all* agreed that this was not the right time to search for SkyClan. No one cat is responsible. All we can do now is send some cats out to look for Twigpaw and bring her home safe."

"I'll go," Tigerheart offered immediately.

"And so will I," Dovewing added.

"Thank you." Bramblestar glanced around at his Clan. "Molewhisker, you will go too," he decided. "You made the first journey with Alderheart, and you know the way to the barn where he saw SkyClan in his vision."

"Sure, Bramblestar." Molewhisker got up and padded over to join Dovewing and Tigerheart.

The three cats dipped their heads to their Clan leader, then headed across the stone hollow and disappeared into the thorn tunnel.

Alderheart watched them go, thankful that they would look out for Twigpaw and bring her home safe. Then his belly twisted with worry as he remembered the huge Thunderpath that lay between their territory and the yellow barn.

She has to go that way, he thought anxiously. *I hope she remembers how to find the tunnel.*

And even if Twigpaw managed to cross the Thunderpath safely, there were more hazards on the other side. A young apprentice, all on her own, just wasn't safe out there.

I know she would do anything to find her kin, but does she really know how terrifying a journey like that can be for a cat?

Alderheart wanted to claw off his own fur when he remembered how distressed Twigpaw had been when they'd discussed SkyClan the night before.

"I could have been more reassuring," he murmured aloud. "And now she's gone."

I've already lost one friend today, he thought, his heart heavy. *Am I going to lose another?*

CHAPTER 8

❧

The sun had only just begun to slide down the sky, but already Twigpaw's injured leg was aching. She couldn't remember ever having been so tired and thirsty before.

Sneaking out of camp through the dirtplace tunnel had felt strange, and at every moment she had expected to be called back by Brightheart, who was on watch. Her feelings of guilt had increased with every stealthy paw step, because she knew that Alderheart and Ivypool would be very worried when they discovered she was missing.

But I might have kin, she had told herself, summoning up the determination to keep going. *Actual blood kin, and I haven't even met them yet. And if Alderheart and Ivypool cared so much about me, they would have made more of an effort to help me, wouldn't they?*

Now Twigpaw picked up her pace, a twinge of pain throbbing through her leg at every paw step. She had long ago crossed the top of the ridge beyond the horseplace, leaving the lake far behind. All the sights and scents were different here, and Twigpaw's fur began to bristle at every unexplained sound in the undergrowth. She desperately tried to remember the route she had taken when Ivypool and Alderheart had gone with her to look for her mother.

I think I know the way to the tunnel under the Thunderpath. But after that . . . ? All I know is that Alderheart said that SkyClan had taken shelter in a barn, which I guess is a Twoleg dwelling. . . .

For a moment, Twigpaw feared she was being completely mouse-brained. She paused, wondering if the sensible thing would be to go back. But then her resolve hardened.

I need my kin more than ever now, because I don't have Violetpaw anymore. I'm not going to think about my so-called sister ever again! I'll have something else now. . . . A father, maybe.

When she was a kit, Twigpaw had thought only of how she had lost her mother. She hadn't considered what it would be like to have a father.

That would be wonderful, too, she decided now.

She set off again, thinking about the relationship Alderheart had with Bramblestar. *Sure, they disagree a lot, but a blind rabbit could see how much they love each other. Alderheart always knows that Bramblestar will be there for him, to look after and guide him.*

Just in front of Twigpaw, a stream crossed her path like a shining snake wriggling through the grass. The surface glittered in the sunlight, dazzling Twigpaw's eyes as she stood on the bank looking down at it.

"I *hate* getting my paws wet," she hissed through her teeth.

Even the shallow stream that divided ThunderClan from WindClan reminded Twigpaw of the time she had nearly drowned in the lake. When she crossed that stream on the way to a Gathering, she had Clanmates around her who could help her if she got into trouble. Now she was alone.

Then Twigpaw imagined that her father was standing beside her. *Come on, Twigpaw,* he might say. *You can do it!*

Twigpaw was so focused on him that she could almost hear his voice.

"Yes, I can!" she replied, and waded out into the water with her head held proudly high.

She flinched at the sensation of cold water creeping through her pelt, rising higher and higher as she ventured deeper. The pebbles underpaw were slippery, and the current tugged at her, so she was afraid of losing her footing and being swept away. She put each paw down firmly, trying to ignore the racing of her heart.

The water grew deeper until it lapped and tugged at Twigpaw's belly fur, then swiftly receded as she climbed up the stream bed on the opposite side. Scrambling out onto the bank, she gave herself a vigorous shake, glittering drops of water spinning away into the air.

"I did it!" she announced, pride flooding through her as she imagined her father's nod of approval.

She could hear the warmth in his voice as he meowed, *I knew you could.*

But Twigpaw had barely taken a pace away from the stream when a sudden noise chased the happy thoughts from her head. It sounded like the barking of a fox—only it was much, much louder. The ground shook with the thundering of many paws.

Twigpaw tensed, and whirled to face the origin of the noise. Her jaws gaped in horror as she saw three enormous creatures bounding across the grass toward her. Their bodies were lean and muscular, with short brindled pelts. Their eyes gleamed with menace, but what terrified Twigpaw most of all were their gaping jaws, with huge tongues lolling from a mouthful of sharp fangs.

For a heartbeat Twigpaw froze. Then she spun around and began to run, ignoring the pain that clawed through her injured leg.

Are those dogs? she wondered, pelting along with her belly fur brushing the grass. She remembered how Ivypool had warned her against the savage creatures that sometimes came with Twolegs into the forest. *I've never seen one before, let alone three. . . .*

And they look very, very hungry!

As she fled, Twigpaw picked up a dull roar ahead of her, growing louder until it rivaled the barking of the dogs. And she spotted the unnatural shiny flicker of monsters speeding to and fro.

The Thunderpath . . . I'll be trapped between it and the dogs!

Casting a terrified glance over her shoulder, Twigpaw saw that the dogs were gaining on her. She imagined that she could feel their hot breath on her hindquarters. Looking ahead again, she could see nothing that might help her except for a tree growing close to the Thunderpath.

Then she remembered Ivypool's words: "Dogs are scary, but they're pretty dumb, and too heavy to climb trees."

I hope these are *dogs,* Twigpaw thought, veering to one side and racing for the tree. *And I hope what Ivypool said was right. There's no time to think of anything else!*

Reaching the tree, Twigpaw hurled herself upward, digging her claws deep into the bark. Scurrying up the trunk as fast as she could, she heard the snapping of jaws below her tail, and whisked it out of reach just in time.

Scrambling onto a forking branch, Twigpaw looked down. All three dogs were at the bottom of the tree, their forelegs reaching upward to rest on the tree trunk. Their deep-chested barking went on and on, and Twigpaw recoiled a little at the vicious threat in their eyes. But she realized that they couldn't climb up to get at her.

I'm safe! she thought. *Thank you, Ivypool!*

Twigpaw's heart was still pounding from fear and the exertion of the chase. To be extra safe, she decided to climb higher, her confidence returning as she bounded from branch to branch. Clustering leaves cut off the sight of the dogs below, though she could still hear their barking.

"Bark on, flea-pelts!" she meowed triumphantly. "You're not eating cat today!"

When Twigpaw finally came to a halt, she could see the land stretching away into the distance in every direction. But most of her view was cut off by leaves.

"I should find somewhere I can see better," she muttered to herself. "I might even be able to spot the barn from Alderheart's vision."

Setting her paws down cautiously, Twigpaw ventured onto a branch that stretched out over the Thunderpath. On the opposite side of the hard black surface she could see trees and undergrowth and Twoleg nests, but nothing that gave her any idea of where to go next.

When she looked down, Twigpaw could see the monsters roaring past her on the Thunderpath. Their fumes rose up to her like smoke, and she gagged on the acrid taste. The noise and the bright, speeding colors confused her, and her head began to spin. She wanted to retreat along the branch, back to the safety of crisscrossing branches and clumps of leaves, but her paws felt clumsy, and the branch kept shifting under her weight.

As she began to edge backward, Twigpaw felt her paws slipping. Letting out a yowl of alarm, she slid out her claws, but they raked uselessly across the surface of the branch. Twigpaw's yowl rose into a panic-stricken screech as she felt herself falling. She bounced off a lower branch, and her shriek was abruptly cut off as she thumped down onto the Thunderpath, the blow driving all the breath out of her body.

Looking up, dazed, Twigpaw saw a huge monster bearing down on her, screeching as it came. Two Twolegs were trapped inside the monster's belly. Their eyes were staring and their jaws wide open as if they were yowling.

They look terrified! Twigpaw thought. *The monster's eaten them, and it's still hungry!*

Her whirling brain had just formed the thought *Those poor Twolegs!* when the monster came rushing up at her, and the whole world vanished into smothering darkness.

CHAPTER 9

Violetpaw shifted uncomfortably in her nest, listening to Needletail as she whimpered and twitched in a bad dream. Gently, she drew her tail across her friend's shoulders, hoping she wouldn't disturb Zelda, who was curled up in a deep sleep at the far side of the den.

"Hush," she whispered to Needletail. "It'll be okay."

But is that true? Violetpaw asked herself.

Over the last few days, ever since the kittypets had come to join the Kin, things had only gotten worse. Darktail had coerced Max, Loki, and Zelda to stay even longer than the day or two they had first agreed to, telling them that they had pledged their loyalty—and that if they left now, they could never come back.

I don't like the way they're being treated, Violetpaw thought, *but what can I do?*

Needletail let out another whimper, and once again Violetpaw stroked her shoulder with the tip of her tail. She guessed that Needletail was dreaming about Rain; she did that almost every night, calling out his name in her sleep.

Or maybe she's having a nightmare about what's going to happen in the morning. Violetpaw shivered. *But I'm not going to let myself think about that.*

Unable to sleep, Violetpaw gazed up at the stars, reflecting how Needletail had changed in the last few days. Rain's death had broken something within her. To other cats Needletail would always insist that Rain was a traitor, and that Darktail had only done what a good leader had to do. "Rain was not the cat I thought he was," she had meowed more than once.

But Violetpaw knew that Needletail's feelings were more complicated than that. Before Rain's death, even when things got tough, she would always have a joke or a cheerful remark for Violetpaw. Now her carefree spirit had vanished, leaving something darker and heavier in its place. It was Violetpaw's turn to take care of her.

And I do it gladly, Violetpaw thought, giving her sleeping friend's ear a lick. *But it's weird and scary, like I'm her mentor or something.*

Another yelp came from Needletail, who thrashed her tail to and fro in the throes of her nightmare. Violetpaw cuddled closer to her friend, but it didn't seem to help.

Eventually weariness began to overcome Violetpaw. She closed her eyes and was beginning to drift into a restless, dreamless sleep when she felt a paw prodding her in the side.

Confused, Violetpaw struggled back to wakefulness. "Needletail . . . ," she muttered.

But when her eyes were fully open, it was Dawnpelt—her former mentor in ShadowClan—who she saw. The she-cat's head and shoulders were thrust through the bushes at the entrance to the den, her pale fur glimmering in the starlight.

"What . . . ?" Violetpaw began.

Dawnpelt raised a paw for silence. "I had to come and tell you," she whispered. "I'm leaving."

Surprised, Violetpaw half sat up; disturbed by her movement, Needletail seemed to rouse for a heartbeat, then fell back into her uneasy sleep.

"I realize now that staying with Darktail and his Kin was a mistake," Dawnpelt went on rapidly. "They're bad cats! So I'm doing what I should have done in the first place: I'm going to ThunderClan to be with Rowanstar and Tawnypelt, and I'm leaving now so that Darktail won't know that I've gone until it's too late."

At first Violetpaw was amazed, though she soon realized she had no reason to be. In the last few days, Birchbark, Lioneye, and Mistcloud had all left the Kin. What had surprised her then was that Darktail had let them go, even offering to escort them off the territory.

"Kinship goes both ways," he had meowed solemnly. "I don't want cats here who will not be loyal."

"Why are you telling me this?" Violetpaw asked.

"I want you to come with me," Dawnpelt replied. "I already sent Juniperclaw and Strikestone on ahead, and we can sneak away tonight, without Darktail seeing."

"Why?" Violetpaw was puzzled. "Darktail took it really well when Lioneye and the others left."

Dawnpelt looked uneasy, scrabbling with her forepaws

among the bracken at the edge of the den. "I just don't trust him," she confessed.

Violetpaw could understand that. "What about Sleekwhisker?" she asked.

Dawnpelt's expression darkened. "Sleekwhisker would never want to leave," she replied. "I haven't even told her."

Violetpaw looked down at the sleeping Needletail, who had curled her tail around Violetpaw's hindquarters as if she was making sure to keep her close.

Would she ever come with me to ThunderClan? Violetpaw asked herself. Then she shook her head. *No, I'm pretty sure she wouldn't.*

Even though Needletail was so unhappy here, Violetpaw couldn't imagine her ever admitting she had been wrong. And that was what she would be doing if she left to go to ThunderClan.

"I'm sorry, but . . . I can't go," Violetpaw mewed softly to Dawnpelt. "I have to stay here with Needletail."

Dawnpelt gave an irritated flick of her ears. "Have you got bees in your brain, Violetpaw? What the rogues are doing here is *not good*. What they're about to do tomorrow goes against everything Clan cats believe in."

"Darktail says we're *not* Clan cats," Violetpaw pointed out.

"Yes, and that's exactly the problem." A low growl came from Dawnpelt's throat. "Clan cats have a code. Clan cats have honor. What do these rogues have?"

She's right . . . But Violetpaw had to thrust that reaction away. *They're the only kin I have now,* she admitted to herself, with another glance at Needletail.

An image of Twigpaw flashed into her mind: the look of dismay and disbelief when Violetpaw had attacked her in the battle. Once, the thought of going to ThunderClan to be with her sister would have filled her with joy, like sunlight striking down into a dark place. But she knew that her decision during that battle had cut her off forever from the light.

"Violetpaw, please come," Dawnpelt urged her again. "You can be my apprentice again in ThunderClan."

With a massive effort Violetpaw pushed away the thought of Twigpaw, and the idea of having a real mentor again in a real Clan. "I'm sorry; I can't," she whispered.

Dawnpelt dipped her head in sad acceptance of Violet-paw's decision. "May StarClan light your path, always," she murmured, and slipped away into the darkness.

With a long sigh Violetpaw curled up again in her nest and closed her eyes. She was just sinking into sleep again when a distant yowling woke her.

What now? she wondered wearily.

Her ears pricked alertly, Violetpaw strained to hear what was going on. She could make out the voices of two cats, and with a sudden chill she recognized that they belonged to Dawnpelt and Darktail.

Darktail must have caught Dawnpelt before she got away!

The cats' tones were angry, though they were too far away for Violetpaw to make out the words. But it was clear that they were arguing.

I wonder why, Violetpaw asked herself. *Darktail just let the other cats go, so why would he be upset about Dawnpelt leaving?*

After a heartbeat the voices moved a little closer. Violetpaw heard Darktail meow, "If you don't want to be with us anymore, then you are no longer our Kin."

Violetpaw relaxed a little with relief. It sounded as if Darktail was letting Dawnpelt go after all.

At last Needletail had sunk into deeper sleep. Violetpaw lay by her side, still trying to overhear what Dawnpelt and Darktail were saying, though now the voices were receding into the distance.

Have I made a mistake by staying? Violetpaw asked herself as she drifted back into sleep. *No,* she decided. *I owe Needletail everything.*

Darktail and Raven had roused Violetpaw and the rest of the Kin as the first pale gleam of dawn crept into the sky. Giving the order for silence, Darktail had led them through the forest, the only sound the whispering of their paws as they padded over the thick layer of pine needles that covered the ground. Now they stood at the edge of the little Thunderpath that separated their territory from RiverClan's.

Glancing around, Violetpaw realized that almost all the Kin were gathered there, the former ShadowClan warriors and the rogues. Thistle, Roach, Pinenose, Sparrowtail, Berryheart, Rippletail, Cloverfoot . . . The line of cats seemed endless. Even the elders, Oakfur and Ratscar, were there, and the three kittypets, Zelda, Loki, and Max.

That's not right, Violetpaw thought. *This is no place for elders or kittypets.*

She was standing with Zelda on one side of her and Loki on the other, with Max just behind them. Violetpaw wished that she could have been nearer to Needletail, but her friend stood several fox-lengths away, closely escorted by Roach and Raven.

They haven't moved from her side since we left camp, Violetpaw thought. *I wonder why.*

"I'm so nervous," Zelda murmured into Violetpaw's ear. "I wish we could have had something to eat before we set out. I'm starving!"

"I'm too nervous to eat," Loki mewed.

"Quiet!" Darktail padded over, and Violetpaw's belly lurched as she realized he had been close enough to hear the kittypets' soft voices. "There'll be plenty to eat *after* we defeat RiverClan. Once we have our victory, we'll have a great big feast."

Zelda gave an excited little bounce. "Oh, I *love* feasts! When I lived with my housefolk, they had feasts sometimes, with scraps of all different kinds of food. They played a game with me: they'd put my feast into the garbage can, and I had to hunt for it. It was fun!"

Violetpaw glimpsed a flash of anger in Darktail's eyes, as if he would have liked to claw the flighty little kittypet's ear off. "Be quiet now," he ordered through gritted teeth. "It's time to claim our new territory."

With a gesture of his tail, Darktail beckoned the three kit-typets a few paw steps away from Violetpaw. Sleekwhisker padded up with the two ShadowClan elders, then stepped back with a nod to Darktail.

"Right," Darktail meowed. "This is the plan. You three kittypets will be going in first, along with the elders."

"Is that a good idea?" Violetpaw asked without thinking. Her belly cramped with fear as Darktail turned a menacing gaze on her, and she realized she shouldn't have questioned her leader. "I—I mean," she stammered, "the kittypets don't have any battle experience, and the elders are . . . well, elder."

Darktail paused before replying. Violetpaw noticed the three kittypets exchanging glances of alarm, while the two elders were listening with grim expressions.

"It's an honor to be the first cats to attack in a battle," Darktail assured them at last.

Violetpaw thought that was a bit strange. *Even if that's true, wouldn't you choose your strongest warriors to honor?* She was sure that Oakfur and Ratscar hadn't fought in a battle for ShadowClan since they'd retired to the elders' den. And when inexperienced apprentices went into battle, they fought beside their mentors. But she didn't dare say anything more to Darktail. *After all, it's different with the Kin.*

"You, Violetpaw, will have the greatest honor of all," Darktail continued smoothly. "You will fight at my side."

Even weirder, Violetpaw thought. *Why does he want me at his side?*

But she had no time to work out what Darktail intended. The bushes at the other side of the Thunderpath rustled, and a group of RiverClan cats stepped out into the open.

By this time the dawn light had strengthened, and a glow in the sky over WindClan territory showed where the sun would rise. There was enough light for Violetpaw to see that the RiverClan leader, Mistystar, was in the lead, her gray-blue fur gleaming except for the dark gash along her side where she had been wounded in the previous battle.

"What's going on?" she demanded. "My dawn patrol reported a large group of cats along our border. What are you doing here?" When Darktail didn't reply at once, she lashed her tail and added, "RiverClan wants nothing to do with you mange-ridden rogues! Be gone!"

In spite of Mistystar's challenging tone, Violetpaw could see confusion in her blue eyes. It made her realize how strange Darktail's behavior was, that it was quite outside a Clan leader's experience.

Still Darktail didn't attempt to answer Mistystar's questions. Instead he let out a deep-throated caterwaul. "Kin! Attack!"

At once Zelda, Max and Loki sprang forward, with the two elders lumbering after them. Violetpaw could tell that the kittypets didn't have much of an idea what they were supposed to do in a fight. Zelda opened her jaws wide, but what came out was more like a squeak than a challenging roar.

Violetpaw wanted to follow her friends and help them, but as she bunched her muscles to hurl herself forward, Darktail blocked her path with his tail.

"Not yet," he mewed.

On the opposite side of the Thunderpath, the RiverClan warriors stared in amazement, exchanging confused glances as if they didn't know what to do about an attack from confused kittypets.

"Time to show what you're made of, my Kin!" Darktail raised his voice again in a yowl. "Time to tell these Clan cats they can't mess with us! The winner of this battle takes the territory!"

Spurred on by his leader's orders, Scorchfur was the first of the Kin to race forward, taking a swipe at Beetlewhisker's nose. Blood sprayed out into the air, and Beetlewhisker let out a screech.

As if at a signal, the RiverClan cats seemed to realize that the attack wasn't absurd after all.

They know it's really happening, Violetpaw thought. *They can see they're in danger of losing their camp.*

Darktail had explained the day before that the RiverClan cats would be at a serious disadvantage: their numbers were about equal since more rogues had come to join the Kin, but RiverClan had taken more serious injuries in the previous battle. Their leader, Mistystar herself, still wasn't fully recovered.

But as the RiverClan cats gave vent to furious yowling and sprang to defend themselves, Violetpaw could see that their courage was as strong as ever, in spite of their wounds. With slashing claws and bared teeth, they fell upon the rogues, driving the less experienced of them wailing into the undergrowth, or leaving them writhing in pain on the hard surface of the Thunderpath.

The three kittypets were doing their best, but they were no match for experienced RiverClan warriors. Violetpaw lost sight of them in the midst of whirling, shrieking bundles of fur.

"Now!" Darktail meowed to Violetpaw. "It's time to have some fun."

Fun? Violetpaw thought, appalled.

Darktail raced forward into the battle, and Violetpaw followed him. At first she wasn't sure she wanted to attack the RiverClan cats. She remembered Dawnpelt's words the night before, how her former mentor was convinced the rogues were evil.

RiverClan attacked us with the others, but they were just trying to help ShadowClan. Can it be right to drive them off their territory?

But she remembered too what Darktail had said, that the Clan cats had always been hostile to the rogues. *And Mistystar called us mange-ridden just now! We should teach her to respect the Kin. . . .*

Violetpaw still hovered on the edge of the battle. Darktail had bounded ahead of her, his claws stretched out to slash at Mistystar. But Reedwhisker, the RiverClan deputy, a lean, black streak of fury, hurled himself between Darktail and his leader. He and Darktail wrestled on the ground, legs and tails flailing.

Roach and Nettle were fighting close together, dealing vicious blows to the RiverClan cats who attacked them. The stench of blood filled the air; Violetpaw gagged on it, wanting to hide under the nearest bush and close her eyes until it was all over.

But she knew she couldn't do that. The Kin seemed to be driving back the RiverClan cats, and she glanced around to see how the kittypets and elders were getting along.

What she saw chilled her from ears to tail-tip. Both elders were badly hurt: Oakfur lay at the edge of the Thunderpath, struggling to stand, while Ratscar stood over him, battling a RiverClan warrior, with blood dripping from a scar across his cheek.

Loki had retreated across a wide area, covered by the same hard stuff as the Thunderpath, that stretched as far as the lake. He was crouched at the water's edge, shivering with fear. Zelda was limping toward him, a huge gash in one of her hind legs, letting out whimpers of pain at every paw step.

For a terrible moment, Violetpaw couldn't spot Max. Then she saw him lying in a clump of long grass on the RiverClan side of the border, the ground all around him clotted with blood. He wasn't moving at all.

Is he dead? A cold wave of horror washed over Violetpaw, and she remembered how the tom had puffed out his chest when he first came into the forest, boasting that he would deal with any cats who dared to attack the Kin. *And this is how he's ended up.*

Violetpaw's horror turned to hot anger. The air seemed to be filled with a red haze, and her mind emptied of everything except the need to hurt the cats who had hurt her friends. She longed to feel her claws slashing through RiverClan pelts.

Hurtling into the undergrowth on the RiverClan side of the border, Violetpaw found herself face to face with Owl-nose. He ducked to avoid the blow she aimed at him, and her claws whipped harmlessly past his ears. He rose up on his hind paws, trying to box her ears with both his forepaws, but Violetpaw barreled forward, keeping her head low, and raked her claws across his unprotected belly. Owlnose backed off, his jaws wide as he gasped in pain.

Violetpaw spun away from him and flung herself back into the battle, hardly aware of which cats she was facing as she whirled around, striking with outstretched claws and letting out fearsome caterwauls. At last she realized that no more opponents were coming forward to challenge her, and she stood still, panting.

A cat loomed up beside her, and she turned, ready to defend herself, then relaxed as she realized it was Needletail. To Violetpaw's relief, though her friend had several scratches down her flanks, she didn't seem to be badly hurt.

"You fought well," Needletail meowed. "But you can stop now. It's over."

Violetpaw pushed her way through a barrier of ferns that separated her from the Thunderpath and looked around. The hard surface and the ground on either side were strewn with the bodies of dead cats. There were so many that at first Violetpaw couldn't identify any of them.

Mistystar stood close by, surrounded by some of her warriors. All of them were seriously injured; Mistystar's wound had opened up again, and blood was trickling down through her blue-gray fur.

The Kin have won, Violetpaw thought, and wondered why she didn't feel more triumphant.

Mistystar bent her head to sniff at the body of a russet tabby tom, who lay stretched out with a gaping wound in his throat. "Foxnose," Mistystar whispered. "You didn't deserve this. Heronwing, too," she added, her voice shaking as she turned toward a gray-and-black warrior whose limp body was huddled nearby. "You fought so bravely."

"Petalfur and Shadepelt are dead, too." A tortoiseshell elder—Violetpaw remembered that her name was Mosspelt—came staggering up, with blood smeared over her white chest fur. She halted beside her Clan leader and pressed her nose into Mistystar's shoulder fur. Violetpaw turned aside, unable to go on witnessing their grief.

Now the sun had fully risen, casting a reddish glow across the landscape. By the light of it, Violetpaw spotted Darktail standing in the middle of the Thunderpath. His white pelt was soaked in blood, scarlet with it, and at first Violetpaw thought that he too must have been badly wounded. But then, seeing his firm stance and the proud angle of his head, she realized that the blood was not his own.

As she watched, Darktail raised one of his paws to his mouth and licked off a clot of thick red blood. He flung back his head and let out a yowl of victory. All around him, the rest of the Kin joined in.

Before the caterwauling died away, Violetpaw noticed a limp, black-furred body lying on the ground close beside her. The dead cat's throat was torn out, and the earth around her was drenched in her blood. With a start of horror, Violetpaw recognized Pinenose, the cat who had fostered her when she first arrived in ShadowClan.

"Oh, Pinenose," Violetpaw whispered sadly, "you never showed me much love, but you took care of me when I was a stranger in your Clan. I'm sorry you had to die."

"Mistystar," Darktail began, while Violetpaw was still staring at her foster mother's body, "it's time to take your *mange-ridden* Clan out of here. This is Kin territory now."

Mistystar glared at him with hatred in her blue eyes. "We'll go," she snarled. "You give us no choice. But we'll be back."

Darktail flicked his tail dismissively. "I'm terrified."

Mistystar called her warriors together, and those who were not so badly injured began helping the seriously wounded cats to stand, with Mothwing and Willowshine quickly packing cobwebs onto the worst of their gashes.

Violetpaw spotted Reedwhisker, who had leaped in to defend his leader and now lay on one side, panting with his eyes half closed. Icewing's white pelt was half clawed off, her wounds showing red and angry, while one of Brackenpelt's ears was shredded, and she held one forepaw off the ground as she tottered upright. Mintfur looked as if he was dead, though he let out a groan when Mothwing bent over him and laid a paw on his neck.

"One moment," Darktail meowed, stepping forward. "Where do you think you're taking these cats?"

Mistystar stared at him as if she found it hard to understand the question. "With us, of course," she replied, "so that Mothwing and Willowshine can treat their injuries. The battle is over!"

"The wounded stay with me," Darktail hissed, his eyes dark and menacing as he gazed at Mistystar. Sliding out his claws, he added, "Unless you'd like to fight us for them."

Mistystar slid out her claws in response, drawing her lips back in the beginning of a snarl. But after a moment's hesitation, facing Darktail with her shoulder fur bristling, she took a pace back. Violetpaw guessed she was considering the poor shape her Clan cats were in, and her own serious wound. None of them were a match for Darktail; the rogue leader seemed to have grown even stronger in the chaos of the battle.

Reedwhisker raised his head, breaking the tense silence. "Leave us," he meowed to Mistystar. "It's not worth another terrible fight. We'll be okay."

Mistystar hesitated a few heartbeats more, then seemed to realize that she had no choice. "Very well," she mewed. "But none of you should worry. We'll come back for you—I promise you that. Meanwhile . . . Darktail, you should at least let us take the bodies of our Clanmates for burial."

Darktail's mouth twisted in mockery. "That carrion? Forget it, flea-pelt."

A growl rumbled from Mistystar's throat as her neck fur fluffed out. Violetpaw thought that she was within a heartbeat of launching herself at the rogue leader.

Oh, StarClan, no!

Before Mistystar could move, the elder Mosspelt stepped forward, thrusting herself between Darktail and her leader. "Don't," she mewed, her voice low and urgent. "That's what he wants."

"But we can't leave our Clanmates here as if they were pieces of crow-food!" Mistystar protested.

"Our Clanmates are not here," Mosspelt persisted. "We can sit vigil for them tonight wherever we happen to be. Not even Darktail can stop their spirits from traveling to StarClan."

Mistystar hesitated for a moment, then bowed her head in acquiescence. "You're right," she whispered. "But it breaks my heart."

Darktail let out a snort, watching with a gloating expression on his face as the defeated RiverClan cats limped off toward the lake. "Feel free to cross my territory on your way to ThunderClan," he sneered. "They're weak and tenderhearted; they're bound to take you in."

Mistystar did not respond, but she did lead her cats away along the lakeshore, through what had once been ShadowClan territory, on the way to ThunderClan. Violetpaw watched them go, half wishing she could go with them but knowing it was impossible.

"Good riddance," Darktail growled, a look of triumph in his eyes. Turning to his followers, he added, "Gather up the prisoners. Gather them up, and find a place to hold them."

CHAPTER 10

❧

"Are you sure that Bramblestar will be okay with this?" Mothwing asked as she and Alderheart slipped through the undergrowth on their way to the lake. Two days had passed since Darktail's group had attacked RiverClan and RiverClan had taken refuge in ThunderClan's camp.

Alderheart felt uncomfortably tense, his ears pricked for the first sounds of a ThunderClan patrol that might stop him and the RiverClan medicine cat and ask awkward questions.

"I'm sure he *won't*," he replied, knowing the huge risk he and Mothwing were taking, "and that's why I didn't ask him."

The golden tabby paused for a moment and turned her amber gaze on Alderheart. "Will you be in trouble?" she asked.

"Probably." Alderheart shrugged. "But it'll be okay. Bramblestar knows that medicine cats sometimes have to make their own decisions about what's right."

Mothwing nodded, then set off again. "I'm so grateful to you, Alderheart," she mewed. "We *have* to know what's going on in the RiverClan camp. But Willowshine is busy with our injured warriors, and I don't think I could do this alone."

Alderheart wasn't surprised. News of the battle had shocked .

him from ears to tail-tip. Darktail had driven Rowanstar and the others from ShadowClan's territory, but that felt different, because so many ShadowClan cats had stayed and taken his side. Now Darktail was attacking Clans who had nothing to do with him? Where would it end? It made Alderheart feel that danger could be lurking behind every rock.

He admired Mothwing for having the courage to set paw on RiverClan territory, now that it was occupied by the rogue leader and his followers. *I must have bees in my brain for agreeing to go with her,* he thought ruefully.

The two medicine cats emerged from the undergrowth and padded down the strip of pebbles that led to the edge of the lake. Mothwing halted again, staring out across the water to the distant trees and bushes of RiverClan territory. Alderheart couldn't believe how tranquil the scene looked, the surface of the lake glittering under the morning sun, when all around, the Clans' territories were in turmoil.

"Which way now?" he asked, standing beside Mothwing. "Through ShadowClan or WindClan?" *Both routes are dangerous,* he reflected. *WindClan has closed its borders, and Darktail's rogues are still patrolling ShadowClan.*

"WindClan," Mothwing replied. "If we go through ShadowClan we're bound to meet the rogues long before we get to RiverClan. A WindClan patrol might give us a hard time, but the rogues will claw our pelts off if they catch us."

"Works for me," Alderheart commented.

"Besides," Mothwing added, "WindClan let Mistystar and her patrol pass yesterday."

"Mistystar went back to RiverClan?" Alderheart felt surprise prickling every hair of his pelt. Since the RiverClan warriors had arrived, he had been too busy patching up injuries in the medicine cats' den to know much about what was happening elsewhere.

"Yes," Mothwing meowed. "She took a patrol over to RiverClan to try to free the prisoners and collect the bodies of our Clanmates for burial, but some of the rogues spotted them when they tried to cross the border. There was a skirmish, and . . ." Her voice was shaking, and she paused to steady it. "Mistystar and our warriors lost. Raven—she was leading the rogues' patrol—let them go, but she told Mistystar that if there was another attempt to steal back the territory, the rogues would kill the RiverClan prisoners."

"That's outrageous!" Alderheart exclaimed, digging his claws into the soft sand of the lake's edge.

"It is." Mothwing blinked unhappily. "But we can't just leave them there and do nothing!"

With a determined flick of her tail, she set off again along the water's edge in the direction of the WindClan border.

"So what's the plan?" Alderheart asked as he padded along beside her.

"Willowshine and I built up a good store of herbs in our den," Mothwing told him. "I thought if I went there and told the rogues I had come to collect them, they might let me into the camp."

"It's worth a try," Alderheart responded. He remembered his quest, when he had discovered Darktail and his rogues in the gorge where SkyClan used to live. Back then, Darktail had seemed fascinated by all the things that medicine cats knew. *I hope that means he'll respect medicine-cat ways now, even though his rogues aren't Clan cats.*

"Of course, I don't care if they let us take the herbs or not," Mothwing went on. "We can always gather more. But once we're in the camp, we might be able to find out how the prisoners are doing, and where they're being kept. If we get really lucky, we might be able to speak to them."

Approaching the stream that marked the border with WindClan, Alderheart opened his jaws to taste the air, and he picked up the powerful fresh scent of WindClan cats. At first he couldn't see any movement on the hillside, but as he and Mothwing splashed through the water and climbed out on the opposite bank, a WindClan patrol rose up out of a clump of reeds and bounded forward to block their way.

"What do you want?" Sedgewhisker, who was in the lead, raked her gaze over both medicine cats. "I hope you're not expecting to visit Onestar. We made it clear enough yesterday that he doesn't want to see any other cats."

Yesterday? Alderheart wondered. Sedgewhisker didn't seem to be talking about Mistystar's patrol just passing along the lakeshore. *I didn't know any cats had tried to visit Onestar.* He pushed his curiosity aside for the moment, swallowing anger at the tabby she-cat's hostile tone. "No," he mewed. "We just want to pass over your territory to get to RiverClan."

At his words, Sedgewhisker relaxed a little, though her companions, Leaftail and Oatclaw, still bristled with suspicion.

Alderheart remembered that his Clanmates always spoke of Sedgewhisker as a reasonable cat; he was relieved that she was the one they had to deal with.

"Well—" she began.

"Don't let them! It's a ThunderClan trick!" Leaftail growled.

Sedgewhisker glanced over her shoulder at her Clanmate. "They're medicine cats, mouse-brain!" Turning back to Alderheart and Mothwing, she added, "Okay, but put one paw more than three tail-lengths from the water and you might find yourself missing your ears."

Alderheart and Mothwing both ignored the threat. "Thank you, Sedgewhisker," Mothwing mewed with a polite dip of her head.

Alderheart could sense the eyes of the patrol boring into his back as he and Mothwing made their way along the lakeshore at the foot of the swell of moorland. "What did Sedgewhisker mean, 'made it clear enough yesterday'?" he asked.

"I forgot you might not have heard," Mothwing replied. "When Mistystar got back from RiverClan, she sent Mallownose and Petalfur to see Onestar and ask for his help. But a WindClan patrol turned them back at the border. Onestar doesn't want to speak to any cat outside his own Clan."

"That's really weird," Alderheart meowed. "When the rogues first arrived, Onestar was so keen to have them driven out. And now . . . things have only gotten worse, but he doesn't seem bothered at all, whether they stay or go."

Mothwing nodded agreement. "I heard how Darktail said

something to Onestar in the first battle. I wonder what it was."

"You and every cat in ThunderClan!" Alderheart responded. "It must have been catastrophic, to affect him like this."

As he and Mothwing drew closer to the horseplace, Alderheart felt uneasy. It was bad enough in ThunderClan's camp: Juniperclaw and Strikestone had arrived recently from ShadowClan, and with the additional warriors from RiverClan, all the cats were treading on one another's tails. And all the newcomers were demanding help to get back their territory. Every cat was stunned that Darktail had invaded RiverClan. His power now extended over half the land around the lake.

Bramblestar had sent out extra patrols, afraid that the rogues could attack ThunderClan at any moment. So far there was no sign that Darktail was planning another invasion, but every cat knew that, sooner or later, it would come. And no cat knew where he was holding the prisoners or how they might be rescued, until Mothwing had come up with her idea.

If her idea even works . . .

"I'm sorry, Alderheart." Mothwing broke the silence as if she had been following his thoughts. "I know this is a mouse-brained plan, but what else can we do?"

"You're right," Alderheart responded, pushing aside his misgivings. "We can't let things go on as they are. Did you hear about Dawnpelt?"

Mothwing shook her head. "What about her?"

"Juniperclaw   and   Strikestone—you   know,   they're

Dawnpelt's kits—came into our camp a few days ago. They asked to join Rowanstar and their other Clanmates, and they said that Dawnpelt was going to follow them, but she never showed."

Mothwing gave Alderheart an uneasy glance. "That's really worrying."

"Juniperclaw and Strikestone don't know what to do. They told us that things were really bad among the rogues, and they're afraid that Darktail has done something to Dawnpelt."

"That wouldn't surprise me," Mothwing mewed.

"It wouldn't surprise any cat. I suppose Dawnpelt might have changed her mind about leaving, but I doubt it."

"Then if we can get into the RiverClan camp," Mothwing suggested, "we might keep a lookout for Dawnpelt, too. If she's there, then at least we can reassure her kits that Darktail didn't hurt her."

And if she's not there . . . Alderheart had a cold feeling in his belly when he thought about Dawnpelt. *I'm sure something bad has happened to her.*

He and Mothwing fell silent again as they passed the horseplace and padded along the stretch of marshland toward the RiverClan border. Glancing up toward the ridge, which Twigpaw had to have crossed on her journey to find the barn where SkyClan was sheltering, Alderheart thought of the other reason he felt tense from his whiskers to his tail-tip.

Dovewing, Tigerheart, and Molewhisker haven't come back with news of her. A quarter moon is an awfully long time to travel to the barn and back.

Alderheart tried to convince himself that as long as the

patrol was still out looking, there was still hope that Twigpaw was okay. But he couldn't manage to banish his fear that he would never see the small apprentice again.

Passing the end of the tree-bridge that led to the island, Alderheart once more made an effort to thrust unwelcome thoughts away. It was time to concentrate on their mission.

When the two medicine cats reached the border, they discovered that the RiverClan scent markers were fading. Alderheart gagged on a mingled, unfamiliar scent, strong and sour, as if the cats who'd left it had never washed themselves since they were kitted. He knew that the reek must come from the rogues.

Are they nearby now? he wondered, his muscles tensing.

Mothwing wrinkled her nose and let out a huff of disgust. "Yuck! They've fouled the whole territory with their stink."

Now she and Alderheart trod warily, taking advantage of the cover that every bush and tuft of long grass offered them.

"It's weird," Alderheart murmured as they paused to rest in a dip in the ground. "Before the battle, a RiverClan patrol would have met us long before now. But we haven't seen a whisker of the rogues."

Mothwing flicked her ears in agreement. "I don't like the silence," she whispered. "But maybe it means Darktail doesn't have enough cats to patrol regularly. After all, he's trying to hold two territories now."

The two cats continued, growing even more cautious as they began to hear the gurgle of running water not far ahead: the stream at the edge of the RiverClan camp. The reek of rogue scent was in the air, growing stronger with every paw step they took.

To Alderheart's surprise, he and Mothwing reached the bank of the stream without meeting any of the enemy cats. But as soon as they set paw in the water and began to cross, three heads appeared over the top of the opposite bank, and three cats came bounding down to the water's edge, where they stood waiting for the medicine cats.

Alderheart couldn't help his heart thumping harder in his chest when he saw that one of the cats was Needletail. Instinctively, he lifted a paw in greeting and stepped forward to meet her. Then he halted as he saw Needletail regarding him with a cold, unrecognizing stare.

We grew to be such good friends when she came with us on my quest, he thought sadly.

It was the cat in the lead, a long-furred black she-cat, who spoke.

"Greetings." Though the word was polite, her voice was harsh. "What are you cats doing here?"

While she was speaking, the third cat stepped out from behind Needletail, and Alderheart got a good look at her for the first time. His heart lurched again as he realized that she was Violetpaw. She looked so much like the missing Twigpaw, and as he gazed at her, Alderheart's compassion swelled up until it almost choked him.

She's trying to look brave and fierce, he thought, *but somehow I can tell that she is just sad and afraid!*

Mothwing dipped her head politely in response to the black

she-cat's question. "Greetings, Raven," she meowed. "Alder-heart and I have come to collect my herb stores."

It was Needletail who replied, the fur on her neck and shoulders rising. "Don't you know this is Kin territory now?"

"Yes, of course we do." Mothwing still kept her even, polite tone. "But medicine cats are supposed to be able to cross Clan boundaries, even after a battle. I gathered those herbs, and we need them for all the extra cats who are living in Thunder-Clan now."

Raven let out a contemptuous snort. "Yeah, well, we're not Clan cats; we are Kin. And the Kin follow no rules but their own," she hissed. "This territory and everything in it are ours now—right, Needletail?"

"Right," Needletail mewed firmly. "We are not Clan cats. Go home now, if you know what's good for you."

As they spoke, Alderheart kept looking at Violetpaw, who had stayed quiet the whole time. She looked upset and unsure of herself, gazing straight ahead as if she didn't want to be near the others as they argued.

I should feel angry with her, for how she attacked Twigpaw in the battle, but she's so young. . . . How can she stand up to all these older cats, telling her what she should do?

Glancing back at Needletail, Alderheart met her gaze, and for a moment the two cats stared at each other. Alderheart could see that behind the strength and anger, Needletail was carrying some hurt deep within her. He remembered that the RiverClan cats had told him that Rain hadn't been seen in the battle.

I wonder if something bad happened to him. Needletail liked him so much. . . .

As he kept gazing at her, something in Needletail's expression shifted. "Okay," she began. "You can come and get the herbs—"

"What?" Raven interrupted, her ears flattened with fury. "Are you completely mouse-brained? They—"

"No, wait. Listen," Needletail meowed. "They can come in, *if* they tell Puddleshine what the herbs are used for."

Raven looked thoughtful, as if she was considering Needletail's suggestion, but Alderheart couldn't understand what his former friend was meowing about.

Puddleshine must know most of the herbs by now, since Yellowfang started teaching him in his dreams. Doesn't Needletail realize that? Her intense expression wasn't giving him any clues. *What is she up to?*

Finally Raven gave an ungracious shrug. "I suppose you might have a point. Okay," she added to the two medicine cats. "You can come into the camp, but if you put one whisker out of line you will be leaving it with a serious limp—that's if you leave it at all."

Alderheart and Mothwing climbed the bank, flanked by Raven and Needletail, with Violetpaw trailing behind. As they crossed the shallow ridge and padded down into the camp, Alderheart's pelt prickled with horror at what he saw. The lush growth of ferns that bordered the clearing and sheltered the dens had been torn apart, and debris was scattered everywhere. The cats themselves looked dirty and hungry, with wild looks in their eyes, as if they expected to be attacked in the next heartbeat. Alderheart scanned the cats for Dawn-pelt, but did not see her.

He tried to look around for the cream-furred she-cat, or to figure out where the prisoners were being held, but Raven hustled him and Mothwing along far too quickly for him to spot any sign of them.

As they hurried across the camp, Violetpaw bounded forward to catch up with Alderheart and trot along by his side.

"How is Twigpaw?" Her mew was soft, as though she didn't want Raven to overhear. "Is her injury healing okay?"

For a moment, Alderheart didn't know how to answer. He could see from the pain in Violetpaw's eyes that she felt terrible about her attack on her sister during the battle. He felt even more pity for her, clearly lost and trapped among these vicious cats.

"Yes," he replied at last, his throat tightening as he spoke the lie. "Twigpaw is recovering just fine."

He hated lying to her, and he wished he could have told her how he had seen in a vision a cat who might be her kin. But there was no time for that, or for the truth about where Twigpaw had gone.

"Thank you," Violetpaw mewed, ducking her head briefly, then wandering off across the camp.

Raven led the way through a line of bushes that enclosed the clearing and down to the other stream that bordered the camp on the opposite side. Here the current had scoured out a hollow underneath the bank, a good-sized cave with a roof supported by tree roots. On a stretch of pebbles at the cave opening, Puddleshine was sitting and sorting herbs into different piles.

"This is your den?" Alderheart asked Mothwing. "It's cool!"

The golden tabby she-cat looked sad. "It *was* my den," she murmured.

Puddleshine sprang up hopefully as Alderheart and the other cats leaped down the bank and landed on the pebbles. "Hi," he meowed, his ears twitching forward in surprise. "What brings you here?"

"Mothwing and Alderheart have come to collect Mothwing's herb stores," Needletail replied. "In exchange, they're going to tell you how to use some of them, like"—Needletail glanced around a little wildly, then grabbed a sprig of watermint in her claws—"like this," she finished.

Puddleshine looked slightly confused. "But that's an easy one. It's watermint, and you use it to treat a bellyache. Yellowfang showed me that in my dreams, along with . . ."

His voice trailed off as he gazed at Needletail and Raven, clearly realizing that something was going on that he didn't understand. Needletail still had the same intense expression, while Raven's eyes suddenly narrowed with suspicion and she slid out her claws.

I hope Puddleshine figures out that Needletail has a plan, Alderheart thought, though he was still wondering what the plan might be.

"Of course, I don't know nearly *everything* yet," Puddleshine went on. "I could definitely use some help with some things. For example, I was just wondering what this is." He nudged a marigold flower closer to Mothwing.

Alderheart's belly lurched. *Every medicine-cat apprentice learns about marigold—it's one of the first herbs we work with! Surely Raven is going to realize that she's being tricked?* But when the black she-cat stayed silent, merely looking on stonily, he breathed a thankful sigh that the rogues knew nothing about medicine cats.

"That's called marigold. We mostly use it to stop infection," Mothwing explained, "though it will help aching joints if you can't get daisy leaves."

Puddleshine nodded, looking as if he was trying to concentrate and remember. To Alderheart's relief, Raven relaxed her suspicious stance and began to clean her claws.

"And this is yarrow," Mothwing continued. "Chewed and swallowed, it will make you vomit, which means it's good for a cat who's eaten something they shouldn't have. . . ."

While the lesson went on, Alderheart nudged Needletail and drew her off to one side. "How are you really doing?" he asked. "Is everything okay? What happened to Rain?"

Needletail flicked her tail, brushing off his concern. "Rain is dead," she told him, "but it's fine. It's a good thing, really."

Alderheart tried to hide his shock at Needletail's indifference toward the death of any cat, especially a cat she had cared for. "And how are you?" he meowed.

"Oh, I'm fine." Needletail seemed to be trying to work up some enthusiasm in her tone, but she wasn't doing a very good job of it. "Everything's fine."

Why does she keep repeating that? Alderheart wondered. *Is she trying to convince herself?*

"Actually," Needletail went on, "I wanted to ask you about Dawnpelt. How is she doing in ThunderClan?"

Alderheart felt his heart sink right down into his paws. But he knew he would have to answer the question. "Dawnpelt isn't in ThunderClan," he replied. "Isn't she still with you and the rogues?"

"No," Needletail explained, her eyes widening in apprehension. "She went to ThunderClan to live with her parents and her littermate."

Alderheart shook his head. "I'm sorry, but she hasn't come to our camp."

As he spoke, the fur on the back of Needletail's neck stood up and terror flashed into her eyes. She looked as if she had suddenly understood something, and it had driven her into the depths of fear.

"What do you—" Alderheart began.

"Well, if something happened to Dawnpelt, it was her own fault!" Needletail interrupted. "She should have been more careful."

Alderheart wanted to protest at Needletail's harsh tone—then he realized that Raven still stood close by, watching and listening carefully. There was no way that Needletail could say what she truly meant. Every hair on his pelt prickled as he began to understand her fear.

I've seen Needletail in a lot of different moods, but never terrified like this. What is going on here with the rogues?

CHAPTER 11

Violetpaw crouched under a bush at the edge of the old RiverClan camp, sharing a fish with Loki and Zelda. Each mouthful of the cold, slimy prey threatened to choke her, and it was an effort to swallow.

"I really don't like fish," she muttered. "I'd give anything for a warm, juicy mouse!"

"Me too," Loki agreed. "Or a bowl of the pellets my house-folk used to give me."

Zelda's only response was a sigh.

The two surviving kittypets had changed since the battle, when Max had been killed. Their excitement and enthusiasm had drained away, and they seemed to realize that they would never be allowed to leave the Kin. Darktail no longer treated them with fake friendliness; he and the other rogues simply ignored them, and Violetpaw was their only friend.

"Well," she mewed, "Darktail says that the fish is ours now, just like the territory, so we all have to get used to it."

"Some of the rogues really like it," Loki pointed out. "I saw Roach and Nettle *fighting* over a fish yesterday."

"Raven, too," Zelda agreed. "And they all leave the nasty

scraps and bones lying all over the camp! Don't they realize they could attract scavengers?"

Forcing down the last of the disgusting fish, Violetpaw sat up to clean her whiskers. On the far side of the camp Raven and Sleekwhisker were bringing the prisoners out of the bramble thicket that had once been the RiverClan nursery. Darktail stood waiting for them in the middle of the clearing.

Almost all the rogues and remaining ShadowClan cats had moved over to RiverClan; Darktail had only left a small group to guard the ShadowClan territory. The camp here was crowded, and keeping the prisoners only made it worse.

Why doesn't Darktail just let these cats go? Violetpaw asked herself. *What does he want with them?*

At sunrise the day before, every cat had realized that Berryheart and Beenose were nowhere to be found. Violetpaw assumed they had gone to ThunderClan, like Dawnpelt, but when she'd tried to ask Needletail about it, her friend had changed the subject.

Why does Darktail let the ShadowClan cats leave, and yet he keeps these prisoners so close? It doesn't make sense.

The prisoners all looked skinny and half-starved, tottering up to Darktail on shaky paws.

"It is time for you to recite the pledge of loyalty to the Kin," Darktail meowed when they were standing in front of him. "Repeat after me: I swear to be a friend to the Kin . . ."

Violetpaw felt a faint tingle of excitement as the prisoners hesitated, exchanging reluctant glances. Darktail had begun demanding the oath from them on the day after the battle, insisting that no cat would be fed unless they proved they were loyal to the Kin. At first the RiverClan warriors had held out—but as the days passed, first one and then another had given in, until Reedwhisker was the only one left who wouldn't repeat the pledge of loyalty to Darktail, proudly refusing to betray his Clan in spite of his hunger and the many wounds he had taken in the battle.

Will he be brave enough to defy Darktail again? she asked herself.

But her small bubble of hope burst as Reedwhisker dipped his head and joined in the oath with his Clanmates, so that all four cats were reciting the words.

He must be too hungry to fight anymore, she thought sadly.

"What was that, Reedwhisker?" Darktail asked. "I didn't quite hear you. Say it again, louder this time."

Looking deeply humiliated, his head and tail drooping, Reedwhisker raised his voice and repeated the words. Violet-paw thought that her heart would break for him.

Once the pledge was finished, Darktail took up a couple of scrawny mice and tossed them at the prisoners, who were herded back into the thicket by Sleekwhisker and Raven.

That's hardly enough for one hungry cat, let alone four of them!

Darktail nodded to the guards and turned away, a satisfied expression on his face.

Thinking about the missing cats made Violetpaw want to go and find Needletail, to try once again to get some information out of her. She started to slip away when Darktail wasn't looking, only to be called back by the rogue leader.

"Violetpaw! Over here! I need to talk to you."

Even though Darktail's voice was warm and friendly, something about it made every hair on Violetpaw's pelt start to rise. *When he uses that voice, that's when he's most dangerous.*

Obediently, she padded over to Darktail and halted a tail-length away from him. She kept her paws neatly together and curled her tail along her side, with her head bent submissively—she knew this was a pose that would please Darktail.

"I've heard that some herbs are missing from the medicine-cat den," Darktail began. "I'm afraid that one of our own cats has stolen them."

Violetpaw risked a glance at him and saw that though his face was calm, there was something malignant in the depths of his eyes.

"If any cat is hoarding herbs for their own use," Darktail continued smoothly, "then I need to know about it. After all, it's not fair for one cat to keep all the herbs for themselves. They're for every cat to share!" Darktail licked one paw and smoothed it over his ear. "I think sharing is very important, as I'm sure you know."

His last words confused Violetpaw. She had seen plenty of evidence that Darktail only shared when it suited his own needs. But she was relieved that she had a good answer to give him.

"No cat stole the herbs or did anything wrong," she assured him. "Alderheart and Mothwing just came to take Mothwing's herbs, since she was the one who collected and stored them."

"Oh, well, yes, of course—*their* herbs," Darktail meowed calmly. "That makes a lot of sense. But I have just one more question . . ."

He paused, and Violetpaw felt her belly lurch with apprehension.

"Which cat exactly told Mothwing and Alderheart that it was okay to come onto our territory to get the herbs?" Darktail asked.

His voice was still friendly, but Violetpaw saw that his eyes were cold and hard. She realized that she was making—no, had *already* made a terrible mistake.

I should have said I didn't know anything about the herbs, she thought, trying to fight down panic. *Maybe Darktail is just pretending not to be angry.*

"I—I'm not sure," Violetpaw stammered. "I mean, no one cat said it was okay. We all just sort of . . . agreed."

Darktail said nothing, just went on staring at her until Violetpaw felt she would never be able to escape from the terrible power of his gaze.

"Am I in trouble?" she asked, her voice no more than a husky whisper.

"Not at all," Darktail assured her. "You and I have an understanding, don't we, Violetpaw? We were both kits that no cat wanted."

"But that's not true!" Violetpaw began to protest. "The ShadowClan cats were very kind to me, and—"

She broke off, trying not to shudder, as Darktail moved

closer to her, so close that she could feel his breath riffling her whiskers.

"I know that feeling well," Darktail purred. "When one feels unwanted, one might do anything—anything at all—to hold on to the cats one cares about. Even lie to protect them. Isn't that so, Violetpaw?"

Violetpaw swallowed hard; she couldn't think of a single thing to say.

"I feel a special connection to you," Darktail went on, "but that doesn't mean that I couldn't make your life very unpleasant if you go on lying to me." When Violetpaw still didn't speak, he added, "And it's not just *you* that I could punish for your lie."

Violetpaw felt an icy claw of fear stab her to the heart. *Why couldn't I have kept my big mouth shut?* she asked herself despairingly. *If I'd told him I didn't know, he'd have believed me.*

"Who *exactly* said this was okay?" Darktail persisted. "Was it Puddleshine? Or some other cat? Was it Needletail?"

Violetpaw took a step back, but Darktail still held her with his intense gaze, as if he could see right into her mind and watch her memory of the encounter when Alderheart and Mothwing arrived in the RiverClan camp.

"It *was* Needletail, wasn't it?" Darktail meowed.

"I—I don't know . . . ," Violetpaw mumbled. "I didn't really see . . ."

But it was far too late for that. Darktail bent his head closer still, until Violetpaw could smell his fishy breath.

"I only want to know the truth," he continued. "I won't punish Needletail—why should I? She has always been loyal to me. She was one of the first cats to join us."

Violetpaw desperately wanted to believe him. *And if I don't tell him now, Puddleshine probably will.* "Yes," she whispered, still unsure that she was doing the right thing. "Needletail did say that they could take the herbs."

"Thank you." Darktail's eyes flashed with anger. His gaze raked the camp until he spotted Needletail, who was just emerging from the bushes with a mouse in her jaws. "Needletail!" he called.

He began striding swiftly across the camp toward the silver-gray she-cat, who started at the sound of his voice and dropped the prey she was carrying.

Violetpaw scurried after him. A wave of panic surged through her as Darktail grabbed Needletail roughly by her scruff and flung her to the ground.

"What were you doing, giving away our herbs?" he yowled angrily. "Are you a spy? Are you loyal to the Kin or not? Are you like your friend, that useless mange-pelt Rain?"

Needletail cowered, terrified, under the barrage of questions. She was clearly struggling to stay calm, but Darktail's furious onslaught had unnerved her.

"You said you wouldn't punish her!" Violetpaw protested.

"She is not being punished," Darktail responded. "She is being shown where she's gone wrong. . . . I am *helping* her." Turning back to Needletail, he added, "If you're not happy with the way I'm leading the Kin, you can leave if you want—just like Dawnpelt did."

Needletail's eyes widened and she looked even more terrified. And realization struck Violetpaw like a flash of lightning.

Could it be that Dawnpelt never made it to ThunderClan . . . because Darktail killed her?

Violetpaw couldn't hold back a shriek of horror. Instantly Darktail spun around, his eyes slitted and full of rage.

"What, do you want to leave too?" he asked in a soft, menacing voice. "I don't want any cats here who don't want to be here."

"She wants to stay," Needletail meowed, scrambling up to stand beside Violetpaw. "We both really, really *want* to stay."

Violetpaw had never been so scared in her life as when Darktail turned a questioning gaze on her. "I want to stay! I promise!" she assured him, her voice quavering.

Darktail nodded. "That's good. You have passed my test, Violetpaw. Because of course, I already knew all of this. Did you think Raven would have kept it from me?"

Of course it was Raven! Violetpaw shuddered with horror at the thought that Darktail had been playing with her, as he might have played with a mouse before he killed it.

"As for you," Darktail went on to Needletail, "because of your betrayal, you must live with our RiverClan prisoners until you earn the right to be one of the Kin again. Roach! Nettle!"

Darktail beckoned with his tail to the two rogues who sat

nearest him, squabbling over the remains of a fish. They padded over, and at Darktail's order grabbed Needletail by her
shoulders, one on each side, and began hauling her toward the
bramble thicket where the RiverClan prisoners were kept.
Needletail struggled for a couple of heartbeats, then let them
take her.

"No!" Violetpaw mewed in anguish. Scared and confused,
she just wanted to be with her friend. "I'll go, too!"

"No, no." Darktail blocked her when she tried to follow,
his voice smooth and friendly again. "You've proved yourself a good and loyal kit. Not like Needletail—and not like
Puddleshine, who gave away herbs that rightfully belonged
to his Kin." He paused, then added, "I said I wouldn't punish Needletail, and I'm not, but Puddleshine . . . now he *does*
deserve punishment."

Darktail stalked off toward the medicine-cat den, and not
knowing what else to do, Violetpaw followed close behind.

Oh, StarClan . . . what have I done?

CHAPTER 12

♣

"So what's the problem?" Alderheart asked, emerging from the herb store to greet the gray tabby tom who had just appeared in the medicine cats' den.

Stormcloud let out a long sigh. "I'm not really sure," he mewed. "I feel guilty for even being here, when so many warriors are badly wounded."

"Don't say that," Alderheart responded. "Any cat who feels unwell is entitled to come visit the medicine cats. Look what happened to Purdy. If he hadn't decided to put up with his bellyache because he thought we were too busy, he might still be here telling stories to us."

Stormcloud nodded sadly. "I really miss Purdy."

He and Alderheart were alone in the den. Briarlight had dragged herself over to the fresh-kill pile with Jayfeather, while Leafpool was helping Mothwing and Willowshine check on the RiverClan cats who were still in poor shape after the battle. Even with five medicine cats in the camp, their resources were being stretched thin.

There are simply too many cats here, he thought. *Even if they were all healthy, they couldn't possibly be comfortable. And some of the RiverClan cats are so seriously hurt that they need care from sunrise to sunrise.*

When RiverClan had first arrived, Squirrelflight had suggested using the abandoned Twoleg nest as an overflow camp.

"We could transfer the worst of the injured over there," she meowed, "and send Leafpool and Willowshine to live with them. There are herbs growing there, right beside the entrance."

Alderheart had thought that was a brilliant idea, but Rowanstar had protested.

"There's no need for that. This is just temporary. ShadowClan and RiverClan will be back in our own territories soon."

Bramblestar had thought for a few moments, then warily agreed with the ShadowClan leader. Alderheart suspected that he and Rowanstar believed that the Twoleg nest would be vulnerable if the rogues attacked.

They could well be right, but that still leaves us with a camp that is full to bursting.

"So, what's the matter with you?" Alderheart repeated to Stormcloud. "Come on, spit it out."

Stormcloud drew one gray tabby paw over his ear. "I can't sleep," he confessed. "And sometimes my chest feels so tight that I can barely take a breath."

"Hmm . . . ," Alderheart murmured. "Have you been upset about anything?"

The tabby tom's ears flicked forward in surprise. "Sure. What *isn't* there to be upset about?" he demanded. "The camp is so crowded, we're treading on each other's tails; Rowanstar and Bramblestar snap at each other every chance they get, and adding Mistystar to the mix has only made it worse. And every cat is terrified that Darktail and his rogues will come for us next."

Alderheart nodded. Stormcloud spoke the truth. Bramblestar was sending out even more patrols, but no cats could agree on the best way of defending themselves. They'd sent more patrols to WindClan, but their borders were still closed, with Onestar refusing even to talk to the other Clans.

"I never had to put up with anything like this when I was a kittypet," Stormcloud went on. "I joined ThunderClan because I believed in what the Clans stood for, but what if—"

He broke off, giving his chest fur a few self-conscious licks.

"What?" Alderheart asked.

Stormcloud shook his head. "Nothing."

Alderheart was pretty sure he knew what the tabby tom had been about to say. *What if there are no Clans soon?* For the first time, Alderheart became aware that this was possible. *If the rogues attack us and win, our whole way of life will just be . . . gone.*

"You should practice taking slow, deep breaths," he told Stormcloud, pushing his fears aside to concentrate on the immediate problem. "Try to relax as much as you can. I'll give you some tansy; that should help."

He padded back into the cleft to fetch tansy leaves from the herb store. While Stormcloud chewed them up, he added, "Tell Squirrelflight that I've excused you from patrols for today. You need to get some rest. Come and see me tonight, before you go to your nest, and I'll give you a juniper berry."

"Thanks, Alderheart." Stormcloud swiped his tongue

around his jaws. "I feel better already."

"Let me know how it goes," Alderheart meowed. "I'm sure everything will work out in the end." *I wish I really believed that, but I'm not sure I do.*

When Stormcloud was gone, Alderheart went back into the cleft to tidy the store and take stock of which herbs were running low. But he had barely begun when he heard yowls and running paw steps coming from the camp. He started up, his pads prickling with apprehension and his fur beginning to bristle.

Is this the attack?

Racing past the bramble screen into the clearing, Alderheart saw cats emerging from the thorn tunnel and recognized Dovewing, Tigerheart, and Molewhisker. At first, relief flooded through him, his shoulder fur lying flat again, but as he ran eagerly toward them, his belly cramped with a different kind of fear. There was no sign of Twigpaw.

Dovewing bounded up to him, with Tigerheart just behind her, while Molewhisker headed toward the tumbled rocks, meowing, "I'll fetch Bramblestar!" as he went.

"Just tell me," Alderheart begged. "I can't wait for Bramblestar. Is she dead?"

Dovewing's green eyes were full of sorrow, which told Alderheart the news that he didn't want to hear. "Bramblestar ought to hear this first," she murmured.

"Please!" Alderheart raked the ground with his claws. "It's like a fox is tearing me apart."

Dovewing bent her head. "I'm sorry." Her voice was so soft

that Alderheart could scarcely hear her. "We think that Twig-paw is probably dead."

As she spoke the words, Alderheart felt something break inside him, like a snapped branch in the frost of leaf-bare. For a moment he couldn't speak; at last he forced out two words in a hoarse voice. "What happened?"

"We don't know for sure," Dovewing replied, her head drooping sadly. "But we found her blood and fur beside the Thunderpath, near the tunnel where she was born."

"Are you *sure* it was her blood?" Alderheart asked, desperately trying to hold on to hope.

Tigerheart nodded. "The scent was faint, but it was Twig-paw's. It looks like she died just as her mother did . . . hit by a monster."

Alderheart's legs felt like they were turning to water; he staggered and slumped to the ground. At the same moment, Molewhisker returned with Bramblestar, deep concern in the Clan leader's face as he strode up to them.

Ivypool bounded over from the fresh-kill pile, and more cats began to gather around, all of them eager for the news.

But Alderheart could hardly bear to listen as Bramblestar began to question the returning patrol. His heart had sunk right down into his paws.

Twigpaw was so young, he thought. *I can't believe she'll never follow me around anymore, or run up and tease me. I can't believe she's really gone.*

As he looked up, struggling to push aside his misery, he realized that even more cats were clustering around Bramble-star, listening to Dovewing in horrified silence.

"We searched the area," the gray she-cat meowed. "We even crossed underneath the Thunderpath by the tunnel and tried to pick up her trail on the other side, but there were no signs of her." Her voice broke. "There was nothing more we could do."

"This is all my fault!" Ivypool exclaimed with a lash of her tail. "I feel so guilty."

Bramblestar stretched out his neck to touch the silver-and-white warrior's shoulder with his nose. "You have nothing to feel guilty about," he assured her.

"Oh, but I do!" Ivypool insisted, her blue eyes dark with grief. "I was her mentor, and I knew how much she wanted to go and look for SkyClan, but I tried to talk her out of it . . . for stupid reasons, really," she added with a glance at her sister, Dovewing.

Dovewing looked up, her whiskers twitching in surprise, while Tigerheart curled his tail protectively around her shoulders. Alderheart saw something flash in Ivypool's eyes, but he had no interest just then in whatever was going on with the three of them.

"*I'm* the one who should be feeling guilty," he confessed. "I also knew how much Twigpaw wanted to go and find her kin, and I knew she'd been upset. Maybe I could have caught up with her if I'd tried to follow her right away." He hunched his shoulders under the burden of his regret. "I was even going to look for her, and then . . ."

"And then what?" Bramblestar prompted, as Alderheart's voice cracked and he broke off.

"And then Purdy died, and I forgot," Alderheart admitted.

Bramblestar took a pace forward and nuzzled his son's neck fur. "We will all miss Twigpaw greatly," he meowed. "Her loss is a tragedy. But you can't blame yourself, Alderheart."

I know he's right, Alderheart thought, *but I can't help it. I forgot about Twigpaw, and now she's dead. . . .*

Stars glittered in a clear indigo sky as ThunderClan gathered to sit vigil for Twigpaw, forming a ragged circle in the middle of the camp. Even though they had no body, the Clan could honor the apprentice and send her spirit out on its journey to StarClan.

Alderheart found it strangely comforting to crouch there in the darkness, with Sparkpelt at his side, silently supportive, and listen to one cat after another offering their memories of Twigpaw. But at the same time there was a weird feeling in the camp, perhaps because of the presence of the Shadow-Clan and RiverClan cats. They had formed an outer circle, listening politely to the ThunderClan ceremony. But Alderheart knew that they couldn't share in his Clanmates' grief for Twigpaw; they had hardly known her.

The last few days have been so confusing, he thought, *I don't suppose many of the others even realized that Twigpaw was gone.*

Ivypool was on her paws now, speaking about when Twigpaw had first become her apprentice, and how she had taken her for her first tour of the territory. "She was so excited, so eager to learn," she mewed. "She would have made a fine warrior."

Dipping her head to Bramblestar, she sat down again and curled her tail around her front paws.

"Thank you, Ivypool," Bramblestar murmured. "Alderheart," he added, turning to his son with amber eyes that gleamed in the starlight, "would you like to say a few words?"

Alderheart stumbled to his paws, but for a moment he had no idea what to say. *When Twigpaw and Violetpaw arrived,* he remembered, *many of us were convinced that they were 'what you find in the shadows' from the prophecy. I believed it myself . . . but now I'm not so sure. And I don't want to start that argument again—not right now.*

As he hesitated, Sparkpelt gave him a gentle nudge in the side, her gaze warm and encouraging. "You can do this," she whispered.

Suddenly Alderheart found that he could. "Like Ivypool said, she was eager to learn," he stammered. "She was . . . she was lively, and she loved life. She felt things so . . . so deeply." At last he came up with the one thing he was sure of, and the only thing that mattered now. "Twigpaw was . . . She was my friend."

Feeling breathless, with no more words, he sat down heavily at his sister's side.

Light-headed after his sleepless night, Alderheart turned to his tasks in the medicine cats' den, hoping that work would help him to push away his grief and guilt. He was helping Briarlight with her exercises, tossing a ball of moss for her to catch, when he heard yowls of outrage coming from the camp outside.

Oh, no! he thought, pausing with the moss ball in his claws. *What now?*

"Go on," Briarlight urged him. "Go find out what's happening—and then come back and tell me about it."

Alderheart brushed past the bramble screen and emerged into the camp to see the dawn patrol padding across the stone hollow from the thorn tunnel. Lionblaze, in the lead, was limping, while blood was trickling from a scratch on Berrynose's shoulder, and Rosepetal had lost a lump of fur on her side. All three of them were bristling with fury.

"Bramblestar!" Lionblaze yowled, gazing up at the Highledge. "We need to report!"

The Clan leader stuck his head out of his den, took one look at the ragged patrol, and raced down the tumbled rocks to speak with them. Squirrelflight spotted them from where she stood with Cloudtail and Brightheart beside the fresh-kill pile; Alderheart heard her let out a shocked meow as she bounded over to her Clan leader's side. Brightheart and Cloudtail ran after her, and more of the Clan emerged from their dens and gathered around the patrol, shooting anxious questions at them.

"What happened?"

"Was it the rogues?"

Alderheart noticed that Rowanstar and Mistystar had also slipped out of the warriors' den and drawn closer with a few of their own warriors around them. They said nothing, but their eyes were watchful.

Jayfeather pushed his way through the crowd and began

sniffing at Berrynose's wound. "Give me some space," he snapped. "These cats need treatment."

"All in good time," Bramblestar responded, waving his tail to keep the rest of the cats back. "First we need to know what happened."

"We ran into some rogues at the ShadowClan border," Rosepetal began.

Bramblestar closed his eyes briefly. "Please tell me you didn't cross," he mewed.

"We didn't!" Berrynose exclaimed. "But those mange-pelts crossed into *our* territory and attacked us."

A murmur of indignation rose from the cats who now surrounded the patrol. Cloudtail drew his lips back in a snarl and clawed at the ground in front of him.

"They drove us off." Lionblaze's tail-tip was twitching furiously; Alderheart could understand the magnificent warrior's anger at having been defeated by a bunch of rogues.

"Because we were way outnumbered," Berrynose added. "But we did give them something to remember us by." He swiped his tongue around his jaws as if he had tasted a particularly juicy piece of fresh-kill.

"One of them—I think it was Nettle—yowled at us," Rosepetal meowed. "He told us that the rogues are coming for ThunderClan next. He said, 'It's only a matter of time.'"

"Of course it's only a matter of time." Rowanstar shouldered his way into the center of the circle that surrounded the patrol. "Until we drive off these rogues, we're all in danger! How long can we go on like this?"

"You're a fine one to talk!" Mistystar slipped up to Rowanstar's side and glared at him, her blue eyes like splinters of ice. "This is all happening because you couldn't manage to drive the rogues out of ShadowClan territory when they first arrived. Now they've not only taken over *your* Clan, but RiverClan as well! It's your fault that we're in this position, and I'm not about to risk the lives of my injured cats just to repair your pride!"

Rowanstar returned glare for glare, his neck fur bristling as he slid out his claws. "The rogues are a problem for all of us," he hissed. "That should be obvious now."

For a moment, the two Clan leaders stood nose to nose, their stiff limbs and fluffed-up fur making Alderheart afraid that they were about to attack each other. *What hope do we have, if we fight among ourselves?*

But before either of the cats could lash out, Bramblestar thrust his way between them. His amber eyes were burning with frustration. "That's enough!" he snapped. "Things are difficult for every cat. Do you think it will help your warriors to see their leaders scrapping like kits?"

Breathing heavily, Rowanstar took a pace backward. "I don't want a fight," he stated, clearly struggling to be calm. "I'm only saying—again—that we have to *do* something. Quickly."

Bramblestar nodded. "I agree with you, but it's not as simple as attacking the rogues outright. Remember, we tried that once—it didn't go well."

Bramblestar gave Rowanstar a hard look, and Rowanstar's

lips pulled back in a snarl. But Bramblestar went on before the ShadowClan leader could argue. "Besides, it's not just that attacking now would put the RiverClan cats at risk"—he dipped his head briefly to Mistystar—"but that even though we still outnumber the rogues, it's by a smaller margin. We can't count on WindClan's help. The RiverClan warriors are still recovering from their injuries; they are nowhere near ready to take on another battle. And Darktail is a *vicious* cat. Even if we could kill him and defeat his followers, we would shed too much blood in doing so. Besides, the rogues now hold two territories. If we retake one, they can always retreat to the other."

In the midst of his anxieties, Alderheart felt warm with pride as he listened to his father's measured, reasonable words. Mistystar was nodding her agreement, and even Rowanstar seemed to relax, his neck fur lying flat again.

"I suppose I can't argue with that," he mewed reluctantly. Then Rowanstar shook his head helplessly. "Why would Onestar allow the other Clans to just wither?" he murmured. "Why would he not fight to keep our way of life alive?"

No cat had an answer to that. Even Bramblestar responded with nothing but a sigh.

While Alderheart and Jayfeather took a closer look at the patrol's injuries, the ThunderClan leader climbed back up the tumbled rocks and raised his voice to address the Clan from the Highledge.

"Let all cats old enough to catch their own prey join here beneath the Highledge for a meeting of the Clans!"

Most of the warriors were already out in the clearing. Alderheart spotted Briarlight dragging herself to the entrance of the medicine cats' den, while Daisy and Leafpool emerged from the nursery, where they were caring for some of the injured RiverClan warriors.

"We need a plan," Bramblestar began, when all the cats were settled in the clearing, looking up at the Highledge. "The rogues have surprised us again by attacking RiverClan, and Rowanstar is right that we can't go on like this. I know that we're overcrowded here, and every cat is uncomfortable and tense. But there are many reasons why we can't mount an attack on the rogues right now. If any cat has an idea of what we might do instead, I'd be happy to hear it."

For a moment no cat responded. Alderheart spotted many of his Clanmates looking blankly at each other. Then he heard Lionblaze clear his throat as the golden tabby warrior rose to his paws.

"Yesterday, Cinderheart and I found out that we're expecting our second litter of kits," Lionblaze meowed, his eyes shining proudly.

Alderheart remembered how excited Leafpool had been the day before when she'd given Lionblaze and Cinderheart the news. But when he glanced over at her now, he saw that her expression was somber. The rest of his Clanmates erupted into yowls of congratulation, but the happy sounds quickly died away and an awkward silence fell.

Every cat has realized just how terrible a time this is to bring kits into the world, Alderheart thought.

"I can't have my kits born when every moment we're expecting to be driven out of our territory," Lionblaze continued fervently, as if he had read Alderheart's mind. "Will the Clans even be here by then? For the first time, it seems possible that they *won't*."

Cinderheart padded quietly up to her mate's side and rested her tail on his shoulder. "What will happen to our kits?" she mewed, looking up at Bramblestar. "What will happen to all of us, if there are no Clans anymore?"

"That . . . that can't happen!" Mousewhisker exclaimed.

"That's right," Poppyfrost agreed with a shudder. "There have *always* been Clans."

Lionblaze shook his head. "Ignoring the problem won't make it go away," he stated. "Remember the prophecy: 'Embrace what you find in the shadows, for only they can clear the sky.' We're no closer to finding out what it means than we were moons ago."

"We've had other things on our minds!" Cloudtail snapped.

Lionblaze dipped his head to the senior warrior. "True, but it seems obvious now that the sky has darkened for all of the Clans. If we don't put our heads together and find a way to clear it, we could lose everything." He lashed his tail. "Everything!"

Alderheart felt a chill pass through him from ears to tail-tip. No cat had spoken so boldly before about what might happen if the Clan cats failed to drive away the rogues. *We need to find SkyClan and bring them back,* Alderheart thought. *I'm sure that would clear the sky! But there's no way to make that happen right now.*

He could feel the tension in the air as his Clanmates shifted uneasily, and from somewhere in the crowd a cat let out a whimper of fear.

The horrified silence seemed to stretch out for moons, until suddenly Mistystar spoke.

"We need time for the RiverClan cats to heal," she meowed. "We can't attack until they're fit to fight. But it troubles me to leave our cats as prisoners for so long."

The crowd grew quiet again, until suddenly Sparkpelt cocked her head and said, "I know! Why don't we see if we can come up with a way to sneak the RiverClan prisoners out, one or two at a time?"

"And how would we even do that?" Berrynose asked with a disdainful sniff. "The rogues must be guarding them pretty carefully. Besides, I heard a rumor that some medicine cats tried to enter the RiverClan camp, and got sent away with a flea in their ear."

As he spoke, Alderheart was aware of Bramblestar turning a hard stare on him; refusing to meet his father's gaze, he studied his paws until he realized with relief that Bramblestar wasn't going to say anything.

Sparkpelt whipped her head around to face Berrynose. "So what's *your* plan, O wise one?" she demanded.

Berrynose shrugged and gave his chest fur a lick.

Before Sparkpelt could say any more, Mothwing rose to her paws and came to stand beside her. "It would be wonderful to rescue our Clanmates," she mewed, "but we would need a cat on the inside to help us."

She glanced across at Alderheart; when he caught the meaningful look in her eyes, he realized she was remembering their visit to the RiverClan camp, when Violetpaw and Needletail had taken them to Puddleshine.

It seemed like Needletail was trying to help us.

"Does any cat here know one of the cats in the rogue camp?" Mothwing asked. "I mean, know them well enough to trust them with a plan?"

Rowanstar let out an annoyed huff. "Obviously, there are ShadowClan cats there," he replied, "but who knows where their loyalties lie now?" He glanced over at Juniperclaw and Strikestone, both of whom looked uncomfortable.

"It's hard to say," Juniperclaw said, not meeting Rowanstar's gaze.

"I know a couple," Alderheart added quietly, still remembering his visit with Mothwing. "But I can't be sure that they would help us."

Up on the Highledge, Bramblestar was looking thoughtful. "I think we ought to consider this carefully," he meowed at last. "Let's sleep on it. It's important to be sure, because we don't want to give away our plan to a cat we can't trust."

As the meeting drew to an end, the crowd of cats broke up into little huddles, anxiously discussing what they should do. Alderheart followed Jayfeather and the injured patrol back to the medicine cats' den. He could still picture Needletail's terrified face as he and Mothwing left the RiverClan camp.

I don't understand what's going on with Needletail, he thought sadly. *She was my friend once, but now . . . I can't be sure.*

Would she help us?

The half-moon floated above the hills as Alderheart headed for the Moonpool. The night was chilly, with a tang of rain in the air, but the clouds thinned out as the medicine cats crossed the border and began to climb.

Leafpool was in the lead, with Jayfeather and Willowshine, while Mothwing and Alderheart had dropped back a few tail-lengths.

"So? Do you think Needletail would help us sneak out the prisoners?" Mothwing asked in a whisper.

Alderheart kept a wary eye on the other medicine cats ahead of them, knowing how sharp Jayfeather's hearing was, but none of them seemed aware of his murmured conversation with Mothwing.

"I have no idea," he replied. "I would need to talk to her."

"Like *that's* going to be easy," Mothwing responded with an irritable twitch of her tail.

When he pushed his way through the bushes at the top of the slope above the Moonpool, Alderheart wasn't surprised to see that neither Puddleshine nor Kestrelflight was waiting for them. Turning, he gazed back the way they had come, but nothing moved in all the landscape. Everything was still and silent under the frosty light.

"We'll give them a little longer," Leafpool decided as she led the way down the spiral path toward the pool. "They might be on their way."

"And hedgehogs might fly," Jayfeather meowed scornfully. "We all know they won't come."

Alderheart sat in silence, watching the glittering reflections of moon and starshine on the surface of the pool, and listening to the sound of the water as it cascaded down the rocks. His heart ached.

It's so peaceful here, and yet the Clans are in such turmoil.

The moon rose slowly in the sky, but still there was no sign of the WindClan and ShadowClan medicine cats. Finally Leafpool rose to her paws again.

"We've waited long enough," she declared. "No cat can say that we haven't given them every chance."

"Then let's get on with it," Jayfeather mewed. "We're wasting moonlight."

Leafpool nodded. "I need to say one thing before we meet with StarClan," she announced. "These are challenging times, and I know that every cat wants to do their best to save the Clans. But I hope that we all have the sense to look after ourselves, and not put ourselves in danger fishing for information. Don't you agree, Alderheart?"

Aware of Leafpool's sharp glance resting on him, Alderheart ducked his head. "Sure, Leafpool," he mumbled.

She must have worked out that Mothwing and I went to the RiverClan camp. She doesn't approve . . . but she hasn't actually told us not to do it again.

Meanwhile, Jayfeather was shifting his paws impatiently. "Are we *ever* going to dream tonight?" he asked. "We need StarClan's guidance more than ever."

"We'll do it now," Leafpool responded. "And may StarClan light our path."

Together with the other medicine cats, Alderheart crouched over the pool and touched his nose to the surface of the water. Icy darkness swirled around him, and when it cleared, he found himself standing on short grass, which stretched away as far as he could see.

He looked around for the spirits of his ancestors, but instead he caught sight of a group of skinny, ragged cats sheltering under some bushes a few fox-lengths away.

"SkyClan . . . ," he whispered to himself.

Pain clawed at his heart as Alderheart recognized the cat who was on watch: the large tom who looked so much like Twigpaw, but with Violetpaw's eyes. He realized once again how much this cat resembled his lost friend.

Then sudden hope sprang up inside Alderheart. *Maybe Dovewing and Tigerheart were wrong! Maybe Twigpaw* did *escape the monster and reach SkyClan after all!*

He padded up to the group of cats, knowing that none of them would realize that he was there. He passed so close to the large tabby tom that their pelts almost brushed.

But though Alderheart thoroughly searched the group of resting cats and peered underneath every bush, there was no sign of Twigpaw, and he couldn't pick up even the faintest trace of her scent.

His hope died, leaving him even more grief-stricken than before. Opening his eyes, he found himself once again crouching beside the Moonpool, but its beauty left his heart cold. *This proves it. If Twigpaw had made it to SkyClan, I would have seen her. She must really be dead.*

CHAPTER 13

Violetpaw crouched over the body of a fat wood pigeon, tearing at the succulent flesh. All around her, Darktail and his Kin were gulping down their prey. The sun felt warm on Violetpaw's back, and from close by she could hear the gentle gurgling of the streams that bordered the RiverClan camp.

It must have been so beautiful here, before Darktail and his rogues attacked.

"Wow, I've never seen a pigeon disappear so fast," Darktail meowed, looking up at Violetpaw from the rabbit he was eating. His eyes gleamed teasingly. "Maybe you'd like some of this rabbit as well."

Scorchfur, one of the last remaining ShadowClan warriors, pricked up his ears and frowned, as if he couldn't believe Darktail's good-humored tone. But he didn't speak, instead running to carry a squirrel to his mate, Snowbird, who was in the nursery with her kits.

Violetpaw had to choke down her mouthful; she trusted Darktail even less when he was being friendly. "No thanks, Darktail. I'm not even sure I can finish this."

"Well, tell me if you change your mind," Darktail responded.

"We can't have you starving, can we?"

As he spoke, Scorchfur came back, hesitated for a moment, and then meowed, "Maybe we should give the leftover prey to the RiverClan prisoners—and to Needletail. They're beginning to look really skinny. After all," he added with a glance toward the center of the camp, where the prisoners were kept, "if we're going to keep them prisoner, isn't it our responsibility to see that they're healthy?"

Violetpaw spotted Darktail narrowing his eyes, his muzzle tensing in anger, then an instant later relaxing. His voice was calm as he replied to Scorchfur.

"Of course I'm feeding the prisoners well. Do you have any reason to think otherwise?"

Scorchfur glared at Darktail, hatred shining visibly in his eyes. Looking from one cat to the other, Violetpaw felt her neck fur prickle with fear. *Don't say it,* she pleaded silently. *Snowbird is still nursing your kits—don't make her struggle for prey while you're punished by Darktail.*

Slowly, Darktail rose to his paws and padded over to Scorchfur, thrusting his face within a mouse-length of the dark gray warrior's.

"Scorchfur," he meowed softly, "do you doubt my ability to lead my Kin? Perhaps you're not truly my Kin. Not every cat is. Perhaps you would be happier somewhere else?"

Scorchfur was silent for a few more heartbeats. "No, Darktail," he blurted out at last. "Of course I don't doubt you. Of course you know what's best."

For a long moment, Darktail did not move, staring into

Scorchfur's eyes. At last, when Violetpaw thought she could not bear the tension any longer, he gave a curt nod and padded back to where he had left his rabbit, close beside Sleekwhisker.

Scorchfur choked down the rest of his vole, then rose and stumbled away, followed by the other ShadowClan warriors who had been eating with them.

"Don't go far," Darktail called after him. "The prisoners' den needs to be cleaned out soon."

Poor Scorchfur, Violetpaw thought. *He should have kept his mouth shut.* Now that there were no apprentices, Darktail saved the worst jobs for cats who had angered him. Poor Puddleshine had cleaned the prisoners' den last. Violetpaw still felt a flutter of guilt when she remembered the terrible confrontation where she'd gotten him into trouble. Fortunately, even Darktail seemed to realize that the Kin needed a medicine cat too badly for Puddleshine to remain on cleaning duty for long.

When Scorchfur and the others were gone, Sleekwhisker let out an exaggerated sigh. "When will *all* the ShadowClan warriors leave? It's obvious they don't understand how you work, Darktail. They're not worthy of your leadership!"

Darktail turned a baleful gaze on her. "Don't forget that *you* were once a ShadowClan cat," he reminded her.

"I haven't thought of myself as ShadowClan for a long time," Sleekwhisker responded boldly. "I'm Kin now, through and through. I was one of the first cats to join you, while these other mange-pelts were ShadowClan right up to the time you took over the territory. And the sooner they leave, the better."

She leaned over so that her pelt brushed Darktail's, but the rogue leader turned a sharp glance on her, making her ease away.

"You shouldn't wish for that!" Darktail snapped. "We need the ShadowClan cats. Even with our kittypet friends and our new Kin, we're still outnumbered by the Clan warriors."

That's Darktail's own fault, Violetpaw thought. *He shouldn't have done whatever he did to Dawnpelt and the others!*

"Wow, I'm stuffed!" she exclaimed, rising to her paws and grabbing up the remains of her pigeon. "I can't finish this," she mumbled through the mouthful of feathers.

Darktail and the rest of his Kin seemed not to be paying any attention to her. Violetpaw carried the pigeon over to the refuse pile and dropped it there, her nose wrinkling at the stink of rotting crow-food.

This is disgusting, she thought. *We never left food to rot in the ShadowClan camp.*

With two territories in which to hunt, the Kin were never short of prey. Violetpaw was revolted by how much they wasted, especially when Darktail kept the prisoners starving.

Glancing over her shoulder to make sure that no cat was watching her, Violetpaw slipped through a clump of long grass and wriggled toward an elder bush where she had stashed a particularly fat vole. She had to claw her way through the tangled stems, taking so long to find it that, for a moment, she was afraid that some other creature had come by and stolen her prey.

Then she relaxed as she spotted the smooth curve of the vole's pelt. Grabbing it in her jaws, she headed for the bramble thicket where the prisoners were guarded.

Violetpaw dropped the vole out of sight behind a rock, then strolled up to Zelda and Yarrowleaf, who were on guard. "Hi," she meowed. "I'll keep watch for a bit, if you want to go eat."

Zelda's eyes lit up, while Yarrowleaf swiped her tongue around her jaws. "Great!" she exclaimed. "My belly thinks my throat's been torn out."

Both she-cats vanished rapidly in the direction of the fresh-kill pile.

When they were gone, Violetpaw retrieved the vole and slid through the bramble tendrils until she reached the clear space in the middle of the thicket where the prisoners lived.

For a moment, none of them realized that Violetpaw was there. Icewing and Mintfur lay stretched out close together; Violetpaw could see every one of their ribs. Icewing's wound showed red and angry, and Violetpaw realized that Puddleshine had not treated it with any medicine. He had not been allowed to. Reedwhisker was curled up asleep. Brackenpelt was trying to groom herself, but the effort of simply turning her head seemed to exhaust her. She flopped down, panting, on her side after a few feeble licks.

Needletail was pacing in the confined space, and as she turned, she spotted Violetpaw. "You again!" she muttered, padding up to her. "You shouldn't take these kinds of risks. Darktail will have your fur off if he finds you here."

"I've brought you some more food," Violetpaw replied, dropping the vole at Needletail's paws. Pain clawed at her heart as she saw how tired and defeated her friend looked.

"And I'm careful. Darktail won't find out. Come on, eat."

Needletail fell on the prey and snatched it up, but instead of starting to eat, she carried it over to the RiverClan prisoners. Violetpaw stared in surprise, her heart warmed by her friend's unselfishness.

"Violetpaw's here again," Needletail mewed. "She's brought you some food."

The RiverClan cats looked up listlessly, their interest suddenly sharpening as they caught the scent of vole.

"Thank StarClan!" Brackenpelt breathed out, her jaws starting to water.

Violetpaw watched as the prisoners devoured the vole; it was gone in a few heartbeats, and they only got a couple of mouthfuls each. She noticed that Needletail didn't take any—she just looked on as the others ate.

"We can't hang on like this," Mintfur meowed when the last scrap of prey had vanished. "Darktail is the cruelest cat I've ever known."

"Hush!" Brackenpelt gave Mintfur a warning prod. "Violetpaw is one of Darktail's cats."

"I don't care!" Mintfur retorted. "Darktail *is* cruel." She glared up at Violetpaw. "Tell him what I said, and let him do what he likes."

"I won't tell him anything," Violetpaw responded. "*I* think he's cruel, too."

"So why do you follow him?" Reedwhisker asked, surprised.

"She *doesn't* follow him, mouse-brain," Needletail pointed out with an irritated twitch of her whiskers. "Would she bring you prey if she agreed with what Darktail is doing?"

"I made a mistake at first," Violetpaw admitted. "I'm try-ing to think of a way to help you, and in the meantime I will keep bringing you food when I can."

The RiverClan cats glanced at one another, and Violetpaw saw the first signs of hope beginning to dawn in their eyes. But before she could say any more she heard sounds from outside the thicket: paw steps and the voices of Zelda and Yarrowleaf.

"I've got to go," she murmured, and slipped quickly out into the open again.

As Zelda and Yarrowleaf came up to her, Violetpaw noticed that Zelda was looking at her with an odd expression. *I wonder whether she heard any of that.*

Only the night before, in the nest they still shared, Violet-paw and Zelda had talked together long after darkness had fallen.

"I still want to go home to my housefolk," Zelda had meowed, "but I don't think that Darktail is ever going to let me."

Violetpaw had been unable to find words to reply, knowing that Zelda was right: she was just as much a prisoner as the RiverClan cats.

Now Violetpaw wondered whether Zelda would betray her to Darktail if she knew that she was feeding the prisoners. *She might, just to get into his favor. I can't risk trusting her.*

Violetpaw met Zelda's gaze, hoping to find some kind of clue in her eyes, but the kittypet's expression was unreadable.

"Violetpaw!" Darktail's voice cut across Violetpaw's

musings, making her jump. "Violetpaw, where are you?"

With a swift nod to Zelda and Yarrowleaf, Violetpaw bounded across the camp to where Darktail was standing with his Kin around him.

"There you are!" he meowed as Violetpaw ran up to him. "The fresh-kill pile is getting low. I want you to hunt."

"Sure, Darktail." Violetpaw kept her expression calm and obedient, but inwardly her heart was surging. *This could be just the break I need!*

Sunhigh was past when Violetpaw returned to the River-Clan camp and slung a rabbit on top of the growing fresh-kill pile. She had already brought back several mice and a squirrel.

One thing about living with the rogues, where every cat is always out for themselves, she reflected, *it's made me a better hunter.*

Even though Clan cats usually hunted in patrols, the Kin often hunted alone so they wouldn't have to share prey. This time, Violetpaw had insisted on going off by herself, knowing that Darktail wouldn't question her. *He's been so nice to me ever since I betrayed Needletail,* she thought with a shudder. *And now that I've caught enough prey to impress him, I've got time for a trip of my own.*

"I'm going to try over in ShadowClan territory," she called out to any cat who might be listening, then bounded down to the lakeshore and headed past the Twoleg half-bridge.

It wasn't ShadowClan territory Violetpaw had in mind. It was time to admit she couldn't fight Darktail alone. She was heading for ThunderClan, and her sister.

I hope Twigpaw isn't too angry with me for what happened in the battle. Because I desperately need her help.

Violetpaw slipped swiftly and silently through the undergrowth, keeping close to the edge of the lake. All her senses were alert for the sound or scent of any rogues who might be hunting in ShadowClan territory, but she did not meet any cat until she splashed through the stream that marked the border with ThunderClan.

Drawing a long breath, Violetpaw began to relax, padding more confidently toward the ThunderClan camp, only to grow tense again as powerful, fresh scents—a mixture of ThunderClan and RiverClan—flowed over her from a bank of ferns just ahead. A moment later the fern fronds waved and three cats pushed their way into the open.

In the lead was a young gray-and-white tom Violetpaw recognized as Dewnose. The other two were less familiar to her, though she had seen them now and then at Gatherings and knew that they came from RiverClan. *I should remember their names. . . . Podlight and . . . yes, Beetlewhisker.*

Violetpaw waited, dipping her head respectfully, as the patrol bounded up to her.

"What are you doing here?" Dewnose asked.

To Violetpaw's relief, he sounded surprised rather than hostile. "I don't mean you any harm," she meowed hastily. "I've come for help—and to see my sister."

"Why should we believe you?" Podlight asked roughly. "How do we know you aren't part of a rogue plan to attack?"

"Oh, come on, Podlight." Dewnose gave the RiverClan tom a shove. "If Darktail wanted to attack, would he warn us by sending an apprentice?"

"I'm here alone," Violetpaw assured them. "Darktail doesn't know. If you don't believe me, you can leave some cat to watch the border while the rest of you escort me in."

Podlight gave her a curt nod, seeming satisfied with that.

"What about the prisoners?" Beetlewhisker asked anxiously. "Are they okay? Will Darktail let them leave soon?"

Violetpaw wasn't sure how to answer that. "They're still alive," she told him after a moment's hesitation. "And they're part of the reason that I'm here. But I need help."

Dewnose nodded, a pleased look on his face. "I'd better bring you to Bramblestar," he mewed.

"And Mistystar," Podlight added sharply.

Dewnose flicked his tail in annoyance. "Sure, and Mistystar," he muttered.

Violetpaw followed Dewnose through the forest, the two RiverClan warriors flanking her on either side. As she emerged into the clearing from the thorn tunnel, she halted for a moment, overwhelmed by the crowds of cats in front of her.

Have all the ShadowClan and RiverClan cats ended up here? Violetpaw hadn't ever given much thought to what had happened to the Clan cats the Kin had displaced. Now she was stunned by just how crowded the ThunderClan camp was.

Over the other side of the camp she caught a glimpse of Juniperclaw and Strikestone, and felt a jolt of relief that at least Dawnpelt's kits had made it here safely. But then she spotted Rowanstar beside them; he had seen her, and the look in his eyes was cold and unfriendly.

Violetpaw cringed inwardly, suddenly more nervous than ever. *Why did I think these cats would greet me as a friend? I hardly know any of them—and the ones I do know probably think I'm a traitor.*

"Come on, Violetpaw." Dewnose touched her shoulder with his tail-tip. "I'll take you to Bramblestar."

Violetpaw hesitated. "Could I possibly talk to Twigpaw first?"

Dewnose's gaze clouded with concern, making Violetpaw feel even more agitated.

"What—" she began.

"I think I know a cat who can help you," Dewnose interrupted her gently.

He hurried off, weaving his way through the groups of cats in the clearing, until he disappeared behind a bramble screen; Violetpaw remembered that was the entrance to the medicine-cat den.

A moment later, Alderheart appeared; at the sight of him Violetpaw felt such a rush of relief that for a heartbeat she was unsteady on her paws. *Alderheart is Twigpaw's friend. Surely he will help me!*

"Violetpaw, thank goodness you're all right!" Alderheart meowed as he bounded up to her. "How are you? And how has Needletail been since I visited with Mothwing? I know she said things were fine—but they didn't *seem* fine."

"Not fine is right," Violetpaw told him. "In fact, they could hardly be worse. I think Darktail has gone a bit crazy since he killed Rain. All he cares about is loyalty, and he punishes any cat he thinks isn't loyal to him. And . . . and that includes Needletail."

Concern flooded into Alderheart's eyes, and for a heartbeat he seemed to gaze into the distance, as if he saw something terrible there. Violetpaw realized that he had been very close to Needletail, and must be upset to think of her being ill treated.

Soon Alderheart's expression grew thoughtful. "Violetpaw, can I trust you?" he asked.

Violetpaw nodded eagerly. "Yes," she assured him. "I know now it was a mistake to stay with Darktail. I should have left along with Rowanstar when the rogues took over Shadow-Clan. But I . . . I wanted to stay with Needletail, and I knew she would never leave." Encouraged by Alderheart's understanding look, she added, "I wanted to believe it would all turn out okay. Have you ever felt like that?"

Alderheart's eyes were full of affection, and Violetpaw almost felt as if he was her kin. *Truly my kin,* she thought, *not like Darktail.*

"Yes, I have," he replied. "Now listen close, Violetpaw. We've been looking for some cat in the rogue camp to help us, because we have an idea. We've come up with a plan. . . ."

As Alderheart explained the plan to her, Violetpaw's pads began to prickle with excitement. She listened, intrigued, and her fur felt warmer as hope kindled within her.

"But for our plan to work," Alderheart finished at last, "we need a cat who can influence Darktail."

"I can!" Violetpaw told him, even more excitement beginning to flow through her, like an icebound stream when the
sun shines on it. "Darktail trusts me. I can do whatever you
want."

Alderheart's gaze was warm as it rested on her. "Thank
you, Violetpaw."

"No, thank *you*—thank ThunderClan." Violetpaw felt a
huge sense of relief. "You're showing me a way out."

"I'd better take you to meet with the leaders," Alderheart
meowed, beckoning her with his tail.

Violetpaw nodded, but before she moved to follow Alderheart, she let her gaze travel around the camp, looking for her
sister among the groups of cats. "Could I talk to Twigpaw
first?" she asked. "I haven't seen her since the battle and I . . .
I feel so terrible about what I did to her. I want a chance to
explain how much I regret it."

As she looked up at Alderheart, Violetpaw felt suddenly
chilled to see his expression change. He almost looked as
though he was in pain.

"I'm sorry," he mewed at last. "Twigpaw left camp half a
moon ago, and she never came back. We think . . . . I'm afraid
we think that she may have been killed by a monster."

Violetpaw stared at him, rigid with disbelief. She felt as
though she had a chunk of ice in her belly, and for a brief
moment black spots swirled over her vision. *No . . . Twigpaw can't
be dead! When we met in the battle, I was attacking her. Oh, StarClan,*

don't let that be the last time I'll ever see her!

"Is this some sort of joke?" she asked. "Why didn't you tell me right away?"

Alderheart shook his head, grief-stricken and confused. "I was so surprised to see you," he replied after a couple of heartbeats. "And I'm struggling with the news myself. I wish I didn't have to believe it."

"But why did she leave camp?" Violetpaw meowed.

Now Alderheart couldn't meet her gaze. "It was my fault," he confessed quietly. "I thought . . . I thought I might have seen one of your kin in a vision."

Violetpaw's tone sharpened. "Our kin?"

"I had a vision of SkyClan," Alderheart began. "They're a Clan who was driven away from the other Clans long ago, back when we lived in the old forest. I saw a tom who looked like both of you."

Her breath coming short and fast, Violetpaw felt as though the ground under her paws was beginning to shake. She couldn't take in everything that Alderheart was telling her.

Does he mean this tom might be my kin? No. The only kin I ever had was Twigpaw, and now Alderheart says that Twigpaw is dead. Violetpaw stood still, her gaze unfocused, while thoughts raced through her mind like clouds in a gale. *No,* she decided at last. *If Twigpaw had been killed, I would have felt it, wouldn't I?*

"You said you *think* she died. No cat saw it happen?" she asked. "No cat saw her body?"

"That's true," Alderheart mewed, "but we're pretty sure, all the same." His gaze rested gently on her. "I'm so sorry,

Violetpaw. Do you still want to help us?"

Violetpaw's heart ached so much that she thought it would crack in two. But the pain only made her more resolved.

I have to believe that Twigpaw is still alive somewhere. I'll do what Alderheart is asking; I'll help get the weaker cats out of Darktail's claws. Then, when my sister comes back, she'll have to forgive me for what happened in the battle. And if she doesn't . . . or if she really is dead . . .

Violetpaw pushed the thought away, refusing even to consider that. "I'll help you," she meowed, meeting Alderheart's gaze steadily. "You can take me to Bramblestar now."

Alderheart took a pace toward the tumbled rocks that led up to the Highledge, then halted. "No, you've been away from your camp for too long," he decided. "I'll talk to Bramblestar; you get back before you're missed. Just remember the plan. . . ."

Violetpaw listened to his rapid instructions, then dipped her head in farewell and left the camp, racing through the forest and along the shoreline until she crossed the border into ShadowClan territory.

I wish I could stay, she thought, *but once our plan works . . . once the rogues are defeated and Twigpaw comes home . . . maybe she and I and Needletail can all live in ThunderClan territory—together.*

The moon shed silver light over the RiverClan camp, the ground blotched with shadows cast by bushes and clumps of reeds. Violetpaw crept furtively from one patch of darkness to the next, her ears pricked for the slightest sound of movement.

When she reached the bramble thicket, she spotted Zelda sitting alone on guard. As Violetpaw watched, the kittypet stretched her jaws in an enormous yawn, then rose and began pacing to and fro, obviously struggling to stay awake.

Violetpaw padded up to her. "Hi, Zelda."

Zelda whipped around, her neck fur bristling, then relaxed as she saw who had spoken. "Violetpaw! You scared me out of my fur! What are you doing here?"

"I want to check on Needletail," Violetpaw explained. "I'm worried about her."

Zelda's eyes stretched wide in dismay. "I can't let you do that! What if Darktail found out? He'd claw my ears off."

"Please . . . ," Violetpaw mewed. "I only want to talk to her. You know she's my friend. What harm could it do?" She paused for a moment, then added, "You could curl up for a nap while I'm in there. I won't let the prisoners escape."

Zelda looked even more distraught. "No! Darktail might see me . . . or one of the Kin would tell him."

"They're all snoring in their nests," Violetpaw told her. "Zelda, please . . . Aren't we friends?"

Zelda slid her claws in and out, tearing at the grass. "Okay, Violetpaw," she mewed at last. "But be quick!"

"Thanks, Zelda." Violetpaw touched her nose to the kitty-pet's ear, then slipped past her and into the thicket, until she reached the clear space in the center.

The RiverClan prisoners were curled up together in a mound of fur, with Needletail close beside them. Violetpaw thought her friend was asleep too; but as she approached, Needletail raised her head and gazed at her, blinking.

"Violetpaw?" Her voice was hoarse.

"I had to talk to you." Violetpaw crouched down beside her friend and spoke softly into her ear. "I've been to Thunder-Clan and spoken to Alderheart. We have a plan to get you and the prisoners out! I promise, all of you are going to be fine."

Needletail listened quietly and did not respond when Violetpaw had finished speaking. Her eyes closed, and Violetpaw thought that she had gone back to sleep. Pity clawed at her heart when she saw how weak her friend was.

Violetpaw was beginning to edge backward, ready to leave, when Needletail stirred again, her eyes opening a slit. "All this that's happening to me . . . it's not your fault, Violetpaw. All the mistakes we made were mine."

"That doesn't matter now," Violetpaw responded, briefly burying her nose in Needletail's shoulder fur. "Don't worry about anything. I'm going to get you out of here."

Needletail shook her head. "Don't take risks for me, Violetpaw. You have to survive, any way you can."

She fell silent again with a small sigh, and Violetpaw realized that this time she really had gone to sleep.

Violetpaw remained crouching beside her for a moment, smoothing her fur with one paw. *Poor Needletail,* she thought. *I've got to make this plan with ThunderClan work. . . .*

Warily she slid out of the thicket with a nod to Zelda, then crept back across the camp in the direction of the elders' den.

I have something to discuss with Ratscar and Oakfur. . . .

CHAPTER 14

Alderheart crouched in the bushes beside the small Thunderpath that separated ShadowClan territory from RiverClan. Sparkpelt and Ivypool were by his side, while Lionblaze, a tail-length or so away, was keeping watch in case any rogues were patrolling on the ShadowClan side.

Two nights had passed since Violetpaw's visit to ThunderClan. Clouds were covering the moon, casting a welcome darkness over the trespassing patrol. The only sound was the faint creaking of branches as a breeze wafted through the trees.

"Do you think Violetpaw is close enough to Darktail?" Sparkpelt whispered, sounding doubtful. "Would he really tell her when the patrols go out?"

"Yes, does she really have that much influence?" Ivypool added. "She's an apprentice, for StarClan's sake!"

"I believe her," Alderheart responded, keeping his voice low. "She told me that a patrol goes by at sunset, and then another at moonhigh. Besides, she doesn't need Darktail to *tell* her that—if she keeps her wits about her, she can see it for herself."

Ivypool nodded slowly, her blue eyes gleaming in the dim light. "After all," she murmured, "this isn't a real boundary anymore, now that Darktail holds both territories. There's not a lot of need for regular patrols."

"True," Alderheart responded. "Besides, I trust Violetpaw. She may be an apprentice, but there's something very capable and serious about her."

"Yes." Ivypool sighed out the word. "She reminds me so much of Twigpaw."

All the cats were silent for a moment; Alderheart knew that his Clanmates were remembering the young cat, sharing in his grief for her.

Then behind him, Alderheart heard Lionblaze spring to his paws. "Look! Across the Thunderpath!" he hissed.

Alderheart saw three dark shapes emerge from the bushes on the RiverClan side. His muscles tensed as he tasted the air, not sure at first which cats were heading toward him over the hard surface of the Thunderpath. Violetpaw's scent flowed between his jaws, and Alderheart relaxed as he recognized her and saw that she was leading the two ShadowClan elders, Oakfur and Ratscar.

Both the old cats let out huge sighs of relief as they reached the bushes and flopped down beside Alderheart and the other ThunderClan cats.

"Good job, Violetpaw," Oakfur meowed. "The plan worked!"

"Great StarClan!" Ratscar huffed. "I thought that mange-ridden Darktail would catch us for sure."

"Shh!" Sparkpelt warned them. "We still have to get you safely through ShadowClan territory."

"Rest for a few moments, and let's have a look at you," Alderheart mewed.

Though there was little light, he could just make out the skinny shapes of the elders and see claw marks scored across their sides. The sweetish scent that rose from them told him that some of the wounds were infected, and he remembered Juniperclaw telling him that Darktail made Puddleshine save all his herbs for the Kin.

"I've chewed up some marigold," he told them as he began to dab the pulp on Oakfur's wounds and then Ratscar's. "That should help, and I'll see to you properly tomorrow in camp."

Oakfur sighed and gave a wriggle of pleasure as the healing juices sank into his wounds. "That feels great, youngster," he rasped.

"I caught some mice for you," Ivypool added, dropping one in front of each of the elders. "Eat up quickly, and then we can go."

The elders didn't need telling, gulping down the prey in huge mouthfuls.

It's like they haven't eaten for a moon, Alderheart thought, disgusted at the state of these honorable cats who had served their Clan so well.

"Is this how Darktail treats elders?" he asked Violetpaw, who was standing close by, her eyes shining with triumph at the success of her first mission.

Violetpaw shrugged. "Darktail always lets the strongest

cats eat first. And they're not allowed to share any prey unless he gives permission."

Alderheart remembered that Darktail had done the same in the gorge when he and his rogues had claimed to be part of SkyClan. *He must have been lying through his teeth when he said he and his rogue friends wanted to be part of a Clan. He just wanted to collect Clan cats to follow him and live by his twisted rules.*

"Are you up for the journey through ShadowClan territory?" he asked the elders. "It's a long way, and it might be dangerous."

"We sure are," Ratscar assured him.

"Yes," Oakfur added. "Anything to get away from those crow-food-eating rogues!"

Alderheart gave each of the old cats a bunch of traveling herbs that he had brought with him from ThunderClan to give them strength for the rest of their journey. Then, while they licked them up, he turned to say good-bye to Violetpaw.

"You've done brilliantly," he meowed. "You're a brave cat, Violetpaw."

The young she-cat ducked her head, embarrassed. "I just want to help," she murmured.

"You've certainly helped us," Oakfur told her. "More than we can ever thank you for."

Ratscar echoed his Clanmate's thanks. "We'll be seeing you again, I hope," he mewed.

"I hope so," Violetpaw responded. "Alderheart, I'll try again three nights from now."

"Okay," Alderheart agreed. "But be careful."

"I will. Good-bye for now, and a safe journey."

For a moment Alderheart wanted to ask Violetpaw about Needletail, but he stopped himself, knowing that, with every heartbeat that the apprentice delayed getting back to Dark-tail's camp, she put herself in more danger.

"Good-bye," he called softly after her as Violetpaw raced back over the Thunderpath and vanished into the bushes on the RiverClan side.

Lionblaze took the lead as the patrol set off toward Thun-derClan territory. Alderheart and Sparkpelt flanked the elders, one on either side, while Ivypool brought up the rear.

The elders were shaky on their paws, and progress was slow, though at first the forest was silent, with no sight or scent of any rogues. Lionblaze led them along the edge of the trees, where the going was easier as the undergrowth thinned out toward the lake.

Alderheart was just beginning to hope that they would get home without any trouble, when suddenly Lionblaze halted. "Fox dung!" he hissed.

"What?" Alderheart craned to see past Lionblaze's muscu-lar form.

A little way ahead, he spotted two cats crouching on the narrow strip of pebbles that separated the forest from the lake. Both of them seemed to be focused on a hole in the bank.

"It's Cloverfoot and that mangy rogue Nettle," Ratscar growled. "It looks as if they're hunting."

Sparkpelt nodded. "There could be voles in there," she murmured.

"And if they're waiting for them to come out, they could be there all night," Lionblaze meowed with an irritated twitch of his tail. "We'll have to take a route farther away from the lake."

Alderheart suppressed a sigh as they set out again, heading deeper into ShadowClan territory. *This is more tiring for the elders . . . and there's more chance of running into rogues.*

His belly began to churn with fear as they made their way through the trees. In this part of the forest, pines had shed their needles over the ground, and while the smooth covering made walking easy for the elders, there was little cover if they needed to hide from a patrol.

Oakfur and Ratscar would never manage to climb a tree, Alderheart thought, wishing that they could move faster, but knowing that the elders were doing the best they could.

At last the pine trees began to give way to oak and beech, and Alderheart realized that they were approaching the border near the clearing where the Twolegs built their pelt-dens in greenleaf.

Perhaps we're going to make it after all, he thought.

They were heading down a slope toward a thick bank of ferns when Sparkpelt raised her tail in warning, then leaped onto a tree stump to get a better view of what lay ahead.

"Rogues patrolling!" she reported in a whisper. "Roach and another cat I don't recognize. I thought I could pick up their stink."

"Head for the ferns," Lionblaze ordered calmly, as Alderheart spotted the two rogues' shapes slinking through the shadows a few fox-lengths away. "And for StarClan's sake, be quiet!"

Sparkpelt and Ivypool bundled the two elders down the slope and into the shelter of the ferns. Alderheart and Lionblaze followed, keeping low with their belly fur brushing the ground, hoping that their movement wouldn't disturb the fern fronds and give them away.

"We must be close," Lionblaze whispered. "I can smell the ThunderClan scent markers."

Just as he spoke, Ratscar let out a hollow cough. From behind them, Alderheart heard Roach's voice. "Loki, did you hear that?"

"Fox dung!" Ivypool snarled.

For a few heartbeats Alderheart was frozen, unsure what to do. He could feel the rogue cats' paw steps vibrating through the ground and knew that within heartbeats they would be discovered.

"Sorry—it's my fault," Ratscar rasped. "Leave me and go on."

"No cat is leaving you," Lionblaze said firmly. "Alderheart, you lead the elders over the border. I'll give the rogues something else to think about."

"No!" Alderheart protested, panic surging through him. "What if they work out what we're doing and use that as an excuse to attack ThunderClan? It's all going wrong!"

"They won't—" Sparkpelt began.

"Then what if they call up more of Darktail's cats? You'll be way outnumbered."

"Alderheart, have you got bees in your brain?" Ivypool's eyes glittered with menace. "Lionblaze has us to help him. Now *go!*" She followed up her words with a violent shove to Alderheart's rump.

Realizing how stupid he was being, Alderheart urged the elders into motion, crawling swiftly through the ferns. ThunderClan scent flowed over them as they crossed the border. At the same moment, Alderheart heard yowling and screeching break out behind him. His paws tugged him back toward the fight, but he knew that his duty was to see the elders safely into the ThunderClan camp.

"Welcome to ThunderClan," he meowed. "Let's go."

Cats poured out of their dens as Alderheart and the elders pushed their way through the thorn tunnel and into the stone hollow, alerted by the joyful caterwauling of Sorrelstripe, who was on watch. Rowanstar and the ShadowClan cats surged across the clearing, surrounding Ratscar and Oakfur, who were almost knocked off their paws by their Clanmates' enthusiastic greeting.

"Take it easy," Alderheart protested, pushing his way through to the side of the two old cats. "They're injured and weak. They should spend tonight in the medicine cats' den."

Reluctantly, the ShadowClan cats gave way, allowing Alderheart to lead Oakfur and Ratscar to the medicine cats' den and pass them over to Jayfeather and Leafpool. His legs were shaky with exhaustion, and he wanted nothing more than to curl up and sleep, but he knew that first he would have to report to Bramblestar.

His father was waiting for him as he emerged past the bramble screen and back into the camp.

"Good job," Bramblestar mewed approvingly. "But where's the rest of the patrol?"

"We met some rogues," Alderheart explained, his pelt beginning to prickle all over with guilt. "Lionblaze and the others stayed to fight them off, while I got the elders across the border."

Bramblestar's ears pricked forward. "Many rogues? Do I need to send a patrol?"

"We only saw two, but—"

Alderheart broke off as more cats appeared from the thorn tunnel. A flood of relief struck him as he recognized Lionblaze in the lead, closely followed by Sparkpelt and Ivypool.

"Are you okay?" he asked, running toward them.

"We're all fine," Lionblaze replied.

"You didn't think those flea-pelts could hurt us, did you?" Ivypool demanded. "That strange cat—what did Roach call him? Loki?—seemed as if he'd never had a fighting lesson in his whole life."

Sparkpelt let out a small *mrrow* of laughter. "We soon chased them off! I've never seen cats move so fast."

To Alderheart's relief, he realized that his Clanmates only had a few minor scratches to show for the skirmish with the rogues.

"Do you think they realized we were rescuing the elders?" he asked.

Lionblaze shook his head. "I told them we were on patrol

and stepped over the border by accident," he explained. "They seemed to accept that."

"Not that we had much time for talking," Ivypool added, examining her claws.

For a few moments Alderheart basked in thankfulness for the news. *I can't remember how long it's been since the Clans had something to be happy about,* he thought. *And now we do. We've rescued our first cats from the rogue camp!*

Then he remembered that not every Clan could share in their triumph. WindClan was still absent.

I wonder what's happening, up there on the moor. . . .

"That sore is healing nicely," Alderheart meowed to Ratscar, dabbing a new dressing of marigold on the elder's hind leg. "You'd better come back tomorrow, though, and let one of us check on it again."

The old cat was looking much stronger and healthier now that he had spent several days in the ThunderClan camp. Alderheart couldn't see his ribs anymore, and his brown pelt was glossy and well groomed.

"I'll do that," Ratscar mewed, "and I can't tell you how grateful we are, me and Oakfur. You know, back in the rogues' camp, Puddleshine did try to help us, but he had to sneak around Darktail. That sorry excuse for a cat didn't want Puddleshine doing us elders any special favors."

"Special favors!" Alderheart felt a sudden jolt of outrage. "Helping sick cats is what a medicine cat is *for.* It's not a favor!"

Ratscar let out a huffing breath. "Try telling that to

Darktail. You know," he continued, "I can't believe how bad things were in that camp. The worst mistake I ever made was not leaving with Rowanstar."

"Why didn't you?" Alderheart asked.

Ratscar shrugged. "I was angry with him for decisions he made while he was ill—but now I know what bad leadership *really* looks like."

"Have you told Rowanstar that?"

"No," Ratscar replied, ducking his head in embarrassment. "Things are still a bit . . . cool, between us."

"Then maybe you should," Alderheart advised.

Ratscar left the den, promising to think about what Alderheart had said.

While he tidied away the herbs he had been using, Alderheart reflected on how well their plan was working. On his second meeting with Violetpaw, she had brought out Snowbird and her two kits. They had settled into the ThunderClan nursery, where there was a bit more space now that most of the injured RiverClan warriors were healed.

Even so, the camp was still hopelessly overcrowded, and tension was in the air. Squirrelflight had suggested once again that they should move some cats out to the abandoned Twoleg den, but no cat wanted to go, and Bramblestar finally had to admit to his worry that they would be vulnerable there if the rogues attacked.

Raised voices sounded from outside the den. *What now?* Alderheart wondered with a sigh.

He padded out from behind the bramble screen to find

Rowanstar and Mistystar standing nose to nose, their legs stiff and their ears laid flat.

Alderheart groaned. *Not this again!*

"I don't know why you're dragging your paws over this," Rowanstar was meowing, his voice tight with fury. "It's obvious we should be attacking the rogues *now*. Any cat can see that we outnumber them, and your precious RiverClan warriors are nearly healed!"

"Yes, but if we attack, Darktail might kill the RiverClan prisoners he still holds," Mistystar said.

Rowanstar lashed his tail in frustration. "I'm nearly ready to go and attack them by myself," he growled. "It's—"

Just then, Bramblestar padded up with a nod for the other two leaders. Alderheart noticed that each of them tried to relax, as if they didn't want to be seen arguing in front of him.

"We need to discuss this," Bramblestar announced, then turned and headed for the tumbled rocks. When he had reached the Highledge, he raised his voice so that it rang out over the stone hollow. "Let all cats old enough to catch their own prey join here beneath the Highledge for a meeting of the Clans!"

Before he had finished speaking, cats were crowding out of the dens and into the clearing. Snowbird and her kits appeared at the entrance to the nursery along with Leafpool and Daisy. Graystripe and Millie, with the two ShadowClan elders, sat outside their den, while Squirrelflight and Jayfeather, with a couple of the RiverClan warriors, looked up from the fresh-kill pile.

Alderheart noticed that most of the ShadowClan cats were clustered around their leader, except for Tigerheart, who was sitting beside Dovewing, with Ivypool looking watchful on her sister's other side.

"Oakfur, Ratscar, Snowbird, we are glad to see you—and the kits, of course—safe here in ThunderClan," the Clan leader began. "This is your home for as long as you need it. It's good that the plan to smuggle cats out of the rogue camp is working, but clearly we can't go on like this forever."

"You can say that again," Rowanstar muttered.

"We need to find a way forward," Bramblestar continued. "It's time to think about our next steps."

Mistystar, who had been sitting near Alderheart outside the medicine-cat den, rose to her paws. "I know you're talking about an attack," she meowed. "But I can only support that when we've gotten all of my cats out. Any other plan is too risky." She lashed her tail once. "And that's final."

Several other cats sprang to their paws as she spoke, yowling their objections. For a few moments it seemed as if the meeting would break up into knots of arguing cats. But then Lionblaze spoke up.

"It seems obvious to me," he stated, dipping his head politely to his leader. "For all of us to be able to agree to an attack, we need to rescue the prisoners. And right now, we're only getting two or three cats out each time. Besides," he added, "so far we've taken elders, a queen and kits—cats we expect Darktail not to miss. No offense," he finished, with a nod to the ShadowClan elders.

"None taken," Oakfur responded. "That's pretty accurate."

"We know from Ratscar and the others," Mistystar went on, "that Darktail keeps the prisoners guarded at all times. It would be too difficult for Violetpaw to sneak them out—and even if she did, Darktail would notice they were missing right away. He might have assumed Ratscar and the others simply ran off, but he would know we were up to something if we started smuggling out the prisoners."

"That's all true," Tawnypelt meowed. "It sounds like we need a plan to get all the prisoners out at once."

Murmurs of agreement rose from all the cats in the clearing.

"But how are we going to do that?" Cloudtail asked.

"We'd have to sneak into the rogue camp," Tigerheart mewed thoughtfully. "And somehow incapacitate the guards . . ."

"Incapacitate Darktail," Snowbird put in from where she sat outside the nursery. As all eyes turned toward her, she added, "He's *very* controlling. He knows everything that goes on in the camp."

"Even with Darktail out of the way," Ratscar added, "you would have to be prepared to fight. The cats who are loyal to Darktail wouldn't just let you stroll out of camp with the remaining prisoners. If nothing else, they'd be terrified of what Darktail would do to them when he found out."

For a moment, the cats were silent. Alderheart thought he saw Snowbird shudder.

"All right," Bramblestar said after a moment. "Let's assume we would be ready to fight. How could we incapacitate

Darktail and his closest allies?"

Alderheart listened as cat after cat chimed in with suggestions.

"We could lure hungry dogs to RiverClan territory!"

"Or lure the cats under a tree and drop rocks on their heads!"

"Maybe if we could just catch ourselves an eagle—*then* we might be able to . . ."

Alderheart sighed, hardly listening anymore as the suggestions became more and more ridiculous. Then an idea slipped into his mind. He rose to his paws.

"I have a plan," he announced, raising his head so that he could see every cat. "I'm supposed to meet Violetpaw again tonight. . . ."

The sun had gone down, but the last traces of scarlet still streaked the sky as Alderheart and Mothwing slipped silently through ShadowClan territory until they reached the small Thunderpath that formed the border with RiverClan. They crept underneath a bush and settled down to wait.

"I wonder if Violetpaw will bring any more cats," Mothwing murmured. "I almost hope she doesn't."

Alderheart nodded agreement. "Every cat she gets out adds to the risk that Darktail will notice what we're doing. We need to concentrate on the prisoners now."

Full darkness had fallen by the time Alderheart spotted the small shape of Violetpaw emerging from the bushes and racing across the Thunderpath. He poked his head out of the bush.

"Over here!" he whispered.

Violetpaw padded up to him and slid underneath the bush to crouch by his side. "I'm sorry," she mewed. "I couldn't bring any other cats. I'm not sure any more which ones I can trust not to give me away to Darktail."

"That's okay," Alderheart responded. "We've got a new plan now."

Rapidly, he explained to Violetpaw what had happened at the meeting, and how they had decided it was vital to rescue the prisoners all at once.

"Mistystar won't attack until all her cats are safe," Mothwing added when he had finished.

"But it's going to be dangerous." Even though they needed Violetpaw desperately, Alderheart knew that he had to warn her. "Are you sure you want to go ahead with this?"

Violetpaw gazed at the two medicine cats, her eyes wide and resolute. "Tell me what you want me to do," she meowed.

"We can't get the prisoners away until we deal with Darktail and his guards," Alderheart continued, "and they have to be out of the way for a good long time. So you're going to put them to sleep."

Violetpaw stifled a *mrrow* of surprise. "But how?" she breathed out.

"Here." Alderheart pushed a small leaf wrap toward Violetpaw's paws. "This is poppy seed. There's enough here for eight cats, and you should try to make sure they get at least three seeds each."

"Are you sure you can feed them to the rogues without Darktail noticing?" Mothwing asked.

"I think so," Violetpaw replied. "I'll hide them in some prey."

"Good," Mothwing mewed. "This is—" She broke off, hesitated, then went on, "We really appreciate you taking this huge risk. RiverClan will never forget what we owe you."

"It's the least I can do," Violetpaw told her. "RiverClan isn't the only Clan with cats they love among the prisoners." She looked down at the poppy seeds. "How long will the cats who eat this be asleep?" she asked.

"It depends on their size and how much they eat," Alderheart told her. "But it should keep them quiet for half the night, at least."

Violetpaw nodded grimly. "Okay. Consider it done."

Alderheart gazed at the young cat, reflecting on how serious she was, and how she had needed to grow up so quickly. *She's so different from Twigpaw. I wonder what would have happened if I'd been able to convince the leaders to let us keep Violetpaw in ThunderClan, back when they were split up at their first Gathering. She's seen so much since that day.*

But Alderheart quickly pushed away any regret, telling himself it had all worked out for the best.

If she weren't living among the rogues, we wouldn't have a cat to help us, he told himself. *And she'll have a good life when we win—and we* will *win. I can't let myself believe any differently.*

He and Mothwing watched Violetpaw as she padded determinedly back across the Thunderpath, the leaf wrap of poppy seeds clamped firmly in her jaws. "That's a brave cat," Mothwing murmured.

When Violetpaw had disappeared into the undergrowth, the two medicine cats rose and headed back toward ThunderClan.

Alderheart was remembering the moment, soon after he'd first found the kits, when he had touched his nose to Twigpaw's and promised himself he would make sure she had a good life.

How did we ever get from there to here?

CHAPTER 15

Twigpaw's belly was yowling for food as she stumbled across a grassy clearing, forcing herself to take one paw step after another. She had never felt so exhausted.

The sun was slipping down the sky, casting long shadows across her path. Around her, trees stretched in every direction; she had no idea where she was or which way she should go. She had begun to despair of ever finding her kin, or even remembering her way home.

Reaching the roots of an oak tree, Twigpaw flopped down to rest. Her rumbling belly told her she should hunt, but she was too weary. The day before, she had even stooped to rubbing up against the legs of a Twoleg, purring and trying to look cute. The Twoleg had put out a hollow thing like a big hard leaf, full of some creamy white stuff. Twigpaw had lapped it up; it had tasted good, but it had made her feel sick for the rest of the day.

When did I last eat real prey? I can't remember....

The days were beginning to blur into one another, so that now she had trouble remembering how long it had been since she'd first left ThunderClan. After she'd lost consciousness when the monster struck her on the Thunderpath, she had opened her eyes to find herself in a strange Twoleg den. It was full of peculiar, acrid scents, and a Twoleg with a white pelt kept forcing round white pebbles down her throat. She slept most of the time—maybe the white pebbles were Twoleg poppy seeds—so she wasn't certain how long she had stayed there. But it must have been at least a quarter moon.

Finally she had started to feel stronger. *Maybe the white-pelted Twoleg was like one of our medicine cats.* He was kind, but Twigpaw knew that she couldn't stay there. She waited for her chance, until one day a second Twoleg opened the door of the den where they were keeping her.

Twigpaw swiped at the medicine Twoleg as he tried to force another pebble into her mouth, dropped to the ground, and fled out of the den. She heard the Twolegs yowling behind her, and their heavy paws thumping along the ground, but she didn't stop until she found refuge underneath a bush beside a Thunderpath.

After that, Twigpaw had begun to search for the yellow barn Alderheart had seen in his vision—but she'd had no idea where she was. She spent several days trekking to and fro around the edges of the Twolegplace, and she had many conversations with kittypets, who all looked at her as if they thought she had bees in her brain.

She'd finally found the barn, but there was nothing there except a faint scent of cats to tell her that she had found the right place. She was too late.

SkyClan might have been there at some point—but they had moved on.

Twigpaw set out to follow the scent trail, but it was faint to start with, and soon it faded altogether. For the last two days, she had been wandering aimlessly, not even knowing how to get home to the lake.

Here and there in the forest she encountered Twolegs, some of them living in pelt-dens, like the ones who came in greenleaf to the clearing on the ShadowClan border. The cats she met were all kittypets, and none of them knew what she was meowing about when she mentioned the Clans or asked if they had seen SkyClan.

Twigpaw was slipping into deeper sleep when she became aware of a gray tom standing beside her, staring down at her with brilliant blue eyes.

"Get up!" he urged her. "You're wasting time! Don't you know that you're our only hope?"

"No, I'm too late . . . ," Twigpaw responded, struggling to her paws. "I got attacked by a monster and messed everything up."

"It's not too late," the gray tom insisted. "Wake up right now, and look for the blood trail in the sky. . . . Follow it until you can see the whole circle of the sun."

Twigpaw startled awake, finding herself still curled up among the oak roots. Looking around, she realized that she was alone in the forest; the gray tom had vanished. But through gaps in the trees she could see the sky and realized that the sun was setting—and just as the gray tom had said, there was what looked like a trail of blood leading to the horizon.

Was that a dream or a vision? Twigpaw wondered. *It had to be a dream . . . I'm not a medicine cat. I don't have visions. But something about that cat was so convincing. . . .*

Even though Twigpaw was exhausted, she forced herself onto her weary paws and began to stumble along, following the trail in the sky.

Shadows were gathering beneath the trees, and Twigpaw could barely force one paw in front of another. There seemed to be no end to the forest, and whenever she caught a glimpse of the sun, it was crisscrossed with branches. It was impossible to get a clear view.

Twigpaw was beginning to despair when the trees ahead of her started to thin out. A fresh spark of hope gave her the determination to bound forward, then thrust her way through a dense bank of ferns and break out into the open. The sky ahead of her was a blaze of scarlet, but the sun had already vanished.

I've failed, Twigpaw thought, letting out a murmur of dismay.

Then she realized that in the direction of the sunset the ground fell away sharply into a rocky cliff. Scampering up to the edge, she was just in time to see the sun, a huge red circle, before it dipped below the horizon of the plain below. Twigpaw stood staring until the last of it sank out of sight and the red trail in the sky began to fade.

So I did what the gray tom said. Now what?

Twigpaw turned around, gazing back through the trees and across the swell of moorland where she had emerged. There was no sign of any cats, and when she tasted the air, she couldn't pick up the faintest trace of cat scent.

It was just a stupid dream, she thought miserably, collapsing in a heap. She was no closer to finding her father than when she'd left ThunderClan, and now she had no more ideas.

It's time to give up. I'll sleep now, and when I wake up, I'll try to figure out a way to get home.

She was curling up in the shelter of a rock, wrapping her tail over her nose, when she spotted something moving through the bushes at the bottom of the cliff. *A gray flash. Is it . . . ?*

New energy seemed to flow into Twigpaw's body as she rose to her paws again and began scrambling down the cliff face toward the place where she had seen the movement. Soon she came to a wide ledge overlooking a shallow valley with a stream at the bottom. And beside the stream . . .

Twigpaw let out a loud meow of delight. *Cats! So many cats, making their camp.* Her gaze devoured them; she could hardly believe what she was seeing. *That's him—the gray flash I saw moving though the bushes. I don't think he's the tom I saw in my dream. But he looks just like me!* Her paws skimmed the rocks as she hurled herself down the rest of the cliff, so eager to meet her kin that she never thought she might be in danger of falling.

At the sound of Twigpaw's meow the cats looked up at her and began to crowd together defensively. For the first time,

Twigpaw could see how skinny and bedraggled they looked . . . even worse off than she was herself.

Among them was a small white she-cat whose belly was so swollen that she must be close to kitting. A larger tabby tom stood protectively beside her. Twigpaw noticed three young cats, too, about her own age, staring at her with a mixture of fear and curiosity.

The cat who looked like her spotted her at last, and his eyes grew huge. "Who are you?" he asked, at the same moment as one of the others demanded suspiciously, "What do you want?"

"I'm sorry," Twigpaw apologized, skidding to a halt. She was hardly able to contain the excitement that was rushing through her from ears to tail-tip. "I didn't mean to scare you. I think I may know who you are. Are you SkyClan?"

The cats exchanged sad glances. "We are what remains of SkyClan," one of them told Twigpaw.

A brown-and-cream tabby she-cat stepped forward and dipped her head to Twigpaw. Though she was as thin and weary-looking as her Clanmates, she held herself with dignity, and her voice was strong as she spoke. "We have been on a long journey, faced great hardship, and lost many friends," she meowed. "But yes, we are SkyClan. How do you know?"

"I come from ThunderClan," Twigpaw replied eagerly. "My name is Twigpaw."

As soon as she mentioned her Clan, astonished exclamations rose from the cats around her. They exchanged excited glances, their suspicion and uncertainty vanishing.

"You come from ThunderClan? We know about Thunder-Clan!" one of them exclaimed. "We've been searching for you for moons and moons!"

Twigpaw blinked as suddenly the cats crowded around her, their words tumbling over each other in their eagerness.

"Echosong had a vision!" one of them was saying. "She said the fire had burned out, but we should find the spark that remains!"

The brown-and-cream tabby let out a purr. "We knew the fire had to be Firestar!" She paused, her eyes rounding with sadness. "But is it true, has he died?"

Other cats broke in before Twigpaw could answer the question, crowding around her until she almost felt she couldn't breathe.

"He came to visit us with a brave she-cat! They gave us back our Clan when it was almost forgotten."

"He showed us how to hunt!"

"He taught us the warrior code!"

"We still teach our kits about him. We will honor his name forever!"

Twigpaw wasn't sure what to say. She'd never met Firestar. "I—I'm sorry," she stammered. "This, um, Echosong's vision was right—Firestar is dead."

The Clan's enthusiastic meows faded somewhat. But they didn't seem surprised. After a moment, the tabby she-cat asked, "How did he die?"

"In a great battle, saving his Clan," Twigpaw replied. "I

wasn't born then, but I've heard so many stories about him! ThunderClan also honors his memory."

"So who is leader of ThunderClan now?" the she-cat mewed.

"He's called Bramblestar. He's a great cat, too."

The tabby she-cat nodded slowly, taking all this in. "My name is Leafstar," she continued at last. "I met Firestar when he came to the gorge and rebuilt our Clan, and I know that ThunderClan is good and honorable. Can you take us back to your hunting grounds? Echosong had a dream where we came to live beside the other Clans—by a large body of water. We would be so grateful if you could take us to Bramblestar."

Twigpaw bowed her head, humbled to think that her Clan was held so highly in the memories of these cats who lived so far away. *But can I even find my way back?* She wasn't sure what to say. *I have to try. They're all counting on me.*

After a moment, the gray tom who looked like Twigpaw stepped forward to stand at Leafstar's side. "My name is Hawkwing," he announced.

"He is the deputy of this Clan," Leafstar meowed. "The deputy Firestar knew, Sharpclaw, was Hawkwing's father. He was killed when a group of rogues attacked us and took over the gorge. We were forced to leave; at first we settled down by a lake not far from here, thinking it might be the water from Echosong's dream—but when greenleaf came, Twolegs moved onto our territory. And so we had to leave our home a second time. We have been wandering through the woods, searching for the spark that remains. And it sounds, Twigpaw, like that is you." Her eyes warmed as she looked down at the young apprentice.

Twigpaw was overwhelmed, but a small part of her registered what Leafstar had said: *a group of rogues attacked us and took over the gorge.* Twigpaw swallowed hard, wondering how to tell these cats, who had already suffered so much, that Darktail was now causing trouble for the other Clans.

Glancing at the gray tom, Twigpaw realized that he was staring at her. For a moment she wondered if he *might* actually be the gray tom from her dream—but that cat's eyes had been the brilliant blue of a clear sky, while Hawkwing's were warm amber.

Just like Violetpaw's!

"Are you alone?" Hawkwing asked her. "Where are your Clanmates? We're not near the lake, are we? What brings you this far from home?"

Twigpaw hesitated, overwhelmed by the questions. "My Clanmates are back on our territory," Twigpaw explained, struggling to find the right words. "There's . . . there's a lot going on back home. There's a group of rogues on the territory, led by a cat you might know. . . ." She swallowed, wondering how the SkyClan cats would react. "A rogue named Darktail."

Leafstar gasped, and Twigpaw saw something dark flash in Hawkwing's eyes.

"Darktail?" he said, as though the word felt strange on his tongue. "Darktail is . . . on *your* territory now?"

As quickly as she could, Twigpaw explained how Alderheart

had had a vision of SkyClan, and had led a quest to try to help them, only to get to the gorge too late. She explained how he and the others had been fooled by Darktail into believing that *he* led SkyClan, only to realize the truth after staying with him for some time.

"They fled and came back to the lake, but Darktail must have followed them," Twigpaw finished. "Because he showed up and began attacking Clan cats not long after they returned. And now . . . well, they're still trying to drive him out."

Twigpaw saw Leafstar and Hawkwing exchange a serious look.

"Well," Hawkwing said, determined. "Now I'm even *more* sure that we have business at the lake."

Twigpaw looked from the older cats to her paws, feeling awkward.

"Were you on the quest, Twigpaw?" Leafstar asked after a moment. "Have you seen the gorge since we left?"

Twigpaw shook her head. "I was too young; I wasn't part of ThunderClan yet. Alderheart found me and my sister Violet-paw on his way back to ThunderClan. We were very young, and it looked as if our mother had abandoned us."

"What cat would do that?" a gray she-cat meowed, while sympathetic murmurs came from several of the others.

"I don't think she meant to," Twigpaw responded, quick to defend the mother she had never known. "Some of my Clanmates and I went to look for her, and we decided that she must have died—we think that she was probably hit by a monster on the Thunderpath." She hesitated. "Then Alderheart had another vision where he saw SkyClan again—and he saw you, Hawkwing. He said you looked . . . just like me." As she mewed the last few words, Twigpaw suddenly felt like she was being stupid. She couldn't meet Hawkwing's gaze anymore, so studied her paws as she added, "I just *had* to come and find you. I had to know whether there was any chance . . ."

For a moment no cat spoke. When Twigpaw dared to raise her head, she saw a stricken look in Hawkwing's amber eyes.

"You're right, Twigpaw." His voice was filled with sorrow. "Your mother must have died, because there's no way that Pebbleshine would ever have abandoned her kits if she were alive. I know, because . . . because she was my mate."

Twigpaw looked up at him, her heart beating so fast she could hardly breathe. "Wait!" she choked out. "Are you saying . . . ?"

"I'm your father, Twigpaw," Hawkwing meowed, and ran forward to nuzzle her close.

With Twigpaw in the lead, along with Leafstar and Hawkwing, the cats of SkyClan straggled along the bank of a narrow stream that wound its way through dense forest. They were traveling toward a high hill Twigpaw could see in the distance—a hill, she hoped and believed, that was one of the same ones she could see from the lake. At last the trees were thinning out, and ahead Twigpaw could see open country, with hills rising in the distance. Three sunrises had passed since she had found SkyClan, and sometimes she was afraid that they would never find the lake again.

Paw steps sounded behind her, and Twigpaw glanced back to see the pale gray tom, Sagenose, hurrying to catch up.

"Are you sure of where you're going?" the SkyClan tom demanded, falling into step beside Twigpaw. "We've been traveling so long I think my paws are going to fall off!"

Twigpaw halted, suppressing a sigh. *How many times have they asked me that question?* "No, I'm not completely sure," she replied. "But I think we're heading in the right direction." As Sagenose let out a disbelieving snort, she added, "You see that hill up ahead? I'm sure I see that on the horizon when I hunt! So we must be getting closer."

Sagenose flicked his ears dismissively. "Is any other cat concerned," he meowed, turning to Leafstar, "that Thunder-Clan hasn't invited us? This one apprentice came looking for us, but she admits she wasn't exactly *sent*."

Twigpaw flinched, looking helplessly at Hawkwing. *Could I possibly have come all this way to find my father, only to have his Clan refuse to follow me home?*

Hawkwing moved closer to her until their pelts brushed. "Sagenose, we've discussed this," Hawkwing responded. "Twigpaw will take us to Bramblestar. When we talk to him, we'll know more about what the future holds."

More cats crowded around as they heard the beginning of the argument.

Sparrowpelt shouldered his way forward and rested his tabby tail for a moment on Twigpaw's shoulder. "Sagenose, we've been wandering for moons, trying to find the right home," he meowed. "And before Echosong died, she told us to follow the blood trail in the sky, and that led us straight to Twigpaw! Echosong even said she'd had visions of a Thunder-Clan cat. Surely that means—"

"We still don't know that we'll be welcome," Sagenose interrupted, glaring at Sparrowpelt.

"I believe it was meant to be this way," Hawkwing cut in. "This is how we were meant to find ThunderClan."

"Of course *you* feel that way," Sagenose snapped. "She's your kit."

"That's enough!" Leafstar thrust her way into the center of the group, her tail raised for silence. "Enough debating! I am your leader, and *I've* decided that we will follow Twigpaw back to ThunderClan. And that's the end of it! Sagenose, do you want to be part of SkyClan or not?"

"Of course I do!" Sagenose blinked, sounding a little hurt. "Well, obviously I do. I've been through enough with you!"

"Fine," Leafstar mewed evenly. "Then no further arguments."

She set out again, striding determinedly along the bank of the stream, and the rest of the Clan followed.

During the argument—and even now that it was over—Twigpaw had been squirming uncomfortably. *I hope I can even find ThunderClan. And that they're willing to take me back . . . not to mention an entire new Clan. . . .* Lilyheart's words echoed in her mind, from the Clan meeting just before she'd run off. *This isn't the right time to find your kin.*

But surely things had improved since Twigpaw had left?

Leaving the last of the trees behind them, the cats struck

out into open country, drawing nearer to the hill Twigpaw thought was close to the Clans' territory. Sunhigh was long past by the time they reached it and trudged up the slope to the top.

As she crested the rise and looked out across the land ahead, Twigpaw halted as if she had just run into a tree. "Oh!" she exclaimed. She had expected to see the Thunderpath and the tunnel where she and Violetpaw had been born. Instead the ground sloped gently away in front of her, covered with bushes and clumps of fern. Down in the bottom of the valley the bushes gave way to dense woodland; here and there Violetpaw caught the glimmer of water.

"Is everything okay?" Leafstar asked, padding up to stand beside her.

"Oh—uh—yes," Twigpaw stammered. She didn't want to tell the SkyClan leader that, once again, she had no idea where she was.

Bracing herself resolutely, she led the way down into the trees.

A narrow stream trickled through the undergrowth, and Leafstar decided that they should hunt and camp there for the night. Twigpaw found it difficult to sleep, shifting restlessly in the nest she had made under an elder bush. She was too worried about the next day's journey.

How long will SkyClan go on following me, if I can't lead them to the lake soon?

Not long after the cats set off the following morning, they emerged from a thick bank of fern onto a strip of grass that bordered the hard black surface of a Thunderpath. Monsters were roaring up and down it in both directions, their bright colors glittering in the sunlight. Twigpaw's belly churned as she remembered the monster that had struck her when she fell from the tree.

"Do we have to cross here?" Hawkwing asked.

Twigpaw nodded. She knew that a Thunderpath lay between the lake and the place where she had found SkyClan; she could only hope that this was the same one. It looked very different from the area where the tunnel was.

But it must *be the right one,* she told herself. *How many Thunderpaths do Twolegs need?*

Twigpaw waited with the SkyClan cats in a line along the grass verge until Leafstar gave the order to cross. Twigpaw could hear the growl of an approaching monster as her paws skimmed across the Thunderpath, but every cat had reached safety on the other side before it swept past on its round black paws.

"Now where do we go?" Tinycloud asked. The pregnant white she-cat was leaning on Sparrowpelt's shoulder, and she looked exhausted. "Is it much farther?"

I hope it isn't, Twigpaw thought, gesturing into the trees with her tail. "This way."

Sunhigh was still some way off when Twigpaw rounded a bramble thicket and halted at the edge of a clearing. In the middle was a cluster of weird rocks made out of flat pieces of wood. Tasting the air, she picked up the faint scent of Twolegs.

"Oh, I don't believe it!" Plumwillow exclaimed as she followed Twigpaw around the bramble thicket. "You have Twolegs near your territory, too?"

"Twolegs are everywhere," Sandynose responded, touching his mate's shoulder with his tail-tip. "We're not staying here, are we?" he asked Twigpaw.

Memories were scrambling into Twigpaw's head. She had never seen this place before, but she remembered Alderheart telling her about his journey to the gorge, and how he had his companions had stopped at a greenleaf Twolegplace and eaten delicious Twoleg food. *This must be the very place!*

"No," she replied to Sandynose, "but it means we don't have much farther to go."

As they left the greenleaf Twolegplace behind, the trees began to thin out. Soon Twigpaw and the SkyClan cats were faced with a steep slope covered with wiry grass and gorse thickets; here and there outcrops of rock poked through the turf. A stiff breeze swept down from the ridge; Twigpaw's whiskers twitched with excitement at the familiar scents it brought with it.

"Don't tell me we have to climb that!" Tinycloud groaned.

"Yes, we do." Twigpaw replied. "But we're very close to the ThunderClan camp now. You'll see!"

Leafstar took the lead as the cats toiled up the slope, while Sparrowpelt and Hawkwing helped Tinycloud. A few tail-lengths from the top, Twigpaw bounded ahead and let out a caterwaul of joy as she reached the ridge, digging her claws into the tough grass.

"Look down there!" she meowed as the SkyClan cats struggled up to join her. "There's the lake—and the horseplace—and you can't see it from here, but the ThunderClan camp is down there, too. We're almost home!"

Yowls of excitement followed her announcement, and Hawkwing gave Twigpaw's ears an approving lick. "I knew you would find the way," he meowed, resting his tail over Twigpaw's shoulders. "I'm very glad Alderheart took you and your sister in," he added.

"So am I," Twigpaw purred.

CHAPTER 16

The sun was setting as Violetpaw led her hunting patrol back into the rogue camp. The rest of the patrol—Loki, Nettle, and Scorchfur—dropped their prey on the fresh-kill pile, grabbed some for themselves, and padded off to eat.

Left to herself, Violetpaw chose several of the best pieces of prey and carried them to a dip in the ground not far from Darktail's den. The shadow of an elder bush sheltered her from the rest of the Kin.

Violetpaw had already hidden the leaf wrap of poppy seeds among the roots of the bush. Now she drew it out and carefully counted out three seeds for each piece of prey before she pushed them inside the fresh-kill.

Darktail and his friends will really *enjoy this,* she thought grimly. Even though her heart was pounding hard at the risk she was taking, she took a kind of joy in the thought that she was playing such an important part in defeating the invaders.

Darktail's den was beneath a jutting rock, screened by overhanging fronds of fern. When Violetpaw was sure all the poppy seeds were well concealed, she padded up to the entrance, trying not to let her legs shake with apprehension.

"Darktail!" she called out. "The hunting patrol is back, and I've picked out some good prey for you."

The fern fronds shook as the white tom brushed past them into the open. "Good," he meowed, swiping his tongue around his jaws. "I'm starving!"

"So am I."

The voice came from behind Violetpaw; she spun around, her belly lurching as if she had swallowed crow-food. Sleek-whisker was standing a fox-length away, her yellow pelt gleaming in the last light of the sun.

How long has she been there? Violetpaw asked herself, fighting against panic. *Did she see what I did to the prey?*

Then Violetpaw forced herself to be calm, telling herself that if Sleekwhisker had spotted her, she would surely have asked what she was doing.

I know she's desperate to catch me doing something wrong, because she can't stand it that Darktail likes me better than her. So, if she hasn't said anything, she couldn't have seen me. . . . I hope.

"The prey is over here." Violetpaw waved her tail in the direction of the elder bush. "Should I fetch it for you, Dark-tail?"

"No, we can eat over there," Darktail replied. Glancing around, he beckoned with his tail to his closest followers, who were stretched out together in a patch of sunlight. "Raven! Roach! Nettle—come over here! It's time to eat."

As the rogues padded over to the prey pile, Violetpaw dipped her head to Darktail. "I'll just go and get some sleep," she mewed.

Darktail twitched his whiskers. "Don't you want to eat with us?" he asked.

"No thanks, Darktail. I had a mouse while I was out," Violetpaw replied, thankful for once that the rogues didn't follow the warrior code, so no cat would be surprised that she had eaten before she brought food back for the Kin.

For a moment, Darktail looked concerned. *Oh, StarClan!* Violetpaw thought, her muscles tensing. *Don't let him order me to share the prey!*

Then Darktail gave her a brusque nod. "Suit yourself," he responded with a shrug, and padded off to join his Kin around the prey pile.

Trying not to let her relief show, Violetpaw slipped away to the new den she had made for herself among some reeds at the edge of the stream, so she could get some privacy from Zelda. *That went well,* she congratulated herself. *Now, I just have to wait. . . .*

Violetpaw lay curled up in her den until night had fallen and the noises outside in the camp had faded into quiet. Expecting that every cat would be asleep, she slid out of her den, shook some scraps of moss from her pelt, and arched her back in a good long stretch. Then, her ears pricked alertly, she headed across the camp to Darktail's den.

He should be in a really deep *sleep,* she told herself with satisfaction. *Along with the other three mange-pelts he calls his closest Kin. Then ThunderClan and I can put our plan into action.*

But as Violetpaw approached the den, Sleekwhisker rose up

out of the shadow of the fern clump. Her green eyes glinted; she was fully awake.

"Oh, good, there you are," she purred.

Disconcerted, Violetpaw took a pace back. "Oh, uh . . . I just went to make dirt," she explained desperately. "I'll get back to my den now."

Sleekwhisker slid out her claws. "I don't think so," she responded, amusement in her voice.

With a hard shove, Sleekwhisker thrust Violetpaw through the screen of ferns and into Darktail's den. It took a couple of heartbeats for Violetpaw's vision to clear in the dim light—but when it did, she felt as if terror had turned her whole body into a block of ice. Darktail and the rest of his close Kin were all there, and every one of them was awake. Their eyes gleamed in the darkness, their baleful gazes fixed on her.

Before Violetpaw could speak, Roach and Raven grabbed her neck fur with one forepaw each. Violetpaw cringed as their claws sank deep into her pelt. The two rogues dragged her forward until she was standing in front of the leader.

"Get off me!" she yowled, trying to dig her claws into the earth floor of the den. "What's gotten into you?"

Darktail gazed down at her, quite calm, his eyes filled with a dreadful gentleness. "Do you have anything you'd like to tell me?" he asked.

"Like what?" Violetpaw tried to sound innocent, desperately wondering if there was any plan that would save her now.

Darktail reached behind him into the shadows and drew out a leaf; on it were the poppy seeds, sticky now from prey juices. "Like what your plan was, exactly, with this little trick," he responded as he pushed the leaf in front of Violetpaw.

Violetpaw felt her blood turn icier still. "I'm—I'm not sure what those are," she stammered.

"Oh, very funny," Darktail meowed. "I wasn't sure, either, so I asked Puddleshine. He was *so* helpful. He explained that these are poppy seeds, and powerful enough to put a cat to sleep." He paused, examining the claws on one forepaw. "Which makes it interesting that several of them were found in the pieces of prey you brought for me and my closest Kin."

Violetpaw shook her head, still trying to cling to innocence. "I'm not sure . . . I didn't . . ."

Darktail suddenly shook off his calm demeanor. "Don't waste our time pretending you didn't do it," he snapped. "Sleekwhisker saw you doing something suspicious to the prey, and she was smart enough to warn us before we could eat it. You know," he went on, a menacing rumble in his throat, "it's almost impressive, how good you are at this: lying, pretending to be a friend when in fact you're an enemy. I suppose it's all the time you spent among those useless Clan cats. I thought you were like *me*—"

"I am—really!" Violetpaw protested, her voice squeaking as if she were a frightened kit.

Darktail ignored her. "No," he continued. "I don't believe that anymore. In fact, I'm beginning to wonder: Is it possible that you had something to do with those former ShadowClan elders and queens who have gone missing? Don't think I haven't noticed. I notice *everything* that happens among my Kin."

Now Violetpaw couldn't stop herself from shaking. She had known that she was taking a risk by agreeing to put the poppy seeds into Darktail's food, but she had never imagined a moment like this, and what it would actually feel like to be caught.

So this is it, she thought. *He's going to kill me.* She realized that if Twigpaw ever did return to her Clan, she wouldn't be there to greet her. She would never have the chance to say that she was sorry and be reconciled with her sister. *Or perhaps Twigpaw is already in StarClan, and I'll see her there.* The thought made a violent shudder pass through her from ears to tail-tip.

"Oh, I'm not going to kill you," Darktail mewed, as if he could read her thoughts. "Killing you wouldn't be enough punishment for the traitorous act you tried to perform tonight—the act you *almost* pulled off."

Before Violetpaw could ask what he meant, Darktail stalked past her out of the den, flicking his tail at Roach and Raven, "Bring her," he snarled.

The two rogues grabbed Violetpaw again and dragged her out after Darktail, with Sleekwhisker padding behind. To her horror, Violetpaw realized that the white tom was heading toward the prisoners' den.

Is he going to throw me inside? she wondered, her legs almost giving way out of fear. She had seen how Needletail and the RiverClan prisoners had been starved and intimidated; she shivered at the thought of having to go through that herself.

Outside the den, Zelda and Nettle were on guard, straightening up and looking alert as Darktail approached. The white tom said nothing to them, simply growling, "Wait here," to Roach and Raven before pushing his way through the brambles and into the den.

Violetpaw was aware of Zelda's scared gaze fixed on her, but she dared not speak to, or even look at, her kittypet friend.

A moment later, scuffling sounds came from among the brambles, and Darktail reappeared, thrusting Needletail in front of him. From behind, yowls of dismay came from the other prisoners.

"What are you doing?"

"What's happening?"

Violetpaw could see every one of Needletail's ribs as her friend staggered to a halt beside her. Her pelt was matted and her eyes were dull, but she tried to hold herself erect and face Darktail.

"Yes, what is happening?" she challenged him. "What do you want?"

"Violetpaw has betrayed me," Darktail replied, his voice a soft, menacing purr. "She tried to put me to sleep by slipping poppy seeds into my prey. Needletail, I'm afraid that *you* are the cat who must pay the price for her treachery, but don't worry. . . . You'll be doing the other prisoners a favor. There'll be more fresh-kill to go around now."

His words ended with a harsh *mrrow* of laughter; Violetpaw thought she had never heard a more evil sound. She didn't know what Darktail meant when he said that Needletail must pay the price, but fear swelled from deep in her belly. *It won't be anything good.*

Needletail cast an alarmed glance at Violetpaw just as Darktail and Sleekwhisker seized hold of Needletail and began dragging her across the camp. At first Needletail tried to fight, writhing in their grip and striking out with all four paws. But she was too weak to win a battle against the two fit, muscular rogues, and soon Darktail and Sleekwhisker held her pinned to the ground until her struggles stopped; then they hauled her up and dragged her onward.

Roach and Raven followed with Violetpaw. As they splashed through the stream that formed the camp border, Violetpaw realized that they were heading toward the lake.

Terror welled up inside her like dark floodwater. *Why would Darktail take us there?* Unbidden, a memory flashed into her mind, of how Dawnpelt had argued with Darktail in the middle of the night. The rogue leader's words echoed in her mind. *If you don't want to be with us anymore, then you are no longer our Kin.*

Icy claws of horror pricked at Violetpaw's belly. *Is he taking us wherever he took Dawnpelt?*

On the lakeshore, Darktail halted and turned to face his prisoners. "Why are you looking so scared?" he asked Violetpaw. "You have nothing to worry about. Your good friend Needletail will take your punishment for you."

Without warning, he leaped forward and sank his claws into Needletail's shoulders, dragging her backward into the lake until the water reached their belly fur. Needletail let out a screech and began striking out at Darktail in an effort to free herself, but as the water rose around them, it was all she could do to stay on her paws.

Then with a powerful spasm of his forelegs Darktail pushed Needletail's head under the surface. Her screeches of alarm were cut off with a choking sound as water flowed into her mouth.

Violetpaw stared in utter disbelief as Needletail's struggles churned up the water. Once, her head broke the surface, and she managed to take a gasping breath. Then Sleekwhisker bounded through the shallows, throwing up splashes that hit Violetpaw in the face. She flung herself on Needletail, pressing her down harder into the lake.

"Stop!" Violetpaw yowled. "Please stop!"

She tried to race down the pebbly shore and into the water, to help her friend, but Roach and Raven held her back while her paws raked helplessly at the ground. Their eyes were mocking as they bared their teeth and dug their claws into her shoulders on either side. With every heartbeat, Violetpaw felt her friend's life slipping away, while she could do nothing to save her.

"Punish me instead!" she begged Darktail, desperation beginning to overwhelm her. *Needletail is the only friend I have left!* "I admit it—I *was* trying to put you to sleep!"

Curiosity flickered in Darktail's dark-rimmed eyes. He relaxed his grip on Needletail and jerked his head, motioning for Sleekwhisker to step back. Needletail staggered to her paws, water streaming from her pelt, her chest heaving as she fought for breath.

"Why did you do it?" Darktail asked Violetpaw.

"I wanted to sneak out the prisoners," Violetpaw confessed.

She was beyond caring about her own punishment, as hope revived within her. *I've managed to stop Darktail hurting Needletail, at least for now.* "It was all me, though. I put poppy seeds in the prey so you and your Kin would eat them. Needletail had nothing to do with it! She didn't even know what I was up to!"

Darktail let out a *mrrow* of mockery. "Is that true?"

Violetpaw nodded vigorously. "It is, I promise!"

Without another word, Darktail signaled to Sleekwhisker, and the two rogue cats seized Needletail and pushed her back under the surface of the lake.

"*No!*" Violetpaw yowled, seeing how weak her friend's struggles were becoming. "Don't—please!"

Darktail turned his malignant gaze on her. "Killing Needletail is a better punishment than if I killed you." The calm in his voice chilled Violetpaw more than savage anger ever could have. "You're so attached to this treacherous cat, you're more afraid of her death than your own. I want you to know what it's like to live with the pain and grief of losing the one cat who befriended you and took care of you."

"Oh, please . . . please, no!" Violetpaw begged again. Every hair on her pelt, every muscle in her body, felt as if it was shrieking in agony.

"I can't believe I once thought you and Needletail would be my loyal Kin," Darktail mewed bitterly. "Needletail was the first Clan cat who gave me any notice. I thought she would help me build something here. But then she got involved with that traitor, Rain—and it's clear to me now that you, Violetpaw, are just as disloyal."

By now Needletail had stopped struggling; the lake was still around Darktail and Sleekwhisker, who stood holding her down in water up to their bellies. Violetpaw felt something break inside her, like a tree branch giving way under the weight of snow in leaf-bare.

Needletail is the closest thing I have to true kin now, she thought, horror gripping her like a badger's claws. *I don't even know whether Twigpaw is alive! What will I do without Needletail?* Memories of her friend crowded in on her. *She sneaked me out of camp to go and visit Twigpaw. She always defended me from Darktail!*

Then Darktail's menacing gaze suddenly softened. "Maybe you're right, Violetpaw," he meowed. "Maybe I should give Needletail another chance. What do you think?"

"Oh, yes!" Violetpaw gave a huge gasp of relief. *Maybe this has just been another one of Darktail's cruel tests!* "Please give her another chance! I'll do anything you want!"

Darktail took a pace back, and nodded to Sleekwhisker to do the same. For a moment there was no movement below the surface. Violetpaw stared helplessly at the spot where her friend had disappeared. *Oh, StarClan, don't let it be too late!*

Then Needletail's head broke the surface, her silver-gray fur darkened by the water and plastered to her skull. Her jaws parted and she coughed up a stream of lake water, then took a wheezing breath. Her terrified gaze sought out Violetpaw, but she didn't speak.

"We've been discussing the situation," Darktail told her, his voice as calm as if they were back in camp, talking over strategy around the fresh-kill pile. "And we have all agreed that we should give you another chance. After all, it's not really fair to punish *you* for Violetpaw's mistake—isn't that right, Needletail?"

Needletail didn't respond. Far from looking relieved, her eyes had widened with a look of deep apprehension, as if she was expecting Darktail to say something horrible.

Darktail waited for a moment, then continued, "I'll be happy to spare your life, Needletail, if you'll do something for me."

"What?" Needletail rasped.

"If you kill Violetpaw yourself."

Violetpaw couldn't believe what was happening. Deep shudders ran through her body, and her belly cramped as if she was going to vomit as she watched Darktail and Sleek-whisker back farther off, to let Needletail crawl, dripping, out of the lake.

Needletail looked once more at Violetpaw, but Violetpaw couldn't read any clue to what she meant to do. It was as if there was no cat at all inside her eyes, just terrible emptiness.

"Bring her to me." Needletail's voice was ragged, but she was standing erect now, as if she was summoning every scrap of strength she had left.

At her words, Darktail exchanged a surprised glance with his Kin, and Roach let out a snort of laughter. Disgusted, Violetpaw realized they had never expected Needletail to obey. It had just been a cruel joke—another way to torture them both.

Roach and Raven propelled Violetpaw forward until she stood in front of Needletail.

She's going to do it, Violetpaw thought, still trying to read her friend's heart in her eyes. *She's going to kill me. And I can't blame her. I sort of deserve it. Needletail should do what she must to save herself. Didn't she give me the same advice?*

Roach and Raven gave her a final shove; Violetpaw stumbled and fell onto her side. Needletail stared at her as she dropped into a crouch. *I wish it could all be over faster,* Violetpaw thought despairingly.

Needletail pounced. She landed on top of Violetpaw, who realized with a shock of understanding that her friend's claws were sheathed. "Run!" she snarled into Violetpaw's ear.

Then, faster than Violetpaw could have believed possible, Needletail swiveled around and leaped at Roach and Raven, all outstretched claws and bared teeth. Taken completely by surprise, the two rogues staggered back, not even trying to defend themselves.

For a moment, Violetpaw stared at them, too stunned to react.

"Run! *Now!*" Needletail screeched at her. "Make this count, Violetpaw!"

As Roach and Raven sprang forward again, Darktail and Sleekwhisker began to splash their way out of the lake. Needletail whirled to attack them, too. Violetpaw's last glimpse of her was of a taut knot of fury, vanishing beneath all four cats at once, her claws still striking out.

She's sacrificing her life for mine, Violetpaw realized. *Of course she is. I should never have doubted her. She's truly the best friend I've ever had, and I can never repay her.*

These thoughts took barely a moment to pass through Violetpaw's mind. Then, feeling as though her heart would break, she turned to run.

Violetpaw dashed along the lakeshore and through the stream that flowed from what had been RiverClan's camp. Once across, she headed farther inland, dodging around trees and through thorn thickets, looking for narrow places she could slip through that might slow down a bigger cat. She was too scared to work out exactly where she was going, but she knew that, somehow, she had to make it to ThunderClan.

Soon Violetpaw realized that some cat was on her trail. The breeze carried Raven's scent to her. Needletail's yowls still split the air behind her, a mixture of rage and pain.

They're killing her! Violetpaw thought. But she had to push away all her pity and grief, or she knew that she would break under the despair.

I have to lose Raven and get to safety. . . . I have to make sure Needletail's sacrifice wasn't for nothing!

CHAPTER 17

❧

Alderheart's pads prickled with nervousness, his heart thumping in his chest as he padded along the edge of the lake, a leaf wrap of herbs in his jaws. He was bringing up the rear of the group of cats who had been chosen to attack the rogues in RiverClan territory. Bramblestar was in the lead, with Rowanstar and Mistystar, followed by many of Alderheart's Clanmates and warriors from ShadowClan and RiverClan.

I hope Violetpaw managed to sneak those poppy seeds into the prey for Darktail and his Kin.

Before they'd left camp, Bramblestar had called out to Alderheart and beckoned him over. "I want you to come with us," he meowed. "We don't know what shape the prisoners will be in, and we'll need to get them to safety quickly. And if the rogues fight back, things become much more complicated. We'll need to hold them off long enough to get the prisoners away." He sighed. "I'll feel better if we have a medicine cat close by."

Alderheart had nodded. "I'm happy to come with you," he'd agreed. "I'll get some herbs ready."

"Good." Bramblestar had blinked in satisfaction. "We leave at sunset."

The last streaks of scarlet had faded from the sky by the time the cats reached the halfbridge and the small Thunderpath that separated ShadowClan territory from RiverClan. They slipped across the hard surface, silent as moving shadows, and crept into hiding in the bushes on the far side, well out of scent-range of the rogues' camp.

"Right," Bramblestar mewed when every cat was crouched around him; his amber eyes glowed in the near darkness. "Remember, as much as we want Darktail's group out, our goal tonight is to free the prisoners."

"And any ShadowClan warriors who are regretting the choice they made to stay with Darktail," Rowanstar reminded him. The ShadowClan leader's tone was faintly resentful; Alderheart guessed he was annoyed that Bramblestar had taken the lead.

Bramblestar dipped his head; if he had noticed the edge to the ShadowClan leader's voice, he gave no sign of it. "Of course," he responded. "The point is, we have come to bring all those cats to safety in the ThunderClan camp. Don't get distracted by the fighting; it's a means to an end. We'll deal with Darktail later. It's a long walk back through ShadowClan territory, so every cat will need their full strength."

"Curse WindClan for closing their borders," Mallownose of RiverClan grumbled. "If they were still talking to us, we could use their camp—it's closer than ThunderClan's."

Alderheart saw Bramblestar's jaws tighten as if he was biting back a sharp retort, and he heard Cloudtail, who was sitting near him, mutter, "Mouse-brain," under his breath.

"There's no point in going over all that again," Mistystar told her warrior with an irritated twitch of her whiskers. "It's just wasting time."

"Besides," Bramblestar added, "it's not too much farther to ThunderClan. And whichever direction we go, we will have to cross a stream."

"I guess so," Mallownose mumbled, giving his chest fur a couple of embarrassed licks.

"So," Bramblestar continued briskly, "we only fight if the rogues resist. I'm hoping that the ShadowClan cats will join us, and without Darktail and his most loyal fighters, the rogues will be outnumbered."

There was a snort of amusement from Cloudtail. "Wouldn't that be lovely," he commented. "But things haven't exactly gone the easy way since Darktail showed up."

Alderheart tended to agree with the senior warrior. Everything he had heard about Darktail—everything he had seen for himself—told him that the rogue leader and his Kin were relentless. *We might pull this off,* he told himself, *but it won't be easy.*

The one thing he was looking forward to was seeing Needletail again. *I hope she's coping okay with being a prisoner.*

"Any questions?" Bramblestar asked, rising to his paws, ready to lead his cats into enemy territory.

Before any cat could reply, a fierce commotion ripped through the quiet of the night. Alderheart could hear yowls, shrieks, and hisses, as if a fight had suddenly broken out. Angling his ears, he could tell that it was coming from the direction of the RiverClan camp.

All the cats sprang up, exchanging startled glances, their neck fur beginning to rise.

"That doesn't sound good," Lionblaze said.

"They shouldn't be fighting yet," Tigerheart meowed. "They were supposed to wait for our move. Something's gone wrong!"

Bramblestar flattened his ears and let out a growl. "Then we need to go!"

Plunging out of the bushes, the attacking cats raced along the lakeshore, then veered inland toward the RiverClan camp. Alderheart grabbed his leaf wrap of herbs and followed.

The cats splashed through the stream that bordered the camp and thrust their way through the fringe of reeds at the water's edge. Scrambling up the slope into the camp, Alderheart spotted the four RiverClan prisoners locked in furious combat with some of Darktail's rogues. A small tabby she-cat was fighting alongside them.

They've risen up! he thought, his heart pounding with excitement. *They weren't meant to fight before we got here—but maybe they're stronger than we thought!* Then he looked more closely and realized that one particular cat was missing from the fight. *Wait—where's Violetpaw?*

He felt a prickle of unease beneath his pelt.

The prisoners were fighting hard, though. They looked desperately skinny and frail, but their eyes glared and their fur was bristling; all their rage against the rogues was pouring out in well-trained Clan battle moves. With a fearsome yowl, the rest of the Clan cats hurled themselves to fight by their side.

As Alderheart hovered at the edge of the fray, ready to drag out any cat too badly wounded to go on fighting, he was pleased to see that Darktail's forces seemed smaller—just as they'd planned. But then he spotted Nettle and one or two others of Darktail's closest Kin, and his excitement ebbed away, to be replaced by bewilderment.

Why are they awake? he asked himself. *They were supposed to get poppy seeds. But Darktail is missing. And so is Violetpaw.*

Had her attempt to drug the cats failed? He searched the screeching crowd of battling cats but couldn't see the young she-cat anywhere. Needletail was missing, too—and she was one of the prisoners. *Darktail must have taken her somewhere.* Fear weighed Alderheart's belly down like a heavy stone. *Does that mean . . . ?* He felt himself tremble as he wondered what would happen if Darktail had caught Violetpaw trying to sneak the poppy seeds into his food. But he forced himself to shake off the fear. *No—I won't believe it. I've lost Twigpaw. I can't bear to lose Violetpaw as well!*

A heartbeat later, Roach and Sleekwhisker appeared from outside the camp and flung themselves into the battle with shrieks of fury. More of the former ShadowClan cats had joined in the fight, too, but Alderheart noticed they were fighting on the side of the prisoners and the other Clan cats. He spotted Scorchfur and a young black tom that he didn't recognize, and Puddleshine hovering behind them, waiting to deal with injuries just as he was.

The rogues are outnumbered, Alderheart thought, his heart racing again. *We're going to win!*

Already the battle was beginning to wane, some of the rogues breaking away and fleeing out of the camp. But Roach, Sleekwhisker, and Nettle kept on fighting furiously, and then at last Darktail appeared, racing up from the direction of the lake.

Alderheart stared at him incredulously. Deep scratches furrowed Darktail's fur, and his white pelt was heavy with water and dotted with blood.

What in the name of StarClan happened to him?

As soon as Darktail appeared, several Clan cats broke away from the main battle to pile on top of the rogue leader, striking out with teeth and claws. For a few moments, Darktail fought back, but he was too badly outnumbered. Struggling free, he yowled, "Kin! Retreat!" and fled out of the camp in the direction of the border with ShadowClan.

His Kin streamed after him. Bramblestar followed at the head of the Clan cats, only to halt at the edge of the camp.

"Let them go," he panted. "They won't be back in a hurry."

"No, those maggot-ridden excuses for cats will be infesting *my* territory," Rowanstar growled.

"We'll clear them out soon," Bramblestar asserted confidently. "After all, you've got most of your warriors back now."

"That's if I *let* them come back." Rowanstar turned to stare balefully at the former ShadowClan warriors, who were clustered together a couple of tail-lengths away, gazing uncertainly at their Clan leader.

"We're sorry, Rowanstar," Scorchfur meowed. "Most of us have wanted to come back for a long time, but Darktail wouldn't let us leave."

"Mouse-hearts!" Rowanstar snorted.

"Oh, come on!" Tawnypelt padded up to her mate and nudged him with her shoulder. "We all know what Darktail and his Kin were like. And none of us realized how much of a threat he was at first—even you."

Rowanstar glared at his mate for a moment longer, then shrugged. "Very well, they can come back," he meowed. "But if they put one paw out of line . . ."

A relieved chorus of sighs came from the ShadowClan cats.

"We won't!"

"Thank you, Rowanstar!"

Alderheart watched with satisfaction as the returning warriors gathered around their leader, then turned to examine the RiverClan prisoners. All four of them lay on the ground, their chests heaving and their paws limp with exhaustion. Alderheart was surprised they had been able to fight so bravely.

Mistystar was crouching beside them, and she looked up anxiously as Alderheart approached. "Are they badly hurt?" she asked.

It was her deputy, Reedwhisker, who replied. "We're fine," he croaked, managing to raise his head a little. "That was the best thing we've ever done, sinking our claws into those mange-pelts."

Looking more closely at each of the RiverClan warriors in turn, Alderheart was relieved to see that none of their injuries were serious. One of Reedwhisker's ears was bleeding, Mintfur and Brackenpelt were both missing small clumps of fur, and Icewing had a long scratch on one shoulder, but it was reassuringly shallow.

"They'll be okay," Alderheart reassured Mistystar. "We'll get those scratches cleaned up and then put on a poultice of marigold."

"But what happened?" The voice was Bramblestar's; he came padding up with Squirrelflight, Scorchfur, and the young tabby she-cat who was a stranger to Alderheart.

"It looked like Violetpaw had planned to put Darktail and his closest kin to sleep with poppy seeds," Scorchfur replied. "But I guess you know all about that. Anyway, her plan didn't work. Darktail got wind of it somehow and dragged her over to the prisoners' den."

"He dragged Needletail out," the tabby she-cat continued. "Then he took both of them—Violetpaw and Needletail— down toward the lake. I . . . don't know what happened to them after that."

Cold dread began to gather in Alderheart's belly. He wanted to race off right away and look for his friends, but he knew he had duties here.

"We heard Darktail say that he was going to punish Needletail for what Violetpaw had done," Reedwhisker mewed hoarsely. "When they'd left, we decided it was time to act. We knew we had to do something to stop Darktail's evil.

So we broke out of our den. Zelda here"—he gestured with his tail toward the young tabby she-cat—"was on guard with Nettle. When we started to fight, Zelda joined in on our side. And so did most of the ShadowClan cats. Then you arrived," he finished with a nod to Bramblestar. "I have never been so glad to see any cats in all my life."

"That's right," Icewing added. "Thanks to you, we've driven Darktail and his rogues out of our territory!"

Alderheart admired the courage of the RiverClan cats, but he felt like he was choking on his worry for Violetpaw and Needletail. *Darktail was covered with scratches. He had blood on his pelt. Whose blood was it?*

His stomach turned.

"Does any cat know what happened to Violetpaw and Needletail?" he asked.

Reedwhisker shook his head, studying his paws. "Darktail said that Needletail would pay the price for Violetpaw's betrayal. He dragged them off—and as far as we know, neither of them has come back to camp."

Alderheart's legs felt weak with foreboding. *They could both be dead! They probably are. . . . And all because I asked Violetpaw for her help!*

Squirrelflight gave him a sympathetic look from deep green eyes, as though she could read his thoughts, and pressed her flank against his. "Stay strong," she encouraged him. "You couldn't have known what would happen, and giving up now will put all these cats at risk."

"We have to look for them," Alderheart whispered.

Squirrelflight gently shook her head. "There's no time right now," she mewed. "We have to get these cats back to ThunderClan, to let the medicine cats treat them properly."

"Excuse me?" Mistystar rose to her paws, looking annoyed. "This is RiverClan territory. There's no way we're going to leave it for Darktail to take over again."

"I don't think you need to worry about that," Bramblestar told her with a respectful dip of his head. "Darktail will have other things on his mind; he'll know we'll be coming for him in ShadowClan next. Besides, your cats need more care than you can give them here, and your medicine cats are still in our camp."

"He's right," Reedwhisker agreed hoarsely. "There's so much work to be done before RiverClan can live here again."

Mistystar hesitated for a moment, a look of deep thought in her blue eyes. "Very well," she meowed at last. "But only for a day or two, until my warriors are fully recovered."

She whisked her tail, beckoning to some of her other Clanmates to help the former prisoners to their paws. Glancing around the camp, Alderheart saw that every cat was getting ready to leave.

The tabby she-cat, Zelda, padded up to Bramblestar and dipped her head politely. The young black tom was with her. "I'm Zelda," she mewed, "and this is Loki. We're kittypets."

Bramblestar's ears angled forward in surprise. "You fight pretty well, for kittypets," he told her, then added, "But what are kittypets even doing here?"

"Darktail brought us into camp," Zelda explained, "and

then he wouldn't let us go. We thought it was fun at first, until we found out what he was really like."

"There was another of our friends with us too," Loki added. "But he was killed when Darktail made us attack RiverClan." He shivered, his eyes full of sorrow.

Bramblestar nodded understandingly. "And now you'd like to go home?"

"Not yet," Zelda meowed. "We want to stay until Darktail is defeated. He's so cruel. . . . We want to be sure that he's gone for good."

Loki nodded vigorously. "Can we come with you?"

"Of course." Bramblestar's eyes gleamed with approval. "Any cat is welcome who wants to fight against Darktail."

The sky was growing pale with dawn, and the last warriors of StarClan were fading from the sky, when Alderheart followed Bramblestar and the rest of the warriors back to the ThunderClan camp.

As they crossed ShadowClan territory, they were careful to stay close to the lake, and every cat was alert for any sign or scent of Darktail and his remaining rogues. But the pine forest remained dark and silent.

I wonder if it's too much to hope for, that the rogues have simply fled, Alderheart thought. *It would be great if they never bothered us again! They've already given us enough trouble.*

But the whereabouts of the rogues weren't Alderheart's main concern. Padding along at the rear of the group, he couldn't put Violetpaw and Needletail out of his mind.

Why would Darktail have taken them to the lake? he asked himself. *Was he going to* drown *them?* Alderheart halted for a moment, his breath catching in his throat. *Could that be what happened to Dawnpelt and the other missing cats?*

Alderheart didn't feel much relief as he and the rest of the cats splashed through the stream that marked the border with ShadowClan. It was good to be back on familiar territory, but his worries still crowded everything else out of his mind. He wondered whether he should ask Bramblestar if he could take out a patrol and go to search for Violetpaw and Needletail.

I could ask him . . . but I don't think he'll agree. He'll want every cat to concentrate on getting ready to drive out the rogues.

Alderheart padded through the thorn tunnel into the camp, surrounded by a fog of misery. Their victory seemed less important than his fears that Violetpaw had sacrificed herself—because of the plan that *he* had made.

But as Alderheart entered the clearing, he halted, gazing around in sudden bewilderment. *Surely there are far more cats here than when we left for RiverClan territory?*

Then he spotted a small gray she-cat, her brilliant green eyes widening as she noticed him.

Twigpaw . . . How can it be?

Alderheart rushed toward her and plunged his muzzle into her shoulder fur, nuzzling her affectionately. "Twigpaw . . . Is it really you?" he choked out. "We all thought you were dead!"

"Oh, Alderheart!" Twigpaw purred. "I'm so glad to see you again. I'm sorry—you must have been so worried about me."

Scolding her for running off was the last thing on

Alderheart's mind. He was too pleased to see her. "Where have you been all this time?" he asked.

"I went to find SkyClan, in the barn you saw in your dream," Twigpaw explained. "Because I wanted to know if the cat you saw was really my kin."

She settled herself on the ground, and Alderheart sat down beside her, reveling in the warmth of her pelt and the scent he had thought never to smell again.

"And you *found* them?" he asked, hearing the surprise and admiration in his voice. *After all the time I've spent wishing we could find them and bring them back . . .* "You found SkyClan, and you brought them here?"

Twigpaw nodded, beaming with pride. "It wasn't easy," she said, "but I did."

Hovering a tail-length away was the dark gray tom he had seen in his dream. He looked exactly like Twigpaw, except that his eyes were warm amber—like Violetpaw's.

Alderheart rose to his paws. "Are you . . . ?" he began.

The gray tom took a pace toward him and dipped his head politely. "I am Hawkwing," he meowed. "I'm Twigpaw's father."

"And he's deputy of SkyClan!" Twigpaw announced proudly.

Alderheart dipped his head in response. "Welcome to ThunderClan," he mewed.

"Thank you." Hawkwing nodded. "It's nice to get a warm welcome," he added hastily.

Alderheart glanced around at the assortment of RiverClan,

ShadowClan, and ThunderClan cats. He realized for the first time that many of them were eyeing Hawkwing and the other SkyClan cats suspiciously. *I guess this is a bit of an awkward time to welcome another Clan into our camp . . . ,* he thought. But he was quickly distracted by Twigpaw.

"Isn't it great?" she asked excitedly, bouncing on her paws. "I've never seen so many cats together before! I was surprised to find RiverClan cats here when I got back. And Shadow-Clan is still staying with us, I see. But—" She broke off, her excitement fading. "Is Violetpaw still with the rogues?"

Alderheart couldn't hide his anxiety and grief at Twigpaw's question, and decided that he couldn't lie to her. *I tried that with Violetpaw, and look how well that worked.*

"I don't know where Violetpaw is right now," he admitted. "It looks like Darktail took her and Needletail out of the RiverClan camp—"

"What?" Twigpaw interrupted. "Why was Darktail in the RiverClan camp?"

"Darktail and his rogues raided RiverClan and drove the Clan out. We just got back from attacking the rogues and taking back the territory."

"So why isn't Violetpaw with you?" Twigpaw asked, deep anxiety in her voice.

"Before we arrived, Darktail took her and Needletail out of the camp to punish them, and no cat knows what happened to them after that."

Twigpaw's eyes stretched wide with horror, and Hawk-wing's gaze was full of concern. "But why would he punish

Violetpaw?" Twigpaw demanded. "What had she done? Why didn't some cat help her? And why—"

"Twigpaw, it's all so complicated—" Alderheart was beginning, when to his relief Bramblestar padded up, with Rowanstar and Mistystar beside him.

"Greetings," Bramblestar meowed, introducing himself and the other Clan leaders. "This is a momentous day for the Clans. I never expected to see SkyClan here, reunited with the rest of us."

"SkyClan never expected it either." A brown-and-cream tabby she-cat joined Hawkwing and gave the leaders a respectful nod. "I am Leafstar, leader of SkyClan. We have come a long way to find you."

More cats were gathering around to listen to the leaders, and Alderheart began to hear uneasy murmurs arising from the crowd.

"Another Clan? What does this mean?"

"Surely there are too many cats in the forest now?"

"Where are they all going to live?"

Bramblestar glanced around sternly, as if he wanted to quell the unwelcoming comments, but before he could speak, Jayfeather stepped forward, gazing at the newcomers with his sightless blue eyes.

"What's the point of twittering like a nestful of blackbirds?" he demanded. "It's obvious what we need to do."

"It might be obvious to you, Jayfeather," Bramblestar meowed.

Jayfeather gave a disdainful sniff. "If you weren't Clan

leader, Bramblestar, I'd call you a mouse-brain. We must seek the advice of StarClan."

A stiff breeze blew into Alderheart's face as he toiled up the last slope toward the Moonpool. Clouds were scudding across the sky where the warriors of StarClan were beginning to appear.

Ahead of Alderheart, Leafpool and Jayfeather scrambled from rock to rock, while Mothwing and Willowshine were just behind him. Puddleshine, once again ShadowClan's medicine cat, brought up the rear.

I wish Kestrelflight could be with us, too, Alderheart thought sadly. *But there's no point even trying to fetch him from WindClan.*

Thrusting his way through the bushes that surrounded the hollow, Alderheart began to follow the spiral path down to the water. His paws slipped easily into the paw marks left there by the ancient cats so many seasons ago.

The moon was only a thin claw-scratch; the water that poured out from the rocks, and the pool below, was dark except for the glimmer of starshine. Alderheart felt the hairs on his pelt rise at how strange and mysterious it seemed without the glow of reflected moonlight they saw at the regular half-moon meetings.

As he and his fellow medicine cats crouched at the water's edge, Alderheart wondered what message the spirits of his warrior ancestors would have for them. He closed his eyes and touched his nose to the surface of the pool, barely biting back a yowl as the chill raced through him from nose to tail-tip.

When Alderheart opened his eyes, he seemed to be still in the hollow beside the pool, but now the surface of the water blazed with reflected light. He raised his head to see that the sides of the hollow were lined with glittering spirit cats, their pelts frosted with starlight and their eyes glowing like countless small moons. He took in a long, awestruck breath.

This is wonderful! he thought, relief bursting in on him like the sun appearing from behind a cloud. *StarClan has barely appeared to any of us since they gave us the prophecy moons ago.*

He waited confidently for the spirit cats to speak. After the long, horrible misadventure with Darktail and his rogues, the Clan cats had finally found SkyClan. . . . Now they had to learn how to "clear the sky."

Leafpool was the first to speak, rising eagerly to her paws. "They're here, finally—we've found SkyClan! Are they 'what you find in the shadows'?"

At the opposite side of the pool, a flame-colored tom also rose; Alderheart recognized Firestar. "They are," he replied. "But there is more to be done."

Alderheart glanced around at the other medicine cats. *How strange for us all to be here together!* He saw the same eagerness reflected in their eyes as they gazed at Firestar.

"What more should we do?" Leafpool meowed. "We found what lies in the shadows—the missing Clan. *Sky*Clan! Now how do we clear the sky?"

"Not every Clan is present," Firestar pointed out. "This was about restoring all five Clans, as it was long ago—long before I came to the forest. SkyClan has no medicine cat, but another Clan is missing from our group, too. . . ."

The starry cats began to fade from Alderheart's sight. As the light died, he and the other medicine cats exchanged uneasy glances.

Mothwing, who had been absent from the vision, looked on curiously. "What happened?"

As quickly as he could, Alderheart explained what they'd seen and heard.

"Of course," murmured Mothwing, her eyes widening with recognition.

"I guess we know what we must do . . . ," Jayfeather mewed reluctantly.

CHAPTER 18

Twigpaw lay stretched on the ground outside the apprentices' den, leaning into the warmth of her father's pelt. Hawkwing was telling her all about SkyClan, about their life in the gorge and their journey to find the other Clans, in much more detail than had been possible while they were still traveling.

I don't think I'll ever get tired of listening to his voice, Twigpaw thought. *It's great to be back home, and it's even better now that I have kin.*

It was very early in the morning, a day after SkyClan had reached the ThunderClan camp. The sun had not yet risen, though rosy tints in the sky showed where it would appear. A breeze carried cool, fresh scents into the camp.

The day before, the clearing had been filled with bustle. Before leaving for the Moonpool and their meeting with StarClan, the medicine cats had tended to the RiverClan prisoners and the cats who had been wounded in the battle.

The SkyClan cats had been invited to share the fresh-kill pile, while Daisy guided Tinycloud into the nursery to rest and recover her strength while she waited for her kits to be born.

"Thank StarClan!" Tinycloud had exclaimed. "I think I have a whole Clan in here, and they're all practicing their fighting moves!"

Now, the camp was peaceful. As soon as the sky began to pale toward dawn, Bramblestar and the other leaders had taken a patrol of uninjured RiverClan warriors, along with a few volunteers from the other Clans, to survey the damage in RiverClan territory and begin the task of rebuilding. Squirrelflight, left in charge of the camp, had sent out the border and hunting patrols, so that the hollow was much less crowded than it normally was these days. *It's almost like there's just one Clan living here again,* Twigpaw thought.

Soothed by her father's voice, Twigpaw could almost have fallen asleep, except for the uncertainty she felt about the future. She felt a strong pull toward this cat who looked so much like her, but she wondered whether they could even live together.

SkyClan will need to find a new territory soon, and where will that be? Is there room around the lake for another Clan?

In the short time since the Clans had been reunited, some of the ThunderClan warriors had discussed the prophecy with her, with a new respect that Twigpaw had never sensed before. *I can see in their eyes that they're taking me seriously, and they listen to what I have to say!*

"You may not be what the prophecy told the Clans to embrace," Squirrelflight had meowed. "But you and Violetpaw are connected to the lost Clan. No cat still thinks it was an accident that you were brought here."

"That's true," Graystripe had agreed. "Maybe it was meant to be? And maybe *embracing* you when you were found is what allowed us to reunite with SkyClan."

Twigpaw hoped that was true. *I felt so useless when no cat knew what I was doing here. But I did bring SkyClan back! I've earned my place here now.*

Movement beside the thorn tunnel attracted Twigpaw's gaze. Berrynose pushed his way into the camp, followed by Cherryfall. And following them was a third cat, a small black-and-white she-cat who was achingly familiar. . . .

"Violetpaw!" she yowled, springing to her paws. "You're alive!"

Twigpaw rushed across the camp to her littermate, relief almost sweeping her off her paws. Violetpaw stood still, staring at her, a flood of joy in her amber eyes, then bounded forward. The two young cats pressed against each other, drinking in each other's scent, purring as if they would never stop.

"I'm sorry we ever fought!" Twigpaw gasped out at last. "I'm so happy, just seeing that you're alive!"

"Alderheart told me you must be dead," Violetpaw responded. "But I never gave up hope. And I'm sorry too: I should never have attacked you in the battle."

"That doesn't matter now," Twigpaw assured her. "Besides, you've more than made up for it. Every cat says that without you, the rogues would never have been driven out of River-Clan territory."

Violetpaw's ears flicked up and her eyes widened in

surprise. "The rogues have been driven out?"

"Yes, but only from RiverClan's territory. The leaders were going to attack once the prisoners were exchanged," Twigpaw told her, "but the prisoners rose up on their own! And with Darktail gone, the Kin were easily chased off. But they've just moved back over to ShadowClan's land. Anyway, the leaders were worried about you. Alderheart said that Darktail took you away, and then came back with scratches and blood on his fur. They thought he'd done something horrible to you—that you might be dead!"

The joy faded from Violetpaw's eyes. "Darktail took Needletail and me down to the lake," she explained. "He was going to drown Needletail as a punishment for what I did, helping cats to escape from him. Roach and Raven and Sleekwhisker were there too." She paused, swallowing, and Twigpaw rested her tail comfortingly on her sister's shoulder.

"Needletail turned on them and attacked them," Violetpaw continued after a moment. "She was so brave! She told me to run, and I did. . . . But I should have stayed and fought beside her!"

"No, you shouldn't have," Twigpaw meowed. "Two of you against four of those vicious cats? You would both have died, and Needletail would have given you a chance for nothing."

Violetpaw nodded reluctantly. "Raven followed me," she went on. "I couldn't think about anything except losing her— and when I finally did, I had no idea where I was." Her head and tail drooped. "It took ages for me to find my way back to the lake, and then I met the ThunderClan patrol on the ShadowClan border."

"Thank StarClan you made it!" Twigpaw leaned forward and nuzzled her sister's shoulder. "Come on," she murmured. "There's a cat I want you to meet."

Leading Violetpaw farther into the camp, Twigpaw saw that the remaining ShadowClan warriors were emerging from their den, having been alerted by Berrynose and Cherryfall. When they spotted Violetpaw, their eyes widened with an expression of awe and deep respect.

"Here she is!" Scorchfur exclaimed, bounding toward them. "Welcome, Violetpaw! You're a hero to us all!"

"You certainly are," Snowbird purred, stroking her tail down Violetpaw's flank. "It's so good to see you alive and well."

Twigpaw let Violetpaw's Clanmates greet her, then gave her a nudge and guided her over to the apprentices' den. Hawkwing had risen to his paws and was waiting for them.

"This is Hawkwing," Twigpaw meowed to her sister, feeling as if her excitement was going to bubble out of her like a mountain spring bursting from the rocks. "He's the deputy of SkyClan—and he's our father!"

Violetpaw halted in front of him, her jaws gaping with astonishment. Hawkwing leaned forward and gently touched noses with her.

"I never hoped to have both my kits close to me," he mewed, his amber eyes shining with delight. "This must be a sign from

StarClan, that kin should stay together, always. You can help me rebuild SkyClan!"

Just as he was speaking, a rush of paw steps sounded behind Twigpaw. Turning, she saw Alderheart dashing up to them, with Leafpool, Jayfeather, and the other medicine cats following him through the thorn tunnel.

"Violetpaw!" he exclaimed. "You're okay!" He pressed his muzzle into her shoulder, then raised his head to look at Hawkwing. Twigpaw could see that his joy and excitement at seeing her sister was mingled with uncertainty.

"Have you discussed this with Bramblestar?" he asked. Clearly, he had overheard Hawkwing's last words.

"Bramblestar isn't here," Hawkwing replied. "He and the other leaders took some cats over to RiverClan. Why—is there a problem?"

"There may be," Alderheart replied, clearly choosing his words with care. "Twigpaw and Violetpaw have allegiance to other Clans."

"But—" Hawkwing began to protest.

"There's no need to worry about that just now," Alderheart went on rapidly. "Violetpaw, you look so skinny and exhausted. You need to come to the medicine-cat den and have some juniper to build up your strength. Twigpaw, can you fetch her something from the fresh-kill pile?"

He padded off with Violetpaw, his tail resting on her shoulders.

Before Twigpaw could go to fetch prey for her sister, Hawkwing asked her, "Do you both have real allegiances to the other Clans? Obviously, you're grateful to ThunderClan and ShadowClan for taking you in and raising you, but . . . *I am your kin. Surely that's more important?*"

At first Twigpaw couldn't think how to reply. She dipped her head, unwilling to meet her father's gaze.

"You have SkyClan blood in you," Hawkwing continued. "You're SkyClan cats. Twigpaw—"

"It's all too much to take in," Twigpaw interrupted desperately. "And I'm not sure what I want to do."

She could hardly bear to see the look of disappointment in her father's amber eyes. She wanted to find the words to console him, but she had no idea how to do that.

"I'd better fetch the fresh-kill," she mumbled, and bounded off before her father could say any more.

As Twigpaw was choosing a vole from the fresh-kill pile, more cats began to pour in through the thorn tunnel, with Bramblestar in the lead. Rowanstar, Leafstar, and the ThunderClan and ShadowClan warriors followed him. All of them looked exhausted.

Squirrelflight, who had been watching over the camp from the Highledge, bounded down the tumbled rocks to meet the returning cats in the center of the clearing. Other warriors gathered around eagerly.

"Is everything okay?" Squirrelflight asked.

"More or less," Bramblestar replied. "We saw nothing of the rogues, but you wouldn't believe the mess they've left behind them in RiverClan! The camp is in a disgusting state—I can't imagine what it was like to live there."

Leafstar shook her head. "It doesn't surprise me," she said. "He and his cats destroyed the gorge after they drove us out. He has no respect for the Clans, or how we live."

Rowanstar shook his head. "Indeed he doesn't."

"Mistystar and her warriors have stayed behind to start rebuilding," Whitewing added. "But they're going to continue living in our camp for a while longer, until they've cleared away the worst of the debris."

Rowanstar stepped forward, puffing out his chest. "I feel responsible for Darktail, that mange-ridden scourge of the forest," he announced. "Now I know what I must do: return to my territory and rid it of that terrible rogue cat once and for all."

Yowls of agreement rose from the rest of the warriors. Twigpaw could see their eyes gleaming with enthusiasm, and their fur bristling with the anticipation of a battle to come.

"But not alone!" Bramblestar raised his voice to make himself heard, and the fervent voices died into silence. "This burden cannot fall on one cat, or one Clan," the ThunderClan leader continued. "All cats, all Clans, must unite and do their part."

"SkyClan is behind you," Leafstar said solemnly. "Many of our cats would welcome the opportunity to fight Darktail again, after everything he's put us through."

Rowanstar nodded at her. "ShadowClan feels the same," he said. "That flea-pelt nearly tore our Clan apart. It's time for him to leave."

"Bramblestar is right." A quiet voice broke into the

discussion, and Twigpaw saw that Alderheart had emerged once more from the medicine-cat den and padded forward to stand beside his father.

"*All* cats, *all* Clans, must unite," he repeated. "According to StarClan, none of our efforts will succeed unless we involve one more Clan. . . ."

CHAPTER 19

A stiff breeze blew across the moorland, bringing with it the distant scent of cats. Violetpaw's fur was flattened to her sides as she climbed the hill, and she felt her eyes begin to water. The chill air of dawn probed deep into her pelt, but her sense of anticipation warmed her through and through.

Another day had passed while the Clan leaders made their plans. "We need to confront Onestar," Bramblestar had meowed, "but we must be very careful how we do it."

"Yes." Rowanstar was in agreement for once. "If Onestar feels we're trying to intimidate him, he'll dig his claws in all the harder."

In the end, the leaders had decided to send the Clan deputies to meet with Onestar. "He won't see us as so much of a threat," Squirrelflight had pointed out. "And as the only leader present, he'll feel more important."

"Why not send Twigpaw and Violetpaw too?" Leafstar had suggested. "They both have stories to tell, and they'll remind Onestar of the prophecy, and how vital it is to clear the sky."

So this morning, Squirrelflight, Tigerheart, Reedwhisker, and Hawkwing had set out, along with Violetpaw and

Twigpaw. Reedwhisker was still recovering from his time in Darktail's prison, but he insisted that he was strong enough for the journey to WindClan.

"My paws will take me anywhere if it means I can help get rid of that mange-pelt Darktail!" he declared.

Violetpaw was immensely grateful to the SkyClan leader for suggesting that she and Twigpaw be part of the mission to WindClan. Her paws wanted to skip along, and she had to keep reminding herself that this was a serious undertaking.

As she padded along beside her father, Violetpaw noticed that he was glancing from side to side, his amber gaze taking in every detail of the moorland.

"Are you worried WindClan will attack us?" she asked him.

"Actually, no," Hawkwing replied. "I was working out how likely it would be for a cat to even *get* attacked on such an open space. You can see so far . . . and there are so few places for an attacker to take cover."

Violetpaw exchanged a glance with Twigpaw, who was walking on their father's other side. She could see from her sister's slightly worried air that Twigpaw was sharing her thoughts.

Is Hawkwing scouting out territory for SkyClan? But surely he won't want to take WindClan's . . . will he?

Before Violetpaw could ask her father what was going through his mind, he suddenly halted.

"Do you think there's something strange going on?" he asked, turning to the older warriors.

Squirrelflight looked puzzled for a moment; then her eyes

widened in understanding. "We haven't come across any WindClan patrols. That's odd. . . . I'd expect the dawn patrol to be out, and one or two hunting patrols. But we haven't even picked up their scent."

As if in response to Squirrelflight's words, a sudden stronger gust of wind swept across the moor, bringing with it the sound of screeching and yowling.

"That's coming from the WindClan camp!" Tigerheart exclaimed. "Are they under attack?"

Instantly Squirrelflight sprang forward, leading the deputies as they raced across the moor. "Stay back!" Hawkwing warned his kits as he followed.

Violetpaw and Twigpaw bounded along at the rear. WindClan's camp lay in a deep hollow on the moor, where the ground fell away near the top of the hill. A thick barrier of gorse and other bushes guarded the edges.

Now the sounds of battle were even louder. Wriggling her way through the thorns, Violetpaw looked down on a mass of fighting cats.

Darktail and his rogues are attacking WindClan! And it looks like they're winning!

She realized that Darktail must have led his Kin across WindClan territory under cover of darkness. That was the only cover they could expect in this bleak landscape. And with the WindClan cats asleep, they would have the advantage of surprise.

Whatever else Darktail may be, he isn't stupid!

The four deputies sprang down the slope into the camp

and flung themselves into the fray. Violetpaw watched as Hawkwing barreled through the battling cats, knocking rogues aside as he headed straight toward where Darktail was wrestling with Onestar. Pride warmed her from ears to tail-tip to see what a strong, fierce fighter her father was.

Before Hawkwing could reach Onestar, the WindClan deputy, Harespring, leaped forward, trying to come to his leader's aid. But Nettle thrust himself between them, his claws out as he aimed a blow at Harespring. Then Hawkwing was there, blocking Nettle and swiping his claws across the rogue's face. Nettle backed off with a screech of alarm.

Violetpaw exchanged a glance with Twigpaw. "We have to help!" she meowed.

With a nod from Twigpaw, both young cats hurtled down into the fight. Violetpaw saw her sister skid to a halt as Raven lunged for her, then dart aside to aim a blow at the back of the rogue cat's head.

Raven spun around so fast that Twigpaw's blow never landed. Her foreleg flashed out at Twigpaw, catching her on the side of her head so hard that she fell to the ground.

Violetpaw sprang to help her, only to be intercepted by Roach, the silver-gray tom, looming over her with death in his eyes. Violetpaw moved to slash at him, only to draw back a pace as if her paws didn't want to obey her.

"Stop!"

An ear-splitting yowl rang out commandingly above the noise of battle. Violetpaw gasped in astonishment as she realized that the voice was Darktail's. Roach turned away from her, staring across the camp, and Violetpaw saw that every fighting cat, friend and foe, had grown as still as if they had been frozen by the cold of leaf-bare.

Every cat's gaze was fixed on Onestar and Darktail. The two cats stood nose to nose, their flanks swelling with their heavy breathing.

"You mouse-hearted excuse for a cat!" Darktail taunted Onestar. "Is that the best you can do? A kittypet fights better! But then . . . you always were a *coward*."

A puzzled murmur ran through the Clan cats. Violetpaw shared their bewilderment. *I don't understand what's going on.*

It was Harespring who voiced the question every cat wanted to ask. "Darktail, you're talking like . . . like you *know* Onestar. How can that be?"

Onestar never took his gaze from the rogue leader as he replied. "This cat's word is not to be trusted. Look at what he's done: raided camps, kept prisoners, killed more Clan cats than we can count. He'll clearly do or say anything in his efforts to steal territory. And that's what this is all about, isn't it?" he challenged Darktail.

An evil gleam lit the white tom's dark-furred eyes. "Of course it's about territory. It's always about territory. And I think you handing some of WindClan's territory over to me would only be fair." His eyes narrowed, and his voice grew more intense and menacing with every word. "Especially after what you did to me!"

Without waiting for a response from Onestar, Darktail turned to address the other Clan cats. "You all think of Onestar as an honorable leader, don't you? Well, I know things about him that would make every WindClan cat's fur stand on end."

Now every cat's gaze was trained on Onestar. "What is he talking about?" Harespring asked.

Onestar's tail stood straight up, while he flexed his claws and ground them hard into the earth. "Why would you listen to him?" he demanded. "You've all seen the kind of cat he is!"

Darktail spun around to face Onestar again. "And they should know what kind of cat *you* truly are," he meowed defiantly. "The Onestar they think they know could not have done what you did to *me!*"

The rogue leader's words ended in a frenzied yowl, and he hurled himself once more at Onestar.

But this time the Clan cats were ready, and as the fighting broke out again, it was clear that the rogues were outmatched. Squirrelflight grabbed Darktail and flung him away from Onestar, aiming a pawful of claws at his throat.

The rogue leader writhed away from her and staggered to his paws. "Retreat!" he screeched.

The Kin broke away, fleeing up the slope and through the bushes, out of the WindClan camp. Darktail was the last to go; at the top of the hollow he turned and looked back, his eyes glaring hatred.

"We're leaving now," he yowled. "But we'll be back! You can count on that, Onestar!"

As he vanished, Violetpaw glanced around at the Clan cats. Their eyes gleamed with victory, but they seemed apprehensive, too, like they knew that Darktail would make good on his threat. A chill ran through her.

This isn't over.

As sunhigh approached, Violetpaw and Twigpaw were sitting with Hawkwing at the bottom of WindClan's hollow. All three of them were sharing a rabbit.

When Darktail and his rogues had disappeared, Onestar had stood silent for a moment, gazing at the cats around him. At last he had straightened up, gathering dignity like an extra pelt.

"Now I must tell the truth," he meowed. "But I will not speak until the Clan leaders are here. This is a matter for them, and I can only bear to explain once."

"Okay," Squirrelflight responded. "Bramblestar, Rowanstar, and Leafstar are—"

"Leafstar?" Onestar interrupted.

Squirrelflight nodded. "Oh, of course . . . you don't know. Leafstar is the leader of SkyClan. They have returned! This cat," she went on, above wondering murmurs from the WindClan warriors, "is the SkyClan deputy, Hawkwing."

Hawkwing dipped his head respectfully. "It's an honor to meet you, Onestar."

Onestar replied with a grunt. "You might not say that when you've heard my story."

Violetpaw thought that sounded ominous; she could see the WindClan cats exchanging worried glances.

"I'll fetch the leaders from ThunderClan's camp,"

Squirrelflight mewed, moving on tactfully from the awkward moment. She bounded up the slope and slipped through the bushes.

When Squirrelflight had left, Onestar retired to his den, while Harespring sent out hunting and border patrols, with orders to keep a sharp lookout for Darktail and his Kin, and to avoid fighting except as a last resort. After that, there was nothing much to do except share the prey the hunters brought back, and wait for the leaders to arrive.

"I wonder what Onestar is going to tell us," Violetpaw remarked, swallowing her last mouthful of rabbit and swiping her tongue around her jaws.

"I don't know," Hawkwing responded, a worried look in his amber eyes. "Onestar has some kind of secret—and it looks as if Darktail thinks it gives him some kind of power over Wind-Clan."

"I wonder if the secret is why Onestar fled from the battle in ShadowClan's territory after Darktail spoke to him," Twig-paw mewed. "And it must be really important to have made him do that."

While she was still speaking, a rustle came from the bushes at the top of the slope, and Squirrelflight appeared, followed by Bramblestar, Rowanstar, and Leafstar. Together they strode down into the bottom of the hollow.

"Where's Onestar?" Rowanstar demanded. "What's all this about?"

"Greetings," Harespring meowed, dipping his head politely as he rose from where he sat a tail-length away from the entrance to Onestar's den. "Onestar is here, but he won't see you until all the leaders have arrived. We must wait for Mistystar."

Rowanstar let out a growl of annoyance, his claws raking the earth of the camp floor. But before he could voice an objection, there was movement in the bushes at the far side of the camp, and Tigerheart emerged with Mistystar.

"Thank StarClan for that!" Rowanstar muttered. "Now maybe we can get this over with."

Bramblestar glanced at the ShadowClan leader with a twitch of his whiskers. "Keep your fur on," he advised. "We've been waiting for StarClan knows how long for Onestar to talk to us. Let's try not to annoy him now."

A bad-tempered snort was Rowanstar's only reply.

Harespring slipped into Onestar's den, and a moment later the WindClan leader emerged. After a curt word of greeting he beckoned the leaders closer with a wave of his tail.

"Maybe we should leave the leaders to it," Hawkwing suggested, rising to his paws and facing the other cats.

"No." Onestar's voice was weary but decisive. "The way you fought today proves that you're a worthy warrior—and besides, every cat should probably hear this."

He remained standing as the four Clan leaders settled themselves around him, and the remaining cats sat in a ragged semicircle a fox-length farther away. Every hair on Violetpaw's pelt was tingling with excitement, and she could see the same feeling in Twigpaw's glittering green eyes.

"*I* am the reason the Clans have been blighted by Darktail

and his rogues," Onestar began. "And the story goes back many seasons, to when we lived in the old forest, when I was called Onewhisker and Tallstar was the leader of WindClan."

The WindClan cats exchanged confused glances at their leader's words. Violetpaw could see that even the senior warriors—the ones who remembered the time Onestar spoke of—had no idea what he was about to say.

"Onestar has kept this secret for such a long time," she whispered to Twigpaw.

"You all know that I never expected to be chosen as deputy, or to become your leader," Onestar continued. "Tallstar appointed me in the last moments of his life, and no cat was more astonished than I was. I felt I was unworthy. . . ." He paused for a moment and bowed his head. "And events have proved that I was right."

"No!" Crowfeather protested from where he sat with his Clanmates. "You've been a noble leader, Onestar."

Looking up again, Onestar shook his head sadly. "When I was a young cat, back in the old forest," he continued, "I carried out my warrior duties, but I also liked to sneak off to explore the little Twolegplace beyond the farm where Barley and Ravenpaw lived. It was fun to spend time with the kittypets there, and tell them stories about what it was like to live in a Clan."

"I never knew that!" Whitetail, a WindClan elder, was looking outraged. "Our *Clan leader* going off to make friends with kittypets!"

"Well, he wasn't leader then," Gorsetail murmured.

"It was easy to impress them," Onestar admitted. He paused to give his chest fur an embarrassed lick. Raising his head, he let his gaze travel over the assembled cats. He opened his jaws to continue, but at first no words came out. Violetpaw could see how much effort it took when he finally began to speak again. "I used to tell them about hunting, and learning battle moves. I was never particularly skilled at those things, but the kittypets didn't know that, because it was all so new and fascinating to them. And if I exaggerated a bit . . . well, it made me feel good. They thought I was wonderful!"

"But what does this have to do with Darktail?" Bramblestar asked.

"I'm coming to that," Onestar replied. "There was one kittypet . . . a young she-cat called Smoke. She had such soft, gray fur, and such brilliant blue eyes . . . It was like I was staring into pools of pure water!"

Squirrelflight rolled her eyes. "I see."

"Smoke and I became . . . more than friends," Onestar admitted. "She loved to hear my stories of Clan life; she couldn't get enough of them. She was happy to be my mate, but of course I only ever saw her in the Twolegplace. There was no way I could have brought her into camp."

Rowanstar exchanged a glance with Mistystar. "You can say that again!" he muttered. "What was the mouse-brain thinking?"

"Obviously he *wasn't* thinking," Mistystar responded tartly.

"Everything was fine," Onestar continued, "until I found out that Smoke was expecting kits. She came to find me on the moor. Thank StarClan that I was out hunting alone, and I came across her not too far from the border of our territory!

"Smoke was almost ready to give birth. She told me that she wanted to join WindClan, so that her kits could be brought up as warriors." He gave a heavy sigh. "You see, I'd told her such wonderful tales of Clan life, as if it was all adventure and massive piles of prey. I had not mentioned all the times we nearly starved to death in a harsh leaf-bare, or how often we might get terrorized by dogs or Twolegs . . . or how heart-breaking it was to lose a Clanmate."

"What did you say to her?" Violetpaw asked curiously, then let out a faint squeak of embarrassment. She had been so caught up in the story that she hadn't stopped to ask herself if an apprentice should be questioning a Clan leader.

"What *could* I say to her?" Onestar didn't seem to realize where the question had come from. "I knew there was no way I could bring a kittypet into WindClan. I would have been in terrible trouble for mating with her in the first place, and even worse, I knew that if Tallstar did let Smoke stay, she would have seen me as I really was. Just an ordinary warrior, not the heroic cat I had made myself out to be. And anyway"—he went on rapidly, as if he was trying to get past the shameful part of the story as quickly as he could—"Smoke was so soft and delicate. . . . She would never have survived a moon out on the moor."

"So you sent her home?" Squirrelflight asked.

Onestar nodded. "I sent her home. I told her to go back to her Twolegs, where she would be safe. Her relationship with me was over. She argued for a while, but at last she left, and I told myself I'd had a lucky escape. I stayed away from the Twolegplace after that, and I never expected to hear from Smoke again."

"But you did," Bramblestar stated.

"Yes, Smoke came to find me one more time," Onestar replied. There was bitter regret in his eyes. "She had a single kit with her, and she told me that after our last meeting, when she was still on her way home, her kits had come. She didn't have any help—not from a cat, not even from a Twoleg. All but one of her kits—*our* kits—had died."

A murmur of pity came from Sedgewhisker, and Onestar flinched as though some cat had struck him a blow.

"Smoke went back to her Twolegs, but only for a short time," Onestar continued. "As soon as her kit was old enough to leave her, she brought him to me. She begged me to at least take *him* into camp, while he was still young enough to learn the ways of the Clans. And I . . . I refused. I was too worried about how I would have to explain to Tallstar."

Violetpaw couldn't help thinking about how ThunderClan and ShadowClan had taken in her and Twigpaw, even though at that time no cat knew who they were.

Onestar could have made up some story, if he'd tried, she thought. *He could have helped the kit.*

"Smoke turned on me then," Onestar continued. "She told me that she would raise the kit by herself, and teach him to hate the Clans who had rejected him." His head drooped, and

Violetpaw could see that he felt great shame at what he had revealed.

"Wait," Bramblestar interjected. "This kit—are you saying that he grew up to be Darktail? That Darktail is *your son?*"

Onestar nodded gloomily. "I tried to tell myself that I was protecting Smoke and her kit," he mewed, raising his voice over the shocked murmurs of the other cats. "I thought that whatever she said when she was angry, she would take him and go back to being a kittypet, and their lives would be better that way."

Violetpaw pressed herself against Twigpaw and felt her sister return the gesture. Both of them gazed at their SkyClan father, and they saw Hawkwing looking back at them with nothing but love.

All our struggles are over now, Violetpaw thought. *We were so lucky that Alderheart found us in the tunnel and brought us back to the Clans. And now that we've found our father, it's even better. He would never have turned his back on us.*

Mistystar broke into Violetpaw's musings. "So," she meowed to Onestar. "Darktail knew that you rejected him."

Onestar gave a weary nod. "Yes, he was old enough to understand. StarClan knows where he went for so long, but wherever it was, he grew into a bitter and resentful cat, full of grief for a father he never knew, and hatred for a way of life he never got the chance to understand."

"You can say that again!" Tigerheart muttered.

If Onestar heard the comment, he ignored it. "He must

have gathered rogues to him as his followers," he went on, "and not long ago, he wandered up the river and found Sky-Clan. He attacked them and drove them out."

Violetpaw saw her father tense for a moment, his neck fur bristling and his claws digging into the ground. She knew that he must be reliving that terrible time. She leaned over to touch his ear with her nose, and gradually he relaxed, blinking gratefully at her from sorrowful amber eyes.

Meanwhile, Onestar was continuing with his story. "When Alderheart arrived on his quest, Darktail got the information that he had been seeking for so long: where I and the other Clans had gone after we left the forest territories. And just like that, he got the chance he'd always craved: to wreak revenge on me—the father who had rejected him—and our whole way of life."

"I'm beginning to understand why you behaved as you did," Mistystar remarked.

Onestar hesitated for a moment, as if he wasn't sure whether the RiverClan leader was expressing sympathy. "When the rogues attacked us here, in WindClan territory," he meowed at last, "and the fighting spilled into ThunderClan—that was the first hint I got that Darktail was my own kit. When he attacked me, he whispered, 'I will destroy you, and all of the Clans, for what you did to me.' At once, I understood the threat that Darktail posed to all of us, and to WindClan in particular. That's why I wanted you, Rowanstar, to drive him out of your territory."

Rowanstar snorted. "It would have helped if you'd told the

truth from the start. I might have understood why you were so furious when I hesitated."

"I know," Onestar admitted. "But I couldn't. All I could do was close my borders. And then," he added, "Bramblestar convinced me to join with the other Clans to expel the rogues from ShadowClan. But in that battle . . ."

Onestar's voice died away. He hunched his shoulders and his tail drooped; Violetpaw thought she had never seen a cat look so ashamed.

"What happened?" Mistystar demanded. "You wanted the rogues off Clan territory so badly, but suddenly you retreated with all of your warriors. Why?"

"I'm not proud of what I did," Onestar replied. "But when I was grappling with Darktail—and I've never battled an enemy with strength so vicious—this cat who was my son leaned into me and whispered something. . . ."

"What?" Squirrelflight asked tensely.

"He said . . . 'What do you think will happen to a cat who rejected, and then killed, his own son? Surely that cat would end up in the Dark Forest. Think of that when you are on your last life!' But what Darktail didn't know was that I *am* on my last life. He made me so afraid. . . ."

A gasp went up from all the assembled cats. Violetpaw knew how shocking it was for a leader to refer openly to being on his last life, and even more shocking to admit that he was worried about where he would go after death. She saw Kestrelflight, the WindClan medicine cat, wince and close his eyes briefly.

"You must be joking!" Rowanstar exclaimed incredulously. "The Dark Forest is not for a leader who saves his Clan from a terror such as Darktail—no matter whose kin he is!"

"That's true," Kestrelflight agreed. "The Dark Forest is for cats who have given themselves to evil. That isn't you, One-star. I could have told you that long ago, if you'd trusted me enough to be honest with me."

Onestar looked down at his paws. "Maybe," he sighed. "I admit that it was a selfish fear. But . . . well, things look a bit different when a leader is on his final life. I started to worry that StarClan would judge me harshly for my mistakes—and StarClan knows, I have made many of those."

Silence followed the end of Onestar's confession. Violet-paw couldn't help feeling sympathy for him: it must have been hard to stand up in front of his Clan and his fellow leaders to admit what he had done. At the same time, she knew— perhaps better than many cats—what disasters had followed Onestar's flight from the battle.

If WindClan had kept fighting with us, we could have defeated Darktail back then. He would never have been able to attack RiverClan. So many cats who are dead would still be alive.

Needletail wouldn't have had to die. . . .

As the silence dragged on, Onestar raised his head again. Suddenly he looked firmer, more decisive—more like a Clan leader.

"We all have the same problem," he meowed. "The rogues go on attacking us, stealing territory, threatening vulnerable cats and kits. I know this problem is of *my* making, and I'm very sorry that I turned away from my friends. I won't do that again; I'm no longer afraid. Darktail and his rogues need to be dealt with, no matter what happens to me—otherwise, they will keep on coming back, and more good cats will perish."

"Then—" Bramblestar began.

"Yes," Onestar affirmed. "WindClan will fight with the other Clans, to drive Darktail off our territory once and for all."

CHAPTER 20

Alderheart crouched at the edge of the Moonpool, ready to touch his nose to the water. The sky was still streaked with the last light of sunset, and there was a reddish tinge to the surface of the pool. He hoped that was not a bad omen.

This may be too soon for us to visit StarClan again, he thought. *But we have to try.*

After Bramblestar and the others had returned to the ThunderClan camp, word of Onestar's confession had spread rapidly through the rest of the Clans. Every cat knew that they would soon be advancing into ShadowClan territory to confront Darktail and his Kin.

This time we'll defeat him, Alderheart mused, *but even so, Clan cats will be injured. . . . Some of us may be killed.*

But before that battle could take place, all the medicine cats from the four lakeside Clans had gathered at the Moonpool to show StarClan that they had carried out their last instructions. All five Clans had reunited.

It's a pity SkyClan has no medicine cat, Alderheart reflected. *That's something we'll have to deal with as soon as possible.*

His thoughts were interrupted by Jayfeather, who shook

out his pelt irritably. "Well, what are we waiting for?"

Alderheart closed his eyes and touched his nose to the surface, bracing himself against the chill. But this time the water was warm and caressing, and when he opened his eyes, he found himself sitting in a forest glade, with sunlight dappling the ground.

All the other medicine cats stood there with him, except for Mothwing. Around the edges of the clearing, under the trees, the cats of StarClan were assembled, their pelts shining with a frosty light and their eyes gleaming. A shiver of mingled relief and excitement passed through Alderheart as he gazed at them: relief because he sensed that they approved of what the Clans were doing, and excitement because there were many cats among them whom he had never seen before.

Can this be . . . ?

"SkyClan ancestors!" Leafpool's delighted mew answered for him. "Now that SkyClan has returned to us, the spirits of their warrior ancestors can walk these skies with our own StarClan."

Alderheart's gaze devoured the newcomers; he knew that each of them would have a story to tell, and he wondered whether he would ever know what those stories were. In particular, he noticed a mottled she-cat who fixed him with an intent look, as if she wanted to ask him something, though she didn't speak.

The air tingled with the happiness that surged through his fellow medicine cats, and for a few moments Alderheart relaxed, content just to enjoy it.

Firestar padded into the middle of the clearing, beckoning with his tail for the medicine cats to join him there. As he stepped forward, Alderheart saw that the flame-colored tom was standing beside a five-pointed leaf that had the same flame color as his pelt. One of the points of the leaf was bent backward.

"Do you know what this means?" Firestar asked, pointing to the bent point with one paw.

"I'm not sure," Alderheart mewed hesitantly when he had studied the leaf for several heartbeats. "The five points stand for the five Clans, right? But why is that point bent?"

"That point stands for ShadowClan." It was Yellowfang who replied, bounding up to stand beside Firestar. "The five Clans must live together, peacefully, on your shared territory. But part of that territory—my old Clan's home—is lost. It must be reclaimed. Do you understand now?"

A murmur of agreement came from all the medicine cats. "Yes, now I do," Alderheart meowed, speaking for them all. "Before we can decide how to live peacefully in the territory we have, we must secure all of that territory. We must reclaim ShadowClan's land."

Firestar nodded. "Exactly. And to do that," he added, "the Clans must remember their names."

Alderheart stared at the former ThunderClan leader, trying to work out what *that* meant. But when he looked to the other medicine cats, he could see that they were just as bewildered as he felt.

Does Firestar mean we should remember our own names? Or does he mean the names of the StarClan cats? Is that where the answer is?

Already the StarClan cats were beginning to fade, their outlines blurring until they looked like patches of mist among the trees, and then were gone. The sunlight in the clearing faded too, and the rustling of the leaves died into silence, until the medicine cats were standing in a dark void.

Alderheart opened his eyes to find himself once more beside the Moonpool, with the other medicine cats waking around him, blinking at one another in a mixture of hope and confusion.

It was Jayfeather who broke the silence, rising to his paws with an impatient lash of his tail. "They've done it again!" he snarled. "Why does StarClan have to be so *vague*?"

A pale sun shone down into the stone hollow, though it gave little warmth, and the air felt damp; Alderheart thought there might be rain to come. It was the day after the medicine cats had met at the Moonpool, and at the first glimmering signs of dawn, Bramblestar had sent out as many hunting patrols as he could muster, with instructions to bring back all the fresh-kill they could find.

"Every cat will need strength today," he had meowed. "Because today . . . this ends."

Now the hunting patrols had returned, and the cats of ThunderClan, ShadowClan, RiverClan, and SkyClan were finishing their prey. Alderheart could feel the excitement thrumming through the camp. Now that the Clans were united again, every cat was hopeful that this time Darktail and his rogues could be dealt with for good.

"Let all cats old enough to catch their own prey join here beneath the Highledge for a meeting of the Clans!"

Bramblestar's voice rang out across the stone hollow. Rowanstar, Mistystar, and Leafstar sat beside him on the Highledge; the cats already in the clearing turned toward them. Leafpool and Jayfeather emerged from the medicine cats' den, followed by Briarlight, who dragged herself into the open to listen. Graystripe, Ratscar, Oakfur, and Millie sat outside the elders' den, while Snowbird and Blossomfall appeared at the entrance to the nursery, their kits frisking around them. Tinycloud, who still hadn't given birth, sank down beside the two queens and tucked her paws underneath her.

Sparkpelt raced across the clearing and plopped herself down beside Alderheart. "This is it!" she exclaimed, her eyes shining with excitement. "Bramblestar *must* give the order to attack."

"Wait and see," Alderheart murmured. "We still don't know what StarClan meant about 'remembering our names.'"

Sparkpelt shrugged, working her claws impatiently into the ground. "Whatever. Now that WindClan has agreed to join us, we have plenty of cats to deal with Darktail!"

"Every time I lead my Clan into a fight," Bramblestar began, when every cat was settled, "I hope that it will be the last that we ever have. And this time, I hope that I'm right. Every cat heard what the medicine cats reported from their journey to the Moonpool: all five Clans have the same problem, Darktail and his rogues. But this time, all five Clans are united against a common enemy. Today we will fight as friends, to protect our very way of life."

A clamor of agreement broke out among the cats in the clearing, enthusiastic caterwauls ringing out to the sky.

"We'll drive them out!"

"For the honor of the Clans!"

"Death to Darktail!"

"Death to the rogues!"

Bramblestar raised his tail for silence, and gradually the noise died down. "I hope you're all fully fed," he continued when he could make himself heard. "Now you need to take a short rest. Conserve your strength. We head out at sunset."

Alderheart still felt a niggling doubt as he paced through the camp, watching the warriors preparing themselves, or concentrating on keeping themselves calm and relaxed.

If we don't need to work out what StarClan meant, then why did they bother telling us?

He was uneasy, too, about his own role in the battle to come. Although he had long ago stopped dwelling on his failed apprenticeship under Molewhisker, he still felt guilty that he couldn't fight alongside his Clanmates.

I'll be there to help the warriors who are injured, he told himself, but it wasn't enough.

Determined to throw off these thoughts, Alderheart padded over to where Violetpaw and Twigpaw were sitting with their father, Hawkwing. Whitewing and Birchfall were sharing tongues close by.

"I'm looking forward to *this* fight!" Twigpaw was mewing as Alderheart approached. "I'd like to claw Darktail's fur off!"

"Me too," Violetpaw agreed, her voice more somber than her sister's. Her face clouded with a dark expression. "Darktail will pay for what he did to Needletail."

"She was a brave cat," Alderheart meowed as he sat down next to her.

His words seemed to give some comfort to Violetpaw. "We all need to watch out for Darktail," she continued after a moment, "especially if the fight takes us anywhere near water. Darktail has a thing about water."

There was a sudden *mrrow* of excitement from Whitewing, who sat erect, her eyes wide. "I have an idea!" she exclaimed.

She scrambled to her paws and raced off to where Bramble-star was curled up with Squirrelflight near the bottom of the tumbled rocks that led up to his den.

Her mate, Birchfall, stared after her. "What's gotten into her?" he muttered.

Hawkwing extended his forepaws and arched his back in a long stretch. "This is enough rest," he meowed. "In SkyClan, we always like to get straight into the fight. The longer you wait, the more time you have to get nervous—and nerves are never good for battle."

Twigpaw blinked up at her father. "Do you know how Sky-Clan got its name?" she asked.

"We were named after a cat who lived a long time ago," Hawkwing replied. "He was Skystar, the first leader of our

Clan. He appeared to Echosong, our medicine cat, many times before she died."

Alderheart felt a shiver of wonder to think that a cat from so long ago could still remain in StarClan to speak to a living medicine cat. "Is that really true?" he asked.

"We think so," Hawkwing told him. "Anyway, however we got our name, we certainly live up to it. We launch attacks from above—from the trees, or tall rocks. Fighting SkyClan must feel like you're being attacked from the sky!"

Understanding lit up Alderheart's mind like a flash of lightning. Springing to his paws, he bolted across the stone hollow after Whitewing, heading toward his father, Bramble-star.

"Leafpool! Jayfeather! Puddleshine! Mothwing and Willowshine! Come here!" he yowled as he went. "I've figured out what StarClan meant!"

CHAPTER 21

❧

Every hair on Twigpaw's pelt tingled with excitement as she padded along behind the gathered forces of her Clanmates. Violetpaw walked beside her, their fur brushing, on their way to ShadowClan territory. WindClan had joined them at sunset, and now the warriors of four Clans were advancing against Darktail and his Kin.

Twigpaw fluffed out her fur against the chilly evening air. Above her head the sky was growing dark, not just because the sun had gone down, but from clouds that were massing above the lake, bulging with rain. Twigpaw could sense that a storm was coming.

That might help the Clans, or it might not, she thought, splashing through the stream that divided ThunderClan from ShadowClan. *All I know is, it's been a long journey to get this far.*

As the Clans advanced into ShadowClan territory, the pine trees stood tall ahead of them, looming in the dim light. Once they entered that part of the forest, Twigpaw knew, they would be fighting almost blind.

The thought brought claws of fear with it, snagging Twigpaw's heart, and she tried to thrust it away. *It will be terrible. . . .*

We'll be relying on scent to help us tell friend from foe.

Once Alderheart had reported his understanding of StarClan's message to Bramblestar, the leaders and deputies had joined together in a quick conference. Then Bramblestar had sent Thornclaw with a message to Onestar, and announced to the cats remaining in the camp what their part in the fighting would be.

Twigpaw's nose twitched, and she opened her jaws to taste the air, almost gagging on the reek of rogue that flowed into her mouth. "We're getting close to the ShadowClan camp," she whispered to her sister.

Violetpaw's eyes narrowed. "This is it," she murmured.

Bramblestar halted, raising his tail to signal to his followers that they should do the same. The warriors of ThunderClan, ShadowClan, WindClan, and SkyClan drew close together— a mass of cats, their paw steps almost silent as they padded over the thick layer of pine needles on the forest floor, their eyes gleaming with eagerness.

"Are you ready?" Bramblestar asked Leafstar.

The SkyClan leader gave him a brisk nod, then leaped up onto the lowest branch of a nearby pine tree. With a whisk of her tail she ordered her Clan to follow her.

That's how SkyClan will attack, Twigpaw thought, her excitement building as she watched. *They'll launch themselves from above, just like Hawkwing said.*

Twigpaw knew that the other Clans would use their special skills, too; that was what StarClan had meant when Firestar told them to remember their names. ThunderClan would attack like thunder: full-on, and with brute force; Shadow-Clan would slip unseen through the darkness of their own territory, with familiarity the rogues could never have; Wind-Clan would dart in and out, quick and elusive.

And RiverClan? For the first time in a long time, Twigpaw felt a prickle of amusement in her belly and chest, tickling her throat. *RiverClan's part is the best! That was such a clever idea of White-wing's!*

A hiss from above broke into Twigpaw's thoughts. She looked up to see Hawkwing crouched on a branch above her and Violetpaw.

"Do you want to join me?" he asked. "I'd feel better, knowing you were close."

At once Violetpaw shook her head. "Thanks, but I'll fight better down here, on the ground," she replied. "I know every paw step of this territory."

"Take care, then," Hawkwing responded. "Twigpaw, how about you?"

In answer, Twigpaw scrambled up the trunk, excitement surging through her as she balanced beside her father on the branch.

But what do I do, now that I'm up here? she wondered, with a questioning look at Hawkwing.

"Just follow me," he meowed, as if she had spoken her thought aloud. "You'll be fine."

With Hawkwing just ahead of her, Twigpaw began moving from tree to tree. When she dared to look down, she could see the ThunderClan, ShadowClan, and WindClan cats creeping along the forest floor, all of them homing in on the camp where Darktail and his rogues were lurking.

This is amazing! she thought after a few moments, marveling at how quickly she was getting used to balancing on thin branches, and how her fear of falling was slipping away.

"Leafstar told us to fan out when we get close," Hawkwing told her after a while. "The cats on the ground will attack in a straight line, so the SkyClan cats will be ready to jump down when the rogues try to run off at an angle."

So he thinks of me as a SkyClan cat, Twigpaw commented to herself. *I don't know about that . . . but now isn't the time to talk about it. Besides, he probably wasn't thinking.*

As these words ran through Twigpaw's mind, a ferocious yowl split the night. The cats on the ground charged up the rock-strewn slope that led to the edge of the ShadowClan camp. Following through the trees, Twigpaw could see beyond the tangle of brambles that surrounded the camp, and into the camp itself.

Rogue cats were tumbling out of their dens; clearly they had been asleep, and were surprised by the force of the attack that was being unleashed against them. Twigpaw caught a glimpse of Darktail, a pale shape in the dim light, snarling orders to his Kin, but in the confusion it didn't seem that any cat was taking notice.

Within a couple of heartbeats, the hollow was filled with screeching, tussling cats. The rogues were hugely outnumbered as Bramblestar's plan unfolded, with the ThunderClan warriors leading the first attack, while WindClan darted in from the edges of the camp to strike and then retreat before their enemies could retaliate. The ShadowClan cats hovered at the top of the slope, hidden in the shadows and prepared to leap out at any rogues who tried to break away from the camp.

SkyClan's plan was working, too. Twigpaw saw Nettle wrench himself free from a fight with Tigerheart and flee, yowling, up the slope. Before he could reach the brambles that surrounded the camp, Hawkwing hurtled down, landing right in front of the rogue tom.

Nettle let out a shriek of shock and fear, doubling back to escape Hawkwing's claws. But Hawkwing was too fast for him, leaping onto Nettle's back and digging his claws into his shoulders. His caterwaul of triumph reached Twigpaw where she still crouched in the tree.

Oh, that worked brilliantly! Twigpaw thought, warm admiration for her father rushing through her.

Above the camp, the sky was growing darker still. The air shook with the sound of thunder, almost drowning the screeches of the battling cats. A fat drop of rain splashed onto Twigpaw's fur as the rain began.

Twigpaw's elation faded. *Rain means heavy fur, and heavy fur makes it harder to fight. And even without wet fur, I can't fight while I'm up here in this tree.*

Looking down, Twigpaw spotted her sister, struggling with a rogue tom who was almost twice her size. Without a second thought, she leaped down from the tree, landing on the soft dirt of the camp floor. "Violetpaw! I'm coming!" she yowled, hurling herself into the fight.

As Twigpaw fastened her claws into the rogue's pelt, dragging him away from her littermate, a flash of lightning lit up the whole forest. By its light, Twigpaw caught a glimpse of Onestar, frozen in sudden stillness as he glared at Darktail.

Then the flash was gone, but there was still enough light for her to see Darktail rearing up and taking a violent swipe at the WindClan leader's face. Onestar was knocked off balance and hit the earth with a screech, his legs and tail waving in the air.

Another peal of thunder rolled out, but Darktail's voice rose above it. "Kin! Follow me! If you're smart enough, retreat with me—you deserve to survive!"

At their leader's command, the rogue cats—Roach, Raven, and a few others—tore themselves away from fighting with the Clans and raced after Darktail out of the camp. Twigpaw realized that Sleekwhisker and some of the other young ShadowClan warriors had remained with Darktail, and now they fled with him, too. The Clan cats stood back and let them go.

In any other battle, Twigpaw would have been dismayed to see their enemies escaping so easily, but now she felt a fierce satisfaction. *It's all going exactly the way we planned it!*

"Follow the rogues!" Bramblestar yowled, pelting up the slope and through the brambles after the vanishing Kin.

Twigpaw swarmed up the nearest tree and began to leap from branch to branch after Darktail and his followers; here and there, she spotted other SkyClan cats doing the same.

Down on the ground, she saw Onestar bounce to his paws

and join in the pursuit. "Bramblestar!" he yowled as he went. "Darktail is mine!"

Darktail and the rogue cats headed toward the lake, with the Clan cats streaming after them. By now the rain was thrumming down, plastering Twigpaw's pelt to her sides and turning the earth beneath the pine trees to glutinous mud. Branches shook down more water onto Twigpaw as she brushed through them, but she didn't hesitate until she leaped into the last tree at the forest edge, above the pebbly shore that stretched down to the lake. She had only just reached it when the rogue cats burst out into the open.

Now! Twigpaw thought.

Dark shapes rose up out of the shallow water at the edge of the lake. Stunned, the rogue cats skidded to a halt, staring in utter disbelief at the RiverClan warriors who had been lying there in wait. Slowly they began to advance, cutting off the rogues' retreat.

The rogues spun around and fled back toward the forest, only to be confronted by Bramblestar and Onestar, with the rest of the Clan cats beside them, ranged in a threatening line along the edge of the trees.

As Onestar leaped forward, with the Clans hard on his paws, most of the rogues broke away with terrified shrieks, dodging and diving under outstretched claws as they tried to escape.

Only Darktail stood still, confronting Onestar. Twigpaw watched, her breath coming short and her heart pounding, as the two toms circled each other. Torrential rain drenched them both, lighting flashing above their heads, glittering across the surface of the lake. The rumble of thunder followed it; Twigpaw dug her claws hard into her branch, feeling as if the whole world might be splitting apart.

"You would never have made it as a warrior," Onestar taunted Darktail. "You would have been better off as a kittypet."

Darktail let out an enraged shriek and sprang at Onestar. The two toms collided in a tangle of soaked fur, claws, and teeth. Locked together, they rolled down the shore and into the waves that lapped the pebbles.

Still wrestling, Onestar and Darktail rolled over in the water—first one on top, and then the other. A jolt of terror struck through Twigpaw, fierce as the lightning.

What if Darktail drowns Onestar, like he drowned Needletail?

Gradually, the two battling cats moved away from the shore, into deeper and deeper water. For a while, Twigpaw could catch glimpses of a head, a tail, or a lashing paw, until at last both cats sank out of sight and did not reappear. The lake rippled and fluttered as rain battered the surface, but no sign of a cat disturbed the water.

Twigpaw heard a single WindClan warrior's voice ring out across the lake. "Onestar! Onestar!"

Rogues forgotten, the Clan cats formed a line along the edge of the lake, the waves lapping at their paws. They gazed toward the place where Darktail and Onestar had been fighting. From the trees, Twigpaw and the SkyClan warriors watched, too.

They waited there for a long time, but neither cat resurfaced.

CHAPTER 22

"I'm really going to miss you," Violetpaw meowed, stretching out her neck to touch noses with Zelda. "Do you *have* to go home?"

The young tabby she-cat nodded. "I'll miss you, too, Violetpaw," she sighed. "But I need to go back to my housefolk."

"Me too." Loki, standing at Zelda's shoulder, ducked his head shyly. "I think they'll be *really* worried about us."

Violetpaw knew that the two kittypets were right. *They were so brave, staying with us until they were sure that Darktail was defeated, but this isn't their place. They'll be happier living with their Twolegs.*

She knew too that the pain of parting wasn't the only shadow that lay over them. Max should have been with them, too, but the older kittypet was gone forever, killed uselessly in the attack on RiverClan.

Loki and Zelda were carefree once, Violetpaw thought. *But they'll never be able to forget what they've seen under Darktail.*

Zelda stepped forward and gave Violetpaw an affectionate nuzzle. "I'll come visit you now and again," she promised. "I'm so happy that you've found your father!"

"You'll be okay?" Violetpaw asked. "You don't want me to come with you?"

"No thanks, we know the way home," Loki assured her. "And there's nothing to be scared of, now that Darktail's gone."

"Good-bye, then," Violetpaw mewed. "And may StarClan light your path."

She stood watching as the two kittypets disappeared through the thorn tunnel.

The sun had risen over ThunderClan's camp. The storm of the night before had passed, leaving a rain-washed sky, pale blue with a few wisps of white cloud. Cats were moving sluggishly around the camp; ShadowClan and RiverClan had returned there too, as their own camps were too damaged for them to be able to rest and recover there. Violetpaw didn't think that any of them had slept well after the fight, even though they were all exhausted.

Neither Onestar nor Darktail had reappeared after they sank, still fighting, into the lake. The WindClan cats had been stunned by grief, especially as they would never be able to bury their leader. When the other Clans had withdrawn, they had remained to sit vigil for him, and Kestrelflight had spoken the words that would guide Onestar toward StarClan.

"He died nobly," the medicine cat had said. "He made up for all his other mistakes when he rid us of Darktail."

Violetpaw hadn't been able to sleep, either. She couldn't stop thinking about how dreadful it was for a Clan leader to lose his final life in such a terrible way.

I have to keep busy, she told herself, heading across the camp and instinctively veering toward the nursery. Alderheart was bustling in ahead of her, on his way to check on the queens and their litters.

It must be almost time for Tinycloud to have her kits.

But before Violetpaw could follow Alderheart into the nursery, she halted at the sound of her sister's voice.

"Violetpaw—come here! The ShadowClan cats are leaving," Twigpaw continued, as Violetpaw bounded over to her. "You should say good-bye."

The ShadowClan cats were gathered together near the entrance to the thorn tunnel, with Bramblestar, Squirrelflight, and some of the ThunderClan, RiverClan, and SkyClan warriors beside them.

"We need to get the stink of Darktail out of our camp," Rowanstar was meowing as Violetpaw and her sister padded up. "And make sure that the rest of his mange-ridden rogues are off our territory."

His tone was friendlier than Violetpaw had ever heard it when he was talking to a ThunderClan cat.

"I hope that everything works out," Bramblestar responded with a dip of his head. "But there's always help in Thunder-Clan, if you ever need it."

"I think we can manage." Rowanstar had a glint in his eyes. "We'll see you at the next Gathering."

He was turning away, with a sweep of his tail to summon the rest of his Clan, when he spotted Violetpaw. "You're welcome to stay here a little while longer," he meowed, "if you want to spend time with your kin."

"I'd really like that," Hawkwing put in, padding forward to

touch his nose to Violetpaw's ear. "Thank you, Rowanstar."

What he really means is, he wants me to stay with him in SkyClan, Violetpaw thought, detecting the longing in her father's voice. She didn't want to say that out loud, but she did put words to her next thought. "Where will SkyClan go now?"

It was Bramblestar who replied. "They'll share our territory for the time being. But soon they will have to work out where they can put their own camp."

Hawkwing's eyes shone as he gazed at Violetpaw and Twigpaw. "I quite like the idea of exploring and discovering new territory."

Bramblestar drew himself up, pride clear in the way he lifted his head and held his tail erect. "I can't believe SkyClan is back where they belong!" he meowed. "We should hold some kind of ceremony to celebrate. Maybe the medicine cats can ask StarClan if there's something we should do."

Squirrelflight gave him a hard nudge. "Don't you dare interrupt Harespring's nine lives ceremony!" she teased him.

Bramblestar gave his chest fur a couple of embarrassed licks. "I can't believe I forgot about that!"

Once again, Rowanstar glanced around at his Clan, gathering them together to leave. Violetpaw noticed that Tigerheart was still sitting a few tail-lengths away; Dovewing was close beside him, and the two cats were talking together. Violetpaw couldn't hear what they were saying, but she could pick up the deep seriousness in their eyes and their voices.

Rowanstar had noticed them too, and watched them for a moment with an odd expression. Then he gave his tail a decisive flick. "Tigerheart!" he snapped. "Get your tail over here! We're going back to camp."

Tigerheart scrambled to his paws and bounded over to the rest of his Clan with a final word to Dovewing. "Sorry," he muttered as he joined his Clan leader.

What was all that about? Violetpaw wondered.

As Rowanstar led the ShadowClan cats out through the thorn tunnel, Hawkwing beckoned his daughters aside, out of hearing of the ThunderClan cats. "When SkyClan establishes its new territory," he told them, "I want you both to come and live with me. You were born in SkyClan, to SkyClan cats. That's where you belong."

Violetpaw exchanged a glance with her sister. *This is all so unexpected,* she thought. *It wasn't that long ago that we thought we had no kin except each other, but now we have a father, and we each have two Clans we could call our own.*

As if he could read Violetpaw's thoughts, Hawkwing leaned forward and gave each of them an affectionate nuzzle. "You don't have to decide right now," he mewed. "All you need to know is that you're growing up to be fine warriors—and there will always be a place for you in SkyClan, if you want it."

Violetpaw stared at Twigpaw, who was looking as confused as she felt. Then she glanced at the last of the ShadowClan cats who were just disappearing down the tunnel.

Can I really go back to ShadowClan and follow Rowanstar, after all that's happened? she asked herself. *Now that Needletail is gone, is ShadowClan really my home?*

The tingle of joy she'd felt at reuniting with her father was replaced by a twinge of dread in her belly. *But would Rowanstar let me go so easily? ShadowClan has been so diminished, they might need every cat they can get.*

Then Violetpaw looked at her father: her kin. It was hard to deny the tug of longing she felt to live with him and Twig-paw. But she sensed that change was looming on the horizon, and she had no idea what the future would bring.

I can only hope that the three of us come out of it okay. After everything that we've been through, we deserve that much. . . .

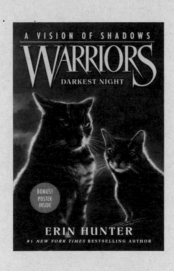

CHAPTER 1

❧

"Hurry up, Twigpaw!" Ivypool's mew rang though the trees.

Hush! Twigpaw flicked her tail irritably. A mouse was snuffling through the freshly fallen leaves of an oak. She could see it in the shadow of a root. It froze as Ivypool's mew shattered the silence. Twigpaw didn't move, relaxing only when the mouse once more began rummaging through the leaves.

She leaped and felt the soft flesh of the mouse beneath her claws as she slammed her paws down. After giving a quick killing bite, she lifted its limp body between her teeth and turned to join the others.

Ivypool was hauling a thrush—an earlier catch—from beneath a clump of ferns. Sparkpelt paced behind Fernsong, and Cherryfall lounged in a patch of late-afternoon sun. As Twigpaw reached them, she tossed the mouse onto the pile of prey they had collected.

Lionblaze sat stiffly, his gaze probing the forest as though searching for danger.

"I don't know what you're looking for." Sparkpelt sniffed at him. "The rogues are gone and all the other Clan cats are in our camp."

1

"Not *all* the Clan cats," Ivypool pointed out.

"ShadowClan went home days ago," Fernsong added.

"But we've still got half of RiverClan and a whole *new* Clan cluttering up our dens." Sparkpelt fluffed out her fur. "I'm sick of sleeping under ferns so a RiverClan warrior can have my nest. In another moon, the ferns will have shriveled and I'll be sleeping in the cold."

"Reedwhisker needs your nest," Fernsong reminded her. "He's still recovering from being held captive by the rogues."

"And he won't be there much longer," Ivypool meowed. "Mistystar says that RiverClan has nearly finished rebuilding their camp. They'll be able to go home soon."

"What about SkyClan?" Sparkpelt challenged.

Lionblaze answered without moving his gaze from the distant trees. "SkyClan will be gone soon too."

"Where? They have nowhere to go." Cherryfall got to her paws.

"The Clan leaders will decide at the next Gathering," Lionblaze told her.

Sparkpelt's fur prickled along her spine. "What are they going to do? Invent new territory for SkyClan to live on?"

"There's not enough room around the lake for an extra Clan." Cherryfall glanced at Twigpaw.

Twigpaw shrank beneath her pelt. Was the ginger she-cat blaming her? *I found SkyClan and brought them here.* This fact, which had made her so proud initially, had begun to peck at her like a crow. The camp *was* overcrowded, and where *would* SkyClan live? *But my father is in SkyClan. I have a family now.*

Despite the happy thought, worry wormed in Twigpaw's belly. *Perhaps I was being selfish by bringing them to the lake. Perhaps there isn't room for another Clan.*

"Who's going to give up territory to make room for them?" Sparkpelt stared at Lionblaze as though the golden tom should have an answer.

He shrugged. "Let StarClan decide."

"StarClan wanted them back." Cherryfall pawed through the day's catch. "Let StarClan find them somewhere to live."

Fernsong shifted his paws. "At least the prey is running well," he meowed. "I just hope we have enough to feed everyone tonight."

"Bramblestar sent out five hunting parties today," Ivypool reminded him. "And RiverClan will bring prey with them when they return from working on their camp."

"*If* they return," Sparkpelt sniffed. "Last night Mistystar and her patrol didn't come back at all."

Twigpaw felt a twinge of irritation. "I thought you *wanted* them gone." Why was Sparkpelt being so crabby? She was usually so positive about everything. "You should be happy they didn't come back."

Sparkpelt flicked her tail dismissively. "Let's take our prey home." She snatched a shrew and a vole by their tails.

"Good idea." Ivypool picked up the thrush.

Twigpaw grabbed her mouse. *At least with her mouth full Sparkpelt won't be able to complain anymore.* Lionblaze, Cherryfall, and Fernsong gathered up the last of the prey, and together they headed back to the hollow.

At the camp entrance, Twigpaw waited for the rest of the patrol to duck through the thorn tunnel. The branches scraped her pelt as she followed them through. On the other side, cats crowded the clearing, chattering like a flock of starlings. Scents swirled around her. RiverClan and SkyClan scent mingled with the smell of her Clanmates. And the faint odor of ShadowClan still lingered on the bushes around the edge of the camp.

As usual, SkyClan's warriors lay around the apprentices' den, soaking up the last of the late-greenleaf sun before its rays disappeared behind the cliff top. Two of their apprentices, Dewpaw and Finpaw, practiced battle moves in the clearing, while Reedpaw jeered fondly at her brothers' clumsy leaps and rolls. Leaf-fall was coming fast; leaves drifted down from the trees at the top of the hollow, falling softly around them.

Twigpaw scanned SkyClan, looking for Hawkwing, Blossomheart, and Violetpaw. Her kin. When ShadowClan had returned to their own territory a few days ago, Rowanstar had allowed Violetpaw to remain behind so that she could spend time with their father and his sister. Twigpaw loved sharing the camp with kin at last, and when she couldn't see their pelts among the others, she wondered, with a prickle of anxiety, where they were. She couldn't let go of the fear that she might lose them again.

Leafstar stood near her Clan. Twigpaw caught her eye. The mottled brown-and-cream SkyClan leader must have seen worry in her gaze, because she nodded toward the medicine den. "Alderheart is checking on Hawkwing," she called over the murmur of voices. "Violetpaw went with him."

Twigpaw's pelt prickled with concern. "Is he okay?"

"Don't worry," Leafstar purred. "Alderheart's checked on all of us today. I think your medicine cat likes making us eat herbs."

Blossomheart, the SkyClan she-cat who Twigpaw had recently learned was her father's littermate, lifted her head. "He says it'll help us build up our strength, but I think he just likes to see the look on our faces as we swallow them."

Outside the nursery, Tinycloud shuddered. "I'm not swallowing any more herbs till I've kitted," she mewed indignantly. She glanced at her bulging belly. "There's hardly room for these kits in my belly, even without herbs."

Blossomfall lay beside her. "Your kits will come soon enough." As she spoke, Stemkit and Eaglekit scrambled over their mother and hurtled after Plumkit and Shellkit, who were darting among the other cats, squealing with delight as they played warrior and prey. Blossomfall purred loudly. "And as you know, once they do, you won't get any peace."

Feeling a pang in her stomach, Twigpaw hurried toward the fresh-kill pile. A group of RiverClan cats sat clustered below Highledge. Reedwhisker, Mintfur, Brackenpelt, and Icewing, who had been held captive by Darktail and his rogues, still looked thin and hollow-eyed after their ordeal. They had been starved in captivity, and their wounds had been left to fester. Now Lakeheart and Mallownose flanked them protectively while Willowshine licked another sticky poultice into Mintfur's scratches.

ThunderClan's patrols were back in camp, too. Berrynose and Poppyfrost were enjoying some prey beside the warriors' den, while Brightheart and Cloudtail shared tongues nearby. Jayfeather was outside the medicine den, helping Briarlight with her exercises. Birchfall stood at the center of the clearing, looking lost. He craned his neck, scanning the countless pelts as though looking for someone, then purred with delight as he caught sight of Whitewing and hurried to join her.

As Twigpaw picked her way between the cats sprawled around the clearing, Graystripe pushed his way out of the elders' den. Behind him, the honeysuckle walls bulged as cats moved inside. Mosspelt, the RiverClan elder, and two cats from SkyClan had made nests there. Graystripe shook out his fur. "Fresh air!" he rumbled, sounding relieved. "It's so stuffy in there, even the fleas are trying to get out."

His mew was swallowed by the chatter of the other cats. But from Highledge, Bramblestar caught the elder's eye and nodded sympathetically.

Finally, Twigpaw reached the fresh-kill pile and dropped her prey.

"Have you seen this?" Molewhisker was already there. "RiverClan brought back *frogs.*" He was staring in disgust at the smooth, fat bodies among the furry forest prey.

Twigpaw wrinkled her nose. "I guess they like the taste."

"Just so long as they don't try to feed them to us," Molewhisker sniffed.

Cherryfall dropped her rabbit onto the pile. "At least they caught *something.*" She glanced pointedly at the SkyClan cats.

"*Some* of our visitors are still too weak to hunt."

Twigpaw bristled. "It's not their fault. They've been through a lot."

Ivypool brushed past and laid her catch on the ground. "Jayfeather said they're supposed to rest until they get their strength back."

Cherryfall grunted. "And who's going to help us get our strength back after we've finished feeding half the forest?"

As Lionblaze and Fernsong laid their prey beside the others', Lionblaze looked sternly at Cherryfall. "Complaining isn't going to help anyone."

"She's allowed to have an opinion." Molewhisker moved closer to the ginger she-cat and glared at Lionblaze. "Besides, are we even sure that SkyClan is a real Clan?"

Cherryfall flicked her tail in agreement. "They might just be another bunch of rogues."

Twigpaw stared at her. How could she *say* that?

She opened her mouth to defend her father's Clan, but Fernsong spoke first. "Bramblestar says they are one of the original Clans. Are you doubting your leader?" The pale yellow tabby tom blinked at Molewhisker.

"Then why hadn't we heard about SkyClan before? How come only Bramblestar knew about them?"

Ivypool flicked her tail crossly. "*StarClan* knew about them," she meowed. "Are you contradicting our ancestors?"

Twigpaw felt a rush of gratitude toward her mentor.

Ivypool went on. "It's not SkyClan's fault they returned to us at such a bad time."

"They *had* to return now," Lionblaze added. "It was part of the prophecy."

"But they didn't return because *StarClan* showed them the way." Cherryfall turned her gaze on Twigpaw. "Some cat *brought* them here because she wanted to find her father."

"That was part of StarClan's prophecy, too," Lionblaze retorted. "We found Twigpaw in the shadows so that she could clear the sky—"

Twigpaw couldn't listen to any more. Cherryfall's words were stinging like nettles. She turned away, hot with shame. Cherryfall was right. She *had* searched for SkyClan because she'd wanted to find her father. Her paws hadn't been guided by StarClan but by her own selfishness.

"Wait." Ivypool hurried after Twigpaw.

Twigpaw stopped, her pelt pricking with worry. "I didn't mean to spoil everything."

"You did a *huge* thing by bringing SkyClan here," Ivypool told her. "This is where they belong. StarClan wanted them to return, and you're the one who found them." She touched her nose to Twigpaw's head. "I am so proud of you. And"—she pulled back and looked Twigpaw in the eyes—"I'm sorry that I didn't support you when you wanted to find your kin."

Twigpaw looked at Ivypool gratefully. It did make her feel better to hear her mentor apologize. If ThunderClan had sent out a search party, Twigpaw wouldn't have had to go out on her own, against Bramblestar's orders. But more than that, it had hurt Twigpaw not to have her mentor's support on something so important to her. "Thank you." She closed her eyes. "But

I'm worried I may have caused more trouble for the Clans by bringing SkyClan here."

"If you have, it's trouble StarClan wants us to have." Twigpaw opened her eyes, and Ivypool met her gaze before she went on. "And it's far less trouble than we've seen in the past moons. Darktail is dead and his rogues are gone. The Clans must find their paws again, and we must find space for Sky-Clan. It may not be easy, but once it's finished, *all* the Clans will be stronger for it." Ivypool dipped her head. "I'm sorry. I wasn't thinking about you or SkyClan."

"What *were* you thinking about?"

Ivypool glanced around nervously. "Tigerheart and Dovewing were quick to volunteer to join the search." She lowered her voice. "I didn't think it was a good idea for them to travel together."

Twigpaw understood. While Tigerheart had been staying in the ThunderClan camp, he and Dovewing had made more and more excuses to hunt and patrol together. They'd even shared prey. Twigpaw had seen the accusing glances exchanged by her Clanmates every time Dovewing and Tigerheart brushed past each other on the way to the fresh-kill pile. Ivypool must be relieved that Tigerheart and the Shadow-Clan cats were gone. How could a relationship between her sister and another Clan's deputy lead to anything but trouble?

BRAVELANDS

For generations, the animals of the African plains have been ruled by the code of the wild: only kill to survive. But when an unthinkable act of betrayal shatters the peace, a young lion, a baboon, and an elephant calf will be thrust together in an epic battle for survival. The fragile balance between predators and prey now rests in the paws of these three unlikely heroes....

CHAPTER 1

Swiftcub pounced after the vulture's shadow, but it flitted away too quickly to follow. Breathing hard, he pranced back to his pride. *I saw that bird off our territory,* he thought, delighted. *No rot-eater's going to come near Gallantpride while I'm around!*

The pride needed him to defend it, Swiftcub thought, picking up his paws and strutting around his family. Why, right now they were all half asleep, dozing and basking in the shade of the acacia trees. The most energetic thing the other lions were doing was lifting their heads to groom their nearest neighbors, or their own paws. They had no *idea* of the threat Swiftcub had just banished.

I might be only a few moons old, but my father is the strongest, bravest lion in Bravelands. And I'm going to be just like him!

"Swiftcub!"

The gentle but commanding voice snapped him out of his

dreams of glory. He came to a halt, turning and flicking his ears at the regal lioness who stood over him.

"Mother," he said, shifting on his paws.

"Why are you shouting at vultures?" Swift scolded him fondly, licking at his ears. "They're nothing but scavengers. Come on, you and your sister can play later. Right now you're supposed to be practicing hunting. And if you're going to catch anything, you'll need to keep your eyes on the prey, not on the sky!"

"Sorry, Mother." Guiltily he padded after her as she led him through the dry grass, her tail swishing. The ground rose gently, and Swiftcub had to trot to keep up. The grasses tickled his nose, and he was so focused on trying not to sneeze, he almost bumped into his mother's haunches as she crouched.

"Oops," he growled.

Valor shot him a glare. His older sister was hunched a little to the left of their mother, fully focused on their hunting practice. Valor's sleek body was low to the ground, her muscles tense; as she moved one paw forward with the utmost caution, Swiftcub tried to copy her, though it was hard to keep up on his much shorter legs. One creeping pace, then two. Then another.

I'm being very quiet, just like Valor. I'm going to be a great *hunter.* He slunk up alongside his mother, who remained quite still.

"There, Swiftcub," she murmured. "Do you see the burrows?"

He did, now. Ahead of the three lions, the ground rose up even higher, into a bare, sandy mound dotted with small shadowy holes. As Swiftcub watched, a small nose and whiskers poked out, testing the air. The meerkat emerged completely, stood up on its hind legs, and stared around. Satisfied, it stuck out a pink tongue and began to groom its chest, as more meerkats appeared beyond it. Growing in confidence, they scurried farther away from their burrows.

"Careful now," rumbled Swift. "They're very quick. Go!"

Swiftcub sprang forward, his little paws bounding over the ground. Still, he wasn't fast enough to outpace Valor, who was far ahead of him already. A stab of disappointment spoiled his excitement, and suddenly it was even harder to run fast, but he ran grimly after his sister.

The startled meerkats were already doubling back into their holes. Stubby tails flicked and vanished; the bigger leader, his round dark eyes glaring at the oncoming lions, was last to twist and dash underground. Valor's jaws snapped at his tail, just missing.

"Sky and stone!" the bigger cub swore, coming to a halt in a cloud of dust. She shook her head furiously and licked her jaws. "I nearly had it!"

A rumble of laughter made Swiftcub turn. His father, Gallant, stood watching them. Swiftcub couldn't help but feel the usual twinge of awe mixed in with his delight. Black-maned and huge, his sleek fur glowing golden in the sun, Gallant would have been intimidating if Swiftcub hadn't known and loved him so well. Swift rose to her paws and greeted the great lion affectionately, rubbing his maned neck with her head.

"It was a good attempt, Valor," Gallant reassured his

daughter. "What Swift said is true: meerkats are *very* hard to catch. You were so close—one day you'll be as fine a hunter as your mother." He nuzzled Swift and licked her neck.

"*I* wasn't anywhere near it," grumbled Swiftcub. "I'll never be as fast as Valor."

"Oh, you will," said Gallant. "Don't forget, Valor's a whole year older than you, my son. You're getting bigger and faster every day. Be patient!" He stepped closer, leaning in so his great tawny muzzle brushed Swiftcub's own. "That's the secret to stalking, too. Learn patience, and one day you will be a *very* fine hunter."

"I hope so," said Swiftcub meekly.

Gallant nuzzled him. "Don't doubt yourself, my cub. You're going to be a great lion and the best kind of leader: one who keeps his own pride safe and content, but puts fear into the heart of his strongest enemy!"

That does sound good! Feeling much better, Swiftcub nodded. Gallant nipped affectionately at the tufty fur on top of his head and padded toward Valor.

Swiftcub watched him proudly. *He's right, of course. Father knows everything! And I will be a great hunter, I will. And a brave, strong leader—*

A tiny movement caught his eye, a scuttling shadow in his father's path.

A scorpion!

Barely pausing to think, Swiftcub sprang, bowling between his father's paws and almost tripping him. He skidded to a halt right in front of Gallant, snarling at the small sand-yellow scorpion. It paused, curling up its barbed tail and raising its pincers in threat.

"No, Swiftcub!" cried his father.

Swiftcub swiped his paw sideways at the creature, catching its plated shell and sending it flying into the long grass.

All four lions watched the grass, holding their breath, waiting for a furious scorpion to reemerge. But there was no stir of movement. It must have fled. Swiftcub sat back, his heart suddenly banging against his ribs.

"Skies above!" Gallant laughed. Valor gaped, and Swift dragged her cub into her paws and began to lick him roughly.

"Mother . . ." he protested.

"Honestly, Swiftcub!" she scolded him as her tongue swept across his face. "Your father might have gotten a nasty sting from that creature—but *you* could have been killed!"

"You're such an idiot, little brother," sighed Valor, but there was admiration in her eyes.

Gallant and Swift exchanged proud looks. "Swift," growled Gallant, "I do believe the time has come to give our cub his true name."

Swift nodded, her eyes shining. "Now that we know what kind of lion he is, I think you're right."

Gallant turned toward the acacia trees, his tail lashing, and gave a resounding roar.

It always amazed Swiftcub that the pride could be lying half asleep one moment and alert the very next. Almost before Gallant had finished roaring his summons, there was a rustle of grass, a crunch of paws on dry earth, and the rest of Gallantpride appeared, ears pricked and eyes bright with curiosity. Gallant huffed in greeting, and the twenty lionesses and young lions of his pride spread out in a circle around him, watching and listening intently.

Gallant looked down again at Swiftcub, who blinked and glanced away, suddenly rather shy. "Crouch down," murmured the great lion.

When he obeyed, Swiftcub felt his father's huge paw rest on his head.

"Henceforth," declared Gallant, "this cub of mine will no longer be known as Swiftcub. He faced a dangerous foe without hesitation and protected his pride. His name, now and forever, is Fearless Gallantpride."

It was done so quickly, Swiftcub felt dizzy with astonishment. *I have my name! I'm Fearless. Fearless Gallantpride!*

All around him, his whole family echoed his name, roaring their approval. Their deep cries resonated across the grasslands.

"Fearless Gallantpride!"

"Welcome, Fearless, son of Gallant!"

His heart swelled inside him. Suddenly, he knew what it was to be a full member of the pride. He had to half close his eyes and flatten his ears, he felt so buffeted by their roars of approval.

"I'll—I promise I'll live up to my name!" he managed to growl. It came out a little squeakier than he'd intended, but no lion laughed at him. They bellowed their delight even more.

"Of course you will," murmured Swift. Both she and his

father nuzzled and butted his head. "You already have, after all!"

"You certainly—" Gallant fell suddenly silent. Fearless glanced up at his father, expecting him to finish, but the great lion was standing still, his head turned toward the west. A light breeze rippled his dark mane. His nostrils flared.

The pride continued to roar, but with a new strange undertone. Fearless wrinkled his muzzle and tried to work out what was different. He began to hear it: there were new voices. In the distance, other lions were roaring.

One by one, the Gallantpride lions fell silent, looking toward the sound. Gallant paced through them, sniffing at the wind, and his pride turned to accompany him. Swift walked closest to his flank.

Overcome with curiosity, Fearless sprang toward the meerkat hill, running to its top and staring out across the plain. His view was blurred by the haze of afternoon heat, but he could see three lions approaching.

They're not from our pride, thought Fearless with a thrill of nerves. He could not take his eyes off the strangers, but he was aware that other lions had joined him at the top of the slope: Gallant, Swift, and Valor. The rest of the pride was behind them, all quite still and alert.

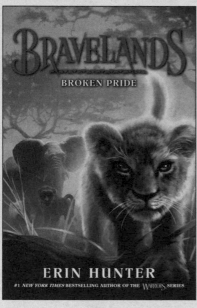

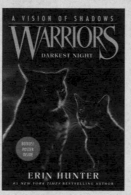

WARRIORS: THE PROPHECIES BEGIN

In the first series, sinister perils threaten the four warrior Clans. Into the midst of this turmoil comes Rusty, an ordinary housecat, who may just be the bravest of them all.

WARRIORS: THE NEW PROPHECY

In the second series, follow the next generation of heroic cats as they set off on a quest to save the Clans from destruction.

WARRIORS: POWER OF THREE

In the third series, Firestar's grandchildren begin their training as warrior cats. Prophecy foretells that they will hold more power than any cats before them.

HARPER ·
An Imprint of HarperCollinsPublishers

www.warriorcats.com

WARRIORS : SUPER EDITIONS

These extra-long, stand-alone adventures will take
you deep inside each of the Clans with thrilling tales
featuring the most legendary warrior cats.

HARPER
An Imprint of HarperCollinsPublishers

www.warriorcats.com

WARRIORS: MANGA

Don't miss the original manga adventures!

WARRIORS: BONUS STORIES

Discover the untold stories of the warrior cats and Clans when you read these paperback bind-ups—or download the ebook novellas!

WARRIORS: FIELD GUIDES

Delve deeper into the Clans with these Warriors field guides.

HARPER
An Imprint of HarperCollins*Publishers*

www.warriorcats.com